Cast of C

Hildegarde Withers. An angular, h͠ with an abundance of common sense and a knack for solving crimes.

Inspector Oscar Piper. Her best friend, a quiet little Irishman who's a veteran of the NYPD homicide division. He thinks the world of Hildy.

Francis X. Mabie. A plump Manhattan alderman who's only modestly on the take. He does all right for himself even without his wife's money.

Adele Mabie. His glamorous new wife. She made a cool million out of her chain of beauty parlors by the time she turned thirty.

Dulcie Prothero. A pretty little redhead whom Adele hired to be her personal maid. She has her own reasons for wanting to come to Mexico.

Julio Mendez. A cheerful blond Mexican who turns up everywhere. His English comes and goes. He's known to all as the Gay Caballero.

Rollo Lighton. A tall, gaunt, blue-chinned newspaperman of questionable credentials who's always on the lookout for a fast buck.

Al Hansen. His short, bulging buddy. He wears a big Stetson, once ran guns for Pancho Villa, and is also always looking to get rich quick.

Michael Fitz. A handsome, smooth-talking, gray-haired promoter who lives in Mexico City and is greatly admired by Lighton and Hanson.

Captain Raoul de Silva. A Mexico City police officer who is, like Hildy, a longtime student of Sherlock Holmes.

Robert Schultz. Known as the Yonkers Matador, he's an American bullfighter whose once-celebrated career is now on the skids.

Mr. & Mrs. Marcus Ippwing. An elderly couple from Peoria who are determined to get the most out of their trip to Mexico.

Manuel Robles. A young customs examiner who happens to be in the wrong place at the wrong time.

Books by Stuart Palmer

Novels featuring Hildegarde Withers
The Penguin Pool Murder (1931)
Murder on Wheels (1932)
Murder on the Blackboard (1932)
The Puzzle of the Pepper Tree (1933)
The Puzzle of the Silver Persian (1934)
The Puzzle of the Red Stallion (1936)
The Puzzle of the Blue Banderilla (1937)
The Puzzle of the Happy Hooligan (1941)
Miss Withers Regrets (1947)
Four Lost Ladies (1949)
The Green Ace (1950)
Nipped in the Bud (1951)
Cold Poison (1954)
Hildegarde Withers Makes the Scene (1969)
Completed by Fletcher Flora

Short story collections featuring Hildegarde Withers
The Riddles of Hildegarde Withers (1947)
The Monkey Murder (1950)
People Vs. Withers and Malone (1963)
with Craig Rice
Hildegarde Withers: Uncollected Riddles (2003)

Howie Rook mysteries
Unhappy Hooligan (1956)
Rook Takes Knight (1968)

Other mystery novels
Ace of Jades (1931)
Omit Flowers (1937)
Before It's Too Late (1950)
as by Jay Stewart

Sherlock Holmes pastiches
The Adventure of the Marked Man and One Other (1973)

The Puzzle of the Blue Banderilla

by Stuart Palmer

Introduction by Tom & Enid Schantz

Rue Morgue Press
Boulder / Lyons

The Rue Morgue Press
P.O. Box 4119
Boulder, Colorado 80306

Printed by
Johnson Printing

PRINTED IN THE UNITED STATES OF AMERICA

The Many Puzzles of Stuart Palmer

SOMETIMES a seemingly ordinary event shapes a person's life, even though it might take years before its significance is recognized. Such an event overtook 12-year-old Stuart Palmer as he was working his way through the pine bookcase in the attic of his family's summer place in rural Wisconsin when he came across a small yellow volume with an intriguing sketch on the cover. It was *The Houseboat on the Styx* by John Kendrick Bangs, a 1896 collection of humorous sketches featuring the "shades" or ghosts of famous literary characters. Among the literary personages making an appearance was Sherlock Holmes, the world's first private consulting detective. Even in that diluted form the character made a lasting impression on Palmer, who wrote years later that "a new comet swam into my ken."

When the Palmer family returned to their winter home in Baraboo, Wisconsin, Stuart rushed to the local library where "the acidulous spinster librarian" handed him, "with a disapproving sniff," Arthur Conan Doyle's *The Valley of Fear*, the second of the four full-length Sherlock Holmes novels. He quickly worked his way through the canon, practically memorizing passages from *The Adventures* and *The Memoirs*, failing only to find a copy of *His Last Bow*. It turns out that the library's copy had been checked out to the town's only ex-convict, who skipped town the next day with his girlfriend. The ex-con was Jack Boyle, whose lone book, *Boston Blackie*, would be filmed many times and many years later. Call it irony or call it coincidence, but the screenwriter for one of those films was Stuart Palmer.

Boyle left behind him numerous unpaid bills and even more empty whiskey bottles, prompting the parents of Baraboo to hold him up to their offspring as an example of the evils of drink and the futility of making a living as a writer. "It was then," Palmer said, "that I definitely chose what was to be my life's work."

But it was Holmes, not Boston Blackie, who inspired Palmer as a writer of detective stories, although his first book, *Ace of Jades*, was a gangster novel more reminiscent of *Boston Blackie* than of "A Scandal in Bohemia." Published in 1931, the book is a notorious rarity in book-collecting circles, a fact for which its author was eternally grateful, since he considered it a terrible book and was known to deny even close friends permission to read his copy.

Fortunately, he published a second book as well in 1931. *The Penguin Pool Murder* introduced the world to Miss Hildegarde Withers, a spinster schoolteacher from Dubuque who taught at Jefferson School in Manhattan. While escorting a class field trip to the aquarium, she spots a body in the penguin tank and meets for the first time Inspector Oscar Piper, to whom she will be both a great friend as well as a thorn in his side for the next thirty-odd years. Set in the autumn of 1929 in the aftermath of the stock market crash, the book was an immediate hit and was quickly sold to the movies, where it became one of the RKO studio's biggest hits of 1932.

Palmer based Miss Withers on several people from his past, including that disapproving librarian from Baraboo as well as a "horse-faced English teacher in the local high school." She got her Yankee sense of humor from Palmer's own father, but the final piece of inspiration came from seeing actress Edna May Oliver on stage during the first run of Jerome Kern's *Showboat*.

Oliver, of course, was picked to play Miss Withers in the first three of six movies that were made based on Palmer's books. Illness was given as the reason Oliver was replaced in the role by first Helen Broderick, then Zasu Pitts, but Palmer obviously thought that wasn't the case at all and never forgave the "great brains of Hollywood" who "in their infinite wisdom" made the decision to replace Oliver. James Gleason, on the other hand, wonderfully portrayed Inspector Piper in all six films. In the final scene of that first movie, Piper and Withers are seen rushing off to city hall to get married. But when audiences—and readers—clamored for more of Miss Withers, it was obvious to one and all the necessity of having these two remain just good friends. If you remember that, however, it makes the last line of the present volume all the more poignant.

The Withers/Piper alliance represents one of the earliest examples in mystery fiction of the amateur female sleuth using her "connections" with a male police officer to butt into murder cases. That formula was to be imitated time and time again. Spinster sleuth Jane Amanda Edwards, the creation of Charlotte Murray Russell beginning in 1935, was a contemporary literary rival of Miss Withers. Jane found her homicide captain, George Hammond, late in life as well, and although he made regular visits to the Edwards dining table, a full-scale romance never developed. Modern readers might be a bit amused to learn that this particular "elderly" spinster was in her mid-forties. Miss Withers appears to be slightly older but acts much older, as many real women of that era did. Inspector Piper, resigned to being jilted, opted to continue their friendship, although there's little doubt that he would have jumped at marriage had a second opportunity ever arisen. If Palmer eschewed romance, it was probably solely for reasons of plot, since he showed every sign himself of being a hopeless romantic at any age, having married five times, the last time only two years before his death at the age of 62 in 1968.

The remarkable success of the first Miss Withers book may partly explain Palmer's lifelong affection for penguins. He adopted them as his personal trademark and often decorated his letters with portraits of the sad-eyed, earthbound birds, perhaps peering under the rim of a deerstalker through a magnifying glass or pinned to the earth by an arrow. Palmer, born in 1905, was a gifted cartoonist, having attended the Chicago Art Institute in the early 1920s before going on to the University of Wisconsin in Madison. Palmer's collection of penguin art went far beyond his own efforts, however. His house was filled with penguins fashioned out of glass, tin, wood, and even soap, picked up in his travels or given to him by friends and fans.

Honors and tributes also filled Palmer's house. *The Penguin Pool Murder* was accorded a place of honor on the shelf of the Haycraft-Queen Definitive Library of Detective-Crime-Mystery Fiction, while two his short story collections, *The Riddles of Hildegarde Withers* (1947) and *The People Vs. Withers and Malone* (1963), written in collaboration with Craig Rice (though how much Rice contributed to the effort is subject to question), were given cornerstone recognition by Ellery Queen in his annotated history of the detective story, *Queen's Quorum.*

Palmer was just as successful writing what he called "B movie melodramas" as he was writing detective stories. When Hollywood bought the Miss Withers books, Stuart Palmer accompanied her to the West

Coast, eventually writing screenplays for 37 movies, including several in the Falcon and Bulldog Drummond series.

World War II interrupted Palmer's career as a mystery writer but not as a screenwriter. Nearly forty when he enlisted in 1944, he was sent to an army base in Oklahoma where he wrote training films for the field artillery. He didn't entirely give up mystery writing. Part of him went back to that 12-year-old boy in Baraboo when he sent off the only fan letter he would ever write in his life, to Arthur Conan Doyle at 221B Baker Street, London, England. He was always grateful that some kindly English postmaster didn't stamp it "Nonexistent address. Return to Sender." During this period in "the wilds of Oklahoma," he wrote two Sherlock Holmes pastiches, one of which was included in Ellery Queen's *The Misadventures of Sherlock Holmes*, a book that was suppressed (after five printings) by the Doyle estate. As a result, Palmer gave up plans to write more pastiches. It's unfortunate, because both were fine stories, especially "The Adventure of the Marked Man," which many critics, ourselves included, consider, along with Vincent Starrett's "The Adventure of the Unique Hamlet," to be the best of all the attempts to write the Sixty-First Adventure. In 1973, we (as The Aspen Press) bundled it and Palmer's story from *The Misadventures*, "The Adventure of the Remarkable Worm," along with "The I.O.U of Hildegarde Withers," in a slim chapbook entitled *The Adventure of the Marked Man and One Other*. The 500-copy edition sold out in a matter of days.

Palmer spent the rest of his time in the service in Washington, D.C., where he acted as liaison between army intelligence and the studios. During this period, he continued to write screenplays, but Miss Withers was shelved for the duration. After Palmer did what was to be his second to last screenplay in 1946, he resurrected Miss Withers in 1947, first in a short story collection, *The Riddles of Hildegarde Withers*, then in the novel, *Miss Withers Regrets*. Over the next twenty years, Hildy would appear in four more novels, with the last, *Hildegarde Withers Makes the Scene*, finished by Fletcher Flora and published in 1969, one year after his death. During this period, he published the final two Withers short story collections, a stand-alone crime novel written under the pseudonym Jay Stewart, and two books featuring Howie Rook, an amply proportioned ex-newspaperman. Palmer put his youthful experience as a clown with the Ringling Brother's Circus to good use in the first of these books.

Many of Palmer's Miss Withers books have been reprinted in recent years, by either International Polygonics or Bantam, but most are once again out of print. *The Puzzle of the Blue Banderilla* hasn't been reprinted in at least 50 years, and possibly longer, but it displays all the charm that made Miss Withers Anthony Boucher's (the namesake of Bouchercon, the World Mystery Convention) favorite female sleuth.

And when you come to the chapter in which Miss Withers duplicates a stunt from a Sherlock Holmes story, thereby earning the respect as well as the aid of a tough Mexican cop, think back to that 12-year-old boy in that musty Wisconsin attic and be grateful for his inspiration. But while Doyle grew tired of Holmes, even killing him off at one point, Palmer never tired of finding new puzzles for the female sleuth he fondly called that "meddlesome old battleaxe" to unravel. And true puzzles they were, in spite of their good humor, filled with clues carefully and subtly inserted, making it possible for the truly observant reader to try and beat Miss Withers to the murderer. Yet Palmer developed his complicated plots in what were actually, for the time, fairly short (60,000-word) books. His years as a screenwriter served him well in honing his skills at setting a scene, and if, in the early days, he loved the exclamation point too much for his own good, it's a small idiosyncracy on the part of one of the most gifted and entertaining mystery writers of his day.

Tom & Enid Schantz
July 2004
Lyons, Colorado

I

That Lonesome Road

A SMALL and excited wire terrier answered the doorbell, paws sliding on waxed floors, whiskers flying. He sniffed at the crack under the door, growled menacingly, and barked. The bell rang again, and the dog raced back through the apartment, scratched at the bathroom door, making the afternoon hideous with sound.

Inside the bathroom his mistress turned off the cold water. "Quiet, Dempsey! Will you be quiet?"

It was the hottest day of the hottest summer that Manhattan had seen for many years, and Miss Hildegarde Withers, weakening in her resolution to improve the vacation time by attending summer school at Columbia, was shamelessly cutting classes.

Beside her tub was a chair, upon which rested a tall glass of iced tea, a heap of assorted thick textbooks dealing with criminology, penology and sociology, and a palm-leaf fan. But the angular schoolteacher had been engrossed in the latest issue of *True Crime* magazine.

Tearing herself from "The Fiend of Johnson's Corners," she hastened to hang makeshift clothing upon her frame and hurried out to answer the summons, Dempsey dashing around her slippered heels in great excitement.

The youth in the blue uniform backed nervously away as she opened the door. "Don't mind the dog," Miss Withers advised him reassuringly. "His mother once frightened a messenger boy, and so he has been trying ever since."

Dempsey wagged his tail, cocked his head, and opened his formidable jaws in a doggish laugh.

His mistress signed for the message, pulled the little dog inside, and closed the door firmly. Then she read the following message:

WOULD A LADY OF TASTE AND RESOURCES CARE
FOR A PERFUME NAMED ELIXIR DAMOUR SOLD
CHAIN DRUGSTORES URGENT ANSWER CARE TRAIN
FORTY MEXICAN NATIONAL RAILWAYS EN ROUTE
LAREDO MEXCITY

OSCAR PIPER

Miss Withers read it over three times, with growing apprehension and wonder. In the past five or six years it had been her habit to interfere regularly in some of the most interesting murder cases of the New York Police Homicide Division. On a number of occasions her help had even been grudgingly requested by the dour and grizzled Irishman at Centre Street. Inspector Oscar Piper was possibly her best friend. Certainly she was his severest critic. But she had never expected to be called upon in a matter of this kind.

"I knew something would happen to that man if he went traipsing off with all those Democrats," Miss Withers said to Dempsey. "On the excuse of opening an international highway, of all things!"

She dressed hastily, hardened her heart to the appeal of the little dog who hopefully brought her his leash and harness at the door, and went hurrying out of the apartment. As she went she murmured "Elixir d'Amour!" Then a sniff. "That man is up to something!"

All that the inspector had been up to was an attempt to fill inside straights. Four men had been trying to forget the heat, the dust, and the blinding sunshine of south Texas by playing penny ante in one of the middle sections of the Pullman, cards and chips strewn over the table hooked under the windows.

And then the conductor, a tall pumpkin-faced *mestizo,* bent above them. "*Señores*, it is not permitted!" was the gist of his potpourri of Spanish-English. His words and manner were apologetic, but there was the faintest twinkle of satisfaction in his dark eyes.

"That's okay, we're honored guests of the Republic," they told him. But the conductor only shook his head. "It is not permitted," he repeated.

When he had gone the four card players looked at each other. Then three turned to face the fourth, a gaunt cadaverish person with a bluish chin, who reminded the inspector somehow of one of the great brown buzzards who had been hovering over the train since they wound out of Laredo fifteen minutes ago.

He had introduced himself as Rollo Lighton, newspaperman of Mexico City. *The* newspaperman, he intimated. Sent up to cover the ceremonies of the opening of the Pan-American Highway.

"Well, that's that," Lighton said. "It seems that the *presidente* has signed an edict forbidding gambling on trains. We're over the Rio Grande now, you know…"

So that muddy ditch had been the Rio Grande! At that moment the train stopped on the edge of nowhere with an unexpected jerk. A stack of white chips slid into the lap of the inspector, who was sitting in the corner next the window, fanning himself with a new straw sun helmet.

"Cripes!" said that worthy gentleman in deep disgust.

The tubby little man beside him stooped to help pick up the chips. He wore shiny black clothes, a large undented Stetson which narrowly escaped being of rodeo proportions, and an innocent and childlike smile.

"You want to watch that *hombre* Hansen, pal," advised Rollo Lighton. "I've heard that money and chips stick to his fingers."

Hansen flashed a wider smile from under the hat. "Only blue chips, friend." He pushed the rescued stack toward their owner. "We're stopped for customs," he explained to the others. "When they get through the baggage we might move into your drawing room where it's private?"

He was addressing the alderman. Francis X. Mabie, Manhattan district leader (and devoutly wishing himself back there at the moment) turned on his warm professional smile. "We'll see, we'll see about that." It was the tone he used in promising to secure a low license number, promising to fix a speeding ticket. "If Mrs. Mabie has no objections… He folded his hands comfortably across his plump facade. Alderman Mabie wore with dignity what the Chinese call "the curve of well-being."

"Your new frau isn't down on poker, is she?" pressed the inspector, presuming a little on the basis of old acquaintance.

"Feeling the heat a little, that's all," Mabie said. They were all feeling the heat. For three days they had been jammed in Laredo with a mob of tourists, lost in a fog of band music and oratory, sweltering in an oven of actual and figurative hot air.

Now that the *presidente* of Mexico and the vice president of the United States had collaborated on the final severance of a sagging ribbon across the International Bridge, the ceremonies were over. Nothing remained except the trip to the Mexican capital as guests of the sunny southern Republic. Most of the captains and the kings had departed over the new highway via the motorcade, but there happened to be a few pessimistic dignitaries who had heard that the lovely old valley of Monterrey basked in a temperature of 115 degrees, that certain hotels in small towns along the new auto route boasted fleas as big as cockroaches and roaches big as mice. It was also pointed out that about eighty miles of the new highway, from Tamuzunchale over the very tops of the highest Sierras Madre, were still unpaved.

These less adventurous souls had chosen the more prosaic if more dependable *ferrocarril,* with its highly recommended *"climas artificiales."* But the cooling system was not yet making any appreciable difference in the dusty heat of the cars, nor did the view of Nuevo Laredo's backyards serve to inspire anyone.

"Those customs boys are taking hell's own time to get through this train," Hansen observed, looking at a large timepiece of yellow gold.

"Anyway, aren't we supposed to receive the courtesy of diplomatic immunity, or whatever it is?" Alderman Mabie demanded.

Lighton rasped his dark chin with a long curved fingernail. "This is just like any other train," he pointed out. "You should have gone on the motorcade if you wanted fanfares and salutes. Anyway, don't worry about customs here. With my drag…"

"Don't tell me anything about customs," Al Hansen put in, pushing his Stetson over one eye. "Say, I once got three bullets through my hide—right there it was too—from these customs boys. Just because I was trying to deliver some goods to a customer of mine south of the river…"

"What sort of goods?" the alderman asked, to fill in the pause.

"Machine guns, for Pancho Villa," Hansen enlightened them. "It was in the spring of 1913, and I had the guns disguised in beer casks, only I forgot to wet the outside of the casks—"

"I'm too dry to listen," the alderman cut in. "Right now I'd like some of this Mexican beer we've heard so much about. But it doesn't seem to be any use punching this bell…"

It wasn't much use. Somewhere else a bell was being rung again and again, so that sharp staccato buzzes came from the porter's closet.

"Portero!" called Lighton hoarsely. Nothing happened.

"PORTER!" Hansen's voice was like a foghorn. A baby down the aisle began to whimper softly, and the old couple from Peoria who wore Texas Centennial hatbands awakened and looked hopefully around for signs of bandits.

Somewhere a door opened, slammed again, and then the porter went past the four men at a jog trot. His swarthy Indian face was impassive as ever, but he seemed to have difficulty in speaking. As he passed he spewed a few words in Spanish over his shoulder and then disappeared toward the front of the car.

Rollo Lighton's jaw dropped open, showing yellow snags of teeth. "He says something about the lady in the drawing room!" he gasped.

"Something that sounded like '*muerte*'," chimed in Hansen. "I know damned little Spanish, but I know that…"

They all tried to stand up at once, struggling out of the cramped seats. Oddly enough it was the quiet little Irishman next to the window who was first into the aisle, somehow gaining stature as he elbowed the others out of his way. The straw sun helmet rolled forgotten under the seat as Oscar Piper, veteran inspector of the Homicide Division, New York City Police, galloped forward like an old fire horse at the clanging of a three-alarm.

Up until this moment his much-anticipated share in the junket of the New York Democratic delegation had turned out to be one unutterable bore, but now, if only "muerte" meant what it sounded like…

Down the aisle, along the narrow washroom corridor, to the door of Drawing Room A. Piper threw it open, then drew sharply back, barring the doorway with his arm to the others. He sniffed, frowning.

"Don't go in there!" he ordered. "Let it clear!"

His keen gray eyes, professionally trained to notice everything, snapped a picture of that Pullman drawing room, a picture in such clear focus that he could have described it under oath in court a year later.

A little room, crowded with much-labeled luggage, a room with two bodies on the floor.

The man was in the dull-gray uniform of a customs examiner for the Republic. His boyishly lean face was of an unearthly ashen-gray color now, and he was staring at the ceiling with wide bloodshot eyes. He looked pitiful and faintly comic, all akimbo as he was—like a dropped and forgotten marionette.

Piper knelt beside him, looked up with a deep crease between his eyebrows. "Dead!" he said softly.

He moved the body slightly from where it lay across an open traveling case, a case which exposed gleaming silver fittings, the glint of crystal bottles… For a moment the inspector turned his back to the frightened, inquisitive people in the half-open doorway…

"Adele!" the alderman was moaning. "Adele!

Oscar Piper bent over the woman who was lying between the two seats, as if flung there by an explosion. She was a more than pretty woman, if a bit thirtyish. Incredibly soft and yet heavy in his arms she was...

"Give me a hand here!" he commanded. There was a moment of hesitation, and then Francis Mabie stepped gingerly over the body of the customs man, took his wife's silken legs...

They got her out of the drawing room, to a seat in the Pullman. Piper forced back the crowd.

"Isn't there anything we can do for her?" Mabie was crying.

There was, and the inspector was doing it. His first-aid methods were so successful that Adele Mabie was sitting up when the porter came trotting back up the aisle, followed by train officials, more customs men, and a bald dumpling of a man with a goatee, who smelled vilely of tequila and carried a small black bag.

The group pushed past them, disappeared through the door of the drawing room.

"I—I guess I must have fainted!" Adele Mabie spoke softly, painfully.

"Quiet, Adele! You mustn't try to..."

The inspector's hand was clenched in his coat pocket. He was an old acquaintance, indeed he had been one of the guests at Adele Mabie's wedding reception, but she did not know him now.

"It would be better to talk," he said softly in her ear. "What really happened in there?"

"Now see here, Inspector!" Mabie was furious.

"Best if she answers," Piper said. "Well?"

"I don't know!" the woman cried. Even in her distraught condition her fingers automatically picked and patted and arranged the loose strands of her dark hair. "I don't know what happened! Just that the customs man—"

"You don't know him? Never saw him before?" Piper demanded.

She shook her head blankly. "Of course not. He was such a nice man, too! Barely looked at my bags, and he didn't say a word about the three cartons of cigarettes or anything. Just smiled and made a joke or two in his funny cute accent, and then..."

She shivered. "I don't remember..."

The others came crowding back around them. There was curious Lighton like a great eager bird, pudgy Hansen with the wide childlike eyes. Behind them were the other passengers of the car, the old couple from Peoria, the Mexican-American family with the three fat-cheeked children, the two giggling *señoritas* with the ample hips, and even an elderly Spanish gentleman with handlebar mustaches and a gold-headed cane.

The inspector scowled at the crowd, and then with sudden decision he took the woman by one arm, motioned her husband to take the other. "Come out on the rear platform," he insisted. "The air will do you good."

The door slammed behind them. "Now please come clean with me, Mrs. Mabie!" he pleaded.

"Listen to me!" cut in the husband angrily. "You forget that you're not in New York now, Inspector!"

"Neither are you, and you're going to find it out," Piper said. "How about it, Mrs. Mabie?"

She drew back against the bulwark of her husband. "I have—nothing to tell you," she said softly. "Nothing."

"You can't tell me anything about why this poor devil in there was holding this gripped in his hand when I found him? With the stopper out?" The stern policeman produced a small amber-colored bottle, shaped like a flattened hexagon. In florid green script it bore the legend "Elixir d'Amour" and beneath in smaller letters "bottled expressly for Longacre Square Pharmacies, N.Y.C."

Mrs. Mabie still shook her head slowly, like one of the trick dolls sold on street corners.

"You don't see anything queer about the fact that somebody just takes one whiff of your perfume and cashes in his checks? And almost takes you along with him?"

She shook her head. "Honestly, Inspector! I have a headache—"

"We'll all have headaches before this is over. If you don't let me help you—"

"It's all a nightmare," the woman whispered. "All a nightmare, and I'm going to wake up in a moment." She nodded as if to clear her head of cobwebs. "You see," she went on, speaking as if to a very small child or to a deaf person, "that bottle isn't mine!"

"I suppose the brownies put it in your traveling bag? I suppose—"

"I never saw it before in all my life!" declared Adele Mabie. "Why, I only use De Markoff's Essence at forty dollars an ounce. And why you imagine that I would plant a drug…"

"I didn't say drug, but I'll go farther. It was poison!" he told her.

"…plant poison in somebody else's cheap perfume bottle, just to kill a poor unoffending little Mexican customs man whom I never saw before in all my life—"

"That's it!" The alderman's voice gained strength. "Why should my wife poison a customs man or enter into a suicide pact with him? You grumble at customs. You don't try to—"

"All right, all right," the inspector cut in. "We'll agree that it was the brownies, after all. But it's going to be a hell of a defense to take into court."

"Into court?" the woman echoed blankly.

"Yes, when you go up for second-degree homicide, or criminal negligence, or whatever it was."

Adele Mabie moaned a little. "She's fainted!" came from the alderman, as he manfully struggled to keep his wife's limp form from sliding to the floor of the platform.

Inspector Oscar Piper opened the door to let two stretcher-bearers through with their burden, a blanket drawn over its face. "And that is that," he said. "We had a chance to do something for her, but she went and fainted. Now we can only hope Mrs. Mabie won't wake up in a Mexican jail."

"But it wasn't her perfume bottle!" Mabie gasped. "Why, they can't do that to her! I tell you, she had no more to do with this than I did!"

"Uh huh," said the inspector. When the train finally hitched its way into the station of Nuevo Laredo, he got down and sent the telegram.

II

Death Smells So Sweet

THE INSPECTOR stood on the station platform in the midst of a crowd of hurrying baggagemen, quaintly clad sellers of fruit juices, slices of pineapple, *chicles* and cigarettes. Everywhere there was a hustling, breathless activity, but nowhere a sign of the police that he expected.

Grimly uncommunicative train officials got off and on the car, but that was all.

It was a pretty problem in ethics which faced Oscar Piper. If he said anything about the bottle in his pocket, the bottle which had spilled most of its strange sweet contents upon the floor of the drawing room, the wife of his friend Francis Mabie was certain to be mixed up in a scandal, perhaps put under arrest.

The inspector was a member of this party because of Alderman Mabie. He had needed a vacation badly, having had none in ten years except one flying trip to Catalina in the course of official business. Since reaching the age of twenty-one Oscar Piper had voted the Democratic ticket, had been what they call a "Tammany cop," although he had always prided himself on making sure that the uniform and not the tiger came first in his loyalties.

It had been as a sort of reward, engineered by the alderman, that he had been offered a place in this junket. Of course, members of the New York delegation had agreed that it would be a good idea to have a police official along—one who knew from years of experience the misguided radicals who might feel inclined to toss a bomb into the midst of the highway-opening ceremonies. But now those vaguely official duties were ended, and he was faced with nothing more than a trip down to a foreign capital he had always wished to visit. Nothing—except that the alderman's new and attractive wife had to go and get mixed up in a homicide.

His loyalties were all for the alderman. And yet Oscar Piper had a deep-rooted dislike for people who act carelessly with little bottles of poison. Potassium cyanide, of course. It was the only thing with that almond odor that could kill with a whiff. The fumes, rising, had filled the drawing room—certainly enough to account for the woman's collapse.

And she denied that it was hers. Denied that she had ever owned the bottle. Well, that was a purely feminine matter. The telegram might help him on that point.

The pumpkin-faced Pullman conductor stepped beside him, held out his large nickel watch warningly. "Only five minoots, *señor!*"

He started. "They're not holding the train, then?"

"Ah no, *señor*. We cannot keep an express train standing in the *estación* just because one poor customs examiner has a heart attack. Very sad, that. But others have finish his work."

"Heart attack, eh?" Piper nodded. Evidently the local doctor wasn't familiar with what the sob sisters call the "acrid scent of bitter almonds."

Far up ahead the engineer gave two blasts upon the whistle. Immediately the platform became a veritable bedlam, people scurrying from the lines of parked cars to clamber aboard or exchange last embraces through the car windows. There was a tumult of farewells, messages, endearments, sidesplitting jokes—all in Spanish. With a faint sense of uneasiness the inspector realized that he was an alien.

Up alongside the second-class coaches there was a quartet of musicians playing "*La Paloma*," sugar sweet and sad…

The conductor was motioning him toward the steps. "Please, *señor!*" He waved his arm, and his voice lifted in a wailing "¡*Vamonos!*"

There was nothing for the inspector but to get back aboard the train, which he proceeded to do. His decision had been made for him. For better or worse, they were off for Mexico City.

He went back through the Pullmans. News of the tragedy had spread, and he had to parry questions right and left. Years of experience had made Oscar Piper an accomplished parrier of questions.

It wasn't quite so easy to deal with Rollo Lighton, back in Pullman car Elysian.

"Look here, Inspector, is it on the level that the doctor says the customs man had a heart attack? Because if it is, then why was the woman—"

"Yeah," Al Hansen cut in. "Heart trouble isn't contagious, is it?"

Piper shrugged. "Maybe she fainted from the shock of seeing a man drop dead in front of her."

"And the smell in the drawing room?"

"A spilled bottle of perfume, I guess." To change the subject Piper pointed to the black headlines of the Mexican newspaper on the seat. "What's that say?"

"¡*Huelga mañana!*" Lighton told him. "Means there's a strike called for tomorrow morning. As if this country hadn't had enough of them. This is going to be a lulu, too."

The inspector wasn't interested in class warfare, except in Union Square. Then suddenly an idea occurred to him, one which would explain many things. "Say, that isn't a police strike, by any chance?"

The two stared at him wonderingly. "Why, no," Lighton said. "It's a strike of electrical unions. Power is going to be shut off in the Federal District tomorrow, probably later in most of the other provinces. Which means that there'll be hell to pay in Mexico City."

The inspector started to go, but Al Hansen caught his arm. "Wait a minute, will you? It's a lousy wind that doesn't blow something into somebody's pockets. We'd like to cut you in on a sure thing, if you can lay hands on some money quick."

They looked at Piper, who stiffened a little. "Dice or horses?"

"Nothing like that. You see," Hansen explained, "I'm on my way down to Mexico City to promote a horse track, but something else has come up. Something red hot."

"And it can't miss!" Lighton put in. "Wait until you hear about it.

Why, I'm risking every dime of my soldier's bonus that I've just been up to the States to collect. You see, we're going to send every cent we can raise down to—"

"Wait," Hansen stopped him. "How about it, Piper? If we let you in, can you lay your hands on a thousand bucks or so? I'll guarantee that you'll get back ten, maybe twenty, grand inside of two weeks."

The inspector kept both hands in his pockets. "Sorry, boys," he said. "I'm just an underpaid cop, without a safety-deposit box to my name. Why don't you try the alderman? He's a gambler."

Al Hansen shrugged. "I just did. He said he had too much on his mind right now."

"Which is my trouble, too," Piper told him and went on back toward the rear of the car. A Mexican waiter in a white jacket was following, carrying a tray with sandwiches and a teapot. The inspector lingered, watched the man enter the door of the drawing room. He caught a glimpse of Adele Mabie inside, dressed in something clinging and soft. She was bearing up well, then.

Piper went on, his objective the rear platform. There had always been something very stimulating to his mental processes in watching two parallel lines of steel rails meet in the distance. But this time, with his hand on the door, he stopped short, drawing instinctively back into the passage.

Through the glass he could see the bulky figure of Francis Mabie leaning against the rear gate of the train. There was a girl with him, a small and exceedingly pretty girl with crisp red curls.

She was excitedly kissing the alderman.

The inspector flattened himself against the wall, shamelessly peeping through the dusty glass. But they were not paying any attention.

Piper regretted with all his heart that he could not read the lips which he saw moving on the other side of the smeared glass door. He never had put much stock in lip reading until, by means of a smattering of that science, Miss Hildegarde Withers had helped him crack one of the most baffling murders of his career at Centre Street.

The alderman and the girl separated, drew closer again. And then, as Piper tried to fit this into his structure of the whole affair, he saw that red-haired miss turn like a cat and strike Mabie, fingers outstretched, across the cheek.

Then she came through the door. The inspector had barely time enough to step back, busy himself with the lighting of a cigar, before the girl burst past him. She had the type of elfin, triangular face, he noted, which looks most attractive when angry. Round chin set hard, wide eyes blazing...

But what interested the inspector most was the fact that as she went past he noticed that she was stuffing money into her handbag—crisp green American currency.

When Piper came out on the platform the alderman seemed honestly glad to see him. "Been looking all over for you," was his greeting.

Somewhat stiffly the inspector inquired after the health of Mrs. Mabie.

"Poor Adele is lying down," Mabie said. "She had a good scare. So did I for that matter. No wonder she fainted, seeing a man drop dead in front of her."

The inspector didn't say anything, and both men listened a moment to the clicking of the wheels along the rails.

"Had an idea all along you'd jumped to the wrong conclusions about that bottle," the alderman continued after a moment. He dropped into one of the camp chairs provided by the Pullman company for its outdoor-loving and dust-loving-passengers. "Eh, Inspector?"

Piper sat down, smiling a stiffish smile. "I can be wrong," he admitted. "Maybe I'm wrong about the bottle. After all, I haven't had it analyzed. Want to draw the stopper and take a whiff of what's left in it?" He produced the flask of Elixir d'Amour.

"Why not?" Mabie said and held out his hand.

The inspector put the bottle back in his pocket. "No, you don't."

The train was rolling across a waste of mesquite, now and then broken by the inevitable adobe hovel, fenced in with organ cactus, in front of which always stood a line of blank-faced Indians in clean faded cotton, drawn up to watch the one event of the day. Big black flies hovered over the huts, swept after the train, and droned endlessly about the two men on the back platform.

Suddenly Piper made a snatch in the air, imprisoned one of the flies in his hand, where it buzzed like a bee. Then he cupped his fist over the upper end of the perfume bottle, loosening but not drawing the cork. He held it there while he counted twenty.

"Look!" he commanded and opened his palm. The fly was still there, moving slowly along what palmists and fortune tellers call the Mount of Venus.

"It's not dead," Mabie said. "See? What did I tell you?"

They both saw. The big black fly suddenly let go the grip of its suction pads, tumbled down the slope of the inspector's palm, and lay motionless, legs in the air, against the base of his thumb.

"Heart failure," Oscar Piper pointed out with a grim smile.

The other man stared at him, haunted eyed. "Will you give me that bottle?" he begged. "Right now, before something else happens?" He pointed over the edge of the rail, down to the stony roadbed and the flickering cross-ties. "Smash the thing!"

Piper shook his head. "That won't do any good. I've got to smash what is behind this. Smash the murderer, not the weapon. Looks as if I pulled the boner of my career by not giving this to the authorities in Nuevo Laredo. Now it's up to me."

"You mean that you still cling to the ridiculous idea that Adele..."

The train whistled lugubriously, a long wailing blast which seemed endless. They were coming toward a station.

They were barely at a full stop before the swarthy porter made his advent, looking inquiringly at the inspector. "*Señor* Piper?"

"Well, what is it?"

"*Telegrama para usted,*" was the announcement. The porter handed over an envelope.

Alderman Mabie stood up as Piper took the message. "Think I'll stretch my legs a bit," he said and climbed over the rail and down the steps to the platform. He walked quickly away.

The inspector wasn't noticing, for the message surprised him. It was not quite what he had expected from Hildegarde Withers. She had wired him:

IF YOU ARE MIXED UP WITH A WOMAN ADVISE STICKING TO CANDY OR FLOWERS DONT PUT ANY- THING IN WRITING STOP PERFUME YOU MENTION WOULD NEVER APPEAL TO A LADY OF TASTE IT IS SOLD HERE FOR FIFTY CENTS AN OUNCE AND IS TERRIBLE BEST REGARDS

                                        HILDEGARDE

It did not occur to the inspector that his tried and trusting sparring partner back in New York had misread his telegram and was imbued with a trace of jealousy. He was too busy with a new train of thought. Adele Mabie was a rich woman, rich in her own right. A woman of taste too. She wouldn't be likely to go in for fifty-cent perfume.

And if that hadn't been her perfume bottle—

He left the platform suddenly, started in through the car. And then he saw that Adele Mabie was coming toward him, rushing along the corridor. She caught his arm.

"Have you seen my husband?"

Piper motioned. "Stretching his legs on the platform, I guess. What's wrong?"

She shook her head. "Oh, nothing, I guess. But it does seem so odd. Probably I'm just jumpy…"

"What seemed so odd, Mrs. Mabie?" Piper demanded.

"It was the tea, the iced tea I had the waiter bring me," she said. "I couldn't drink it, because it was so bitter. And then just as we stopped I thought I saw a face at the train window. I don't know who it was, or if I imagined it all. But it makes me wonder—"

"It should make you wonder," Piper snapped. "Come on, show me that tea."

"It's still on the tray," she said. "In the drawing room. I didn't want to send it back until someone else had looked at it. I may be imagining things, but still…"

Back they went to the door of the drawing room again. And Adele stopped in the doorway, pointing.

A little one-legged table was hooked under the windows, between the seats. On the table was a flat silver tray with a napkin and the remains of a sandwich. But there was no glass of tea.

There had been a glass. The shivered fragments strewed table and carpet, and everywhere pieces of ice melted soppily amid bits of tea leaf.

"But what happened?" Adele cried. "Why, only this minute I stepped out of the door! There hasn't been time for anyone to do this!"

The windows, still left open to clear away the faint sweet odor of perfume and bitter almonds, faced away from the noisy life of the station platform, faced full upon a little wilderness of freight cars, oil tanks, and the distant purple mountains. There was nothing alive within the view of the inspector except a starved yellow dog, who immediately streaked out of sight.

Piper dropped to his hands and knees, surveying the floor. It took him only a moment to find the bullet, which was embedded not too deeply in the upholstery of the settee. It was .38 caliber, a most baffling bit of lead. It had smashed the glass of bitter tea, smashed it so thoroughly that fingerprints and contents were alike beyond analysis. That much was obvious to the inspector.

"But I don't see how it could have happened!" Adele repeated.

Piper stood up. His finger drew an imaginary line in the air, from the bullet hole in the upholstery to the tray on the table, then out through the window.

"I'll tell you," he said. "The bullet was fired from a noiseless gun, because there was no sound of a shot. The gun had no barrel, because there are no rifling marks on the slug."

"But who?" she implored. "Who could have done it?"

"There you have me," Piper said. "All I know is that the person who fired that shot must be more than nine feet tall." He shook his head after sniffing at the remains of the glass of iced tea. "No chance to find out if it was poisoned or not," he told her. "But it would seem that somebody didn't want us to look into the matter."

Adele Mabie shivered a little. "I—I think I'll go and find my husband," she said.

"Good idea. And when you find him, stick to him and stay in the middle of the crowd until the train starts up again," Piper advised her. He watched her out of sight.

Then he locked the drawing-room door behind him, drew the shades of the windows, and turned on the light. He went through the baggage of Mr. and Mrs. Francis Mabie with what is usually known as a fine-tooth comb. Luckily all of the much-labeled bags were unlocked, presumably left so as a result of the second customs examination.

Through hatboxes, Gladstones, briefcases, and overnight bags, he went, searching for he knew not what. In one black leather case devoted to lingerie he found a small book bound in rough cloth—*Your Trip to Mexico*. It was well-worn, and he would have liked more time to examine it, having learned that often such things can serve as excellent keys to the character of their owners.

He thumbed through the little book, found two back pages stuck. Between them someone had left a snapshot, one of the cheap horrors snapped at amusement parks and sold for a dime. The chemical coating was peeling from the thing, but Piper could see Adele Mabie's face, a face younger and happier than she was wearing today. She was seated in a "prop" roller coaster, marked "Luna Park," with a man. Unfortunately the face of her companion had been neatly cut away with fingernail scissors. What to deduce from this evidence of some trip to Coney Island the inspector could not decide. So he pocketed it and went on with his search.

Investigating every jar of cold cream, every container of shaving soap, every flask of cleansing lotion, he found no weapon and no trace of poison—nothing that didn't belong. He even squeezed the tube of toothpaste, sniffed cautiously, and touched it to the tip of his tongue. No, nothing had been planted here. Nothing but an incongruous bottle of perfume that nobody owned. He replaced everything exactly as he had found it.

Then, as he moved toward the door, someone knocked from the outside. It was an odd, timorous knock. Piper turned out the light, waited for the knob to click…

But there was another knock.

Certainly this wasn't the Mabies. On an impulse he threw off the catch and opened the door. The red-haired girl in the yellow dress, the prettiest girl on the train, stood there. Her eyes were still fiery.

"Here!" she said, thrusting thirty dollars into his hand.

III

A Jump at the Moon

"OH," blurted the girl, "I've made a mistake!" She reached for the money.

Piper drew back, gazing appraisingly at the cropped red curls, hot brown eyes, bright yellow dress. "Maybe you have," he admitted. "The question is how much of a mistake?"

"It's so dark in there," she said.

It was dark, but the inspector optimistically thought that things were growing just a bit lighter. He held the drawing-room door open invitingly. "Want to come in and wait?"

Red hair tossed, red lips curled. "Not tonight, Josephine!" She was going to say something else, but suddenly she cocked her head like an insolent bird and stared at him. "Haven't I seen you before? On the train coming down from New York, perhaps?"

Oscar Piper flashed his gold badge, watched for some effect on the girl's face. Did he imagine it, or was she swiftly withdrawing into her shell, like a startled clam? "I'll ask all the questions," he told her, in his best inquisitorial manner. "Who are you, what are you doing on this train, and why are you returning this money to Francis Mabie?"

The girl gave a soft and tremulous smile. Her quick softening gave Piper the momentary impression that this was going to be duck soup. Then she spoke. "We're below the border, aren't we?"

"What of it? I want to know—"

"And isn't there a full moon tonight?"

The inspector didn't care a hang if there was. He couldn't believe, being a modest man, that this pert young thing was hinting at an assignation on the back platform in the light of the full moon.

The soft smile flashed again. "There *is* a moon, so will you please go and take a running jump at it, Mr. New York Copper?" And then she turned on her heel, went hurrying away toward the front of the train. Outside sounded the mournful chant of "¡*Vamonos!*"

So she had won the round on points, eh? The inspector was close to losing his temper. "Hey, you!" he called out and rushed after the girl.

And then the way was barred by a new addition to the passenger list, in the person of a tall blond young Mexican in a blue beret. He carried a guitar under his arm, in each hand a big bag in heavy alligator, with the heads left on and fitted with artificial eyes.

"Damn sorry!" the youth insisted, but all the same the inspector tripped over a bag, cursed, and gave up the chase. It was hard for him to remember that below the Rio Grande his bright gold shield meant just about as much as one of the tin "Chicken Inspector" badges sold at Midwestern county fairs. The other passengers were pouring back onto the car from either end. Here was the old couple from Peoria, dragging with much ado a whole fresh pineapple big as a half-bushel basket. Hansen and Lighton, their heads together. And Adele Mabie, her arms loaded.

It was evident that she had sought forgetfulness of the afternoon's tragedy in the purchase of a pair of deerskin sandals, a set of crudely carved doll furniture fastened to a sheet of cardboard, three packages of Mexican burned-milk candy in round tiers of bright red boxes, two riding crops of jointed cowhorn, and a pair of large fire-opal earrings. Behind her the alderman was loaded down with two *serapes,* great home-woven blankets in demoniac colors and designs.

Piper followed them back into the drawing room, closed the door. Mabie dropped his burdens, faced him. "Now what's all this about the tea glass and a shot and—"

"I'll tell you both," the inspector said. "Mrs. Mabie, have you any enemies?"

She almost dropped the doll furniture. "Any *what?*"

"Anyone who would like to kill you?"

For a moment there was a look in her eyes as if she had heard some obscene four-letter word. "To kill me?"

"That's what I said. Look back into your past!"

She smiled faintly. "Really, I'm afraid I haven't had a Past! Why, no, I can't think of anyone who would like to kill me. If it were the other way around..."

"I'm serious," Piper said. "Mrs. Mabie, you're a rich woman, aren't you?"

She nodded.

"And I'm her only heir," the alderman cut in swiftly. "If that's what you're driving at. Piper, are you crazy?"

Adele linked arms with her husband. "Go on, Mr. Piper."

"Well..." he hesitated. "Any cousins or anything like that who might resent your being left all this money?"

"But—but I wasn't! I mean, I made it. Don't you know, Inspector, that I once owned the biggest chain of beauty shops in the country? And that I sold out for one million dollars when I was thirty—well, a couple of years ago. Then I went around the world and came back to New York where I met Francis and one thing led to another—"

"You can ask anybody if we're not the perfect couple!" Mabie put in. "We get on like rye and ginger ale, don't we, dear?"

"I'm not accusing you," Piper said. It was his private opinion that Alderman Mabie would never murder for money, not when he could handle bridge and harbor contracts. A man sticks to his racket.

"No triangle stuff, then? No former sweetheart with a grudge?"

Mabie opened his mouth to speak, but Adele spoke first. "A woman making a million dollars has no time for anything else, Mr. Piper. It wasn't until I came back to New York and met my handsome rising politician that I realized I'd been missing something...so you see!" Suddenly her face changed, a little drawn. "You mean by all this that somebody is trying to kill me?"

Piper shrugged. "Your dressing case is usually unlocked, Mrs. Mabie?"

She nodded, wondering.

"One more question. What would a woman do who found a strange bottle of perfume in her luggage?" He looked at Mabie.

"Toss it out, of course."

But Adele cut in. "She would not! She'd sniff it to see if it was any good! No woman on earth could resist the temptation."

Piper nodded, pleased. "That's what you were meant to do, instead of the unlucky devil of a customs man—and one good sniff of prussic acid is all anybody needs. It's good-bye in any language."

Nobody said anything for a moment. Mrs. Mabie's pink fingertips toyed with the wrappings of the Mexican candy she had bought. "Somebody must hate me terribly," she said. "To go to all this trouble…"

"Looks that way," Piper agreed. He rose to go. "And you can't help me any, eh?"

Adele Mabie hesitated, looking intently at the tip of her shoe. "Why—why, no, I can't think of anyone. Unless—Francis, it couldn't be that girl, could—"

Piper intervened. "What girl?"

Adele said, "Oh, just a silly idiot of a maid in Laredo who tried to put an end-curl in my hair and did this!" She showed the inspector a singed strand and then tucked it back into her smooth coiffure.

"Yeah? What about this maid?"

Adele Mabie flashed a sidelong look. "Why, Mr. Piper! You ought to know, because I saw you trying to pump her, right outside this room. How Miss Dulcie Prothero got onto the train I haven't the slightest idea, but—"

"Wait a minute, wait a minute!" Piper put in. "That girl—why, she didn't look like a maid."

Adele laughed bitterly. "Well, she didn't *act* like a maid! It turned out that all the experience she talked about when she answered my ad in the New York paper for a traveling maid was a great big lie. She hadn't the slightest idea of what a lady's maid is supposed to do, not the slightest. Why, I found out—she actually admitted, mind you—that she'd been working in a soda fountain!"

"Where?" broke in the inspector, jubilant.

"Oh, Amsterdam and Seventy-second, or some terrible place on the West Side"—as if this were an especially sore point. "The fuss that girl made when I discharged her, after she ruined my hair! It seems that she had her little heart set on a trip to Mexico City, and the things she said!"

"Well, you did fire her a little roughly," put in Mabie. "And without any notice."

For an instant Adele's eyes blazed. "Yes, Francis, stand up for a pretty girl! I suppose I'm just a cruel and unreasonable woman because I wouldn't put up with being b-burned!"

The alderman moved toward her, but she shook her shoulders discouragingly. "That insolent, hotheaded little fool!"

"I'll be going," Piper said. "Got to question the boy who brought you that tea, though it's not likely we'll get anything out of him. You'd better take all the precautions you can from now on."

There was a strange, dazed look in Adele Mabie's eyes. "But, Inspector, if somebody on this train wants to kill me, what can you or anybody do?"

"I don't know," said Piper honestly. "But I'm going to do it."

He spent the next half-hour in trying to get something out of the porter and waiters, without any luck. Language difficulties aside, they seemed to view him as a meddlesome gringo to whom one should answer "¿Quién sabe?" and nothing else. But he did find out that Adele Mabie's dressing case had been used to prop open the door of the drawing room as they pulled out of Laredo station. Where anybody passing could see it, Piper reminded himself.

The train roared and rattled along its bumpy roadbed, climbing, dropping, winding on. The inspector, conscious of the fact that he had a lot of loose ends that needed tying or braiding or whatever it is that is done to loose ends, dropped into a chair at the rear of the combination club- and dining-car. Calling for a bottle of amber Moravia, he sipped it in silence.

Up ahead, in one of the dining booths, Hansen and Rollo Lighton were playing checkers on a table which had not yet been set with linen and silver for dinner. Their voices now and then drifted back in snatches.

They were still talking about the strike scheduled to darken the lights and stop the wheels of Mexico City on the morrow. And they seemed to be speaking as if that strike were distinctly an act of Providence. "It's an ill wind that can't blow something into the right pockets!" was a pet remark of Al Hansen's. He repeated it two or three times.

Hansen was looking at his watch. "Ought to be getting the message about now…" He mumbled something else indistinguishable.

"Don't worry about him," Lighton said. "Mike is an old hand at this sort of thing. When corners need cutting, he's the one to cut 'em. Been down there for ten years. I was with him when he promoted that Washington to Mexico City auto race a couple of years ago. Wrote the publicity. Mike Fitz made a good thing out of it too, believe me, even if the race never came off. His backer backed out on him."

Hansen said something about "more cash."

"Sure he will. He's a dependable guy, and this sort of thing is right up his alley. If you want something promoted—business or red-hot telephone numbers—he's the man. Ten to one he'll come through with some of his own money—and he's got plenty."

Far to the south, in the great city hung on a sky-high plateau, Mr. Michael Fitz was frying his supper, in the shape of a solitary egg and two strips of bacon, when the doorbell rang.

Fitz instantly closed the kitchenette door, crouched beside a chair in the square living room to put on his too-tight shoes. Then, after a quick and critical glance at the tanned handsome man with grayish waved hair who stared back at him from his pocket mirror, he answered the door.

It was only a messenger boy, after all. He took the telegram, automatically reached into his trouser pocket, and found there a solitary *tostón*. On second thought Mike Fitz left it there. It was no time for expensive habits.

The boy lingered hopefully for a moment, then started down the apartment stairs. He was almost to the bottom when a voice hailed him from above, in a jubilant summons. "Hey, *muchacho!*" And a silver *tostón* came flying down to tinkle on the bottom step.

Mike Fitz read the telegram again, read the official form which the company had added at the bottom. Merrily whistling the lilting notes of "*Adelante*, Maria Theresa," he waltzed into the kitchenette, turned off the electric stove, and threw the egg and bacon into the garbage pail.

He looked at his watch—or, rather, at the white place on his tanned wrist where his watch had been until last week. Then he shrugged. It was still early, plenty of time to get to the telegraph office, grab some chicken with rice at Prendes, and then...

"Even in Mexico City luck has to turn sometime!" he told himself gaily, as he put on his raincoat and fared forth onto the Paseo.

The train swung and swayed as it raced southward toward the ancient mountains of the Aztecs and the Mayas at the dizzy speed of thirty-some miles per hour. In the club/dining car a few passengers were already eating. Inspector Oscar Piper turned down a pressing invitation to join Mr. and Mrs. Ippwing in a slice of their pineapple. "Like nothing you ever tasted in your life, honestly!"

But he had other fish to fry. "Thanks just the same," he said and pushed on. A moment later he stood in the door of the first-class day coach, his mind made up as to what had to come next.

Here was another world, a scene of life and color entirely foreign to anything within his ken. At the farther end of the car three boys were softly harmonizing with violin, mouth organ and guitar. It was some wailing, melancholy song that must have come straight down from Granada and the Moors. Whole families shared basket dinners or supplies purchased from the train windows at Villaldama. Many already slept, curled two-deep in a section, wrapped in gay blankets. Some of the luggage in this car was of fine leather, some consisted of blanket rolls, bags tied with rope, paper sacks and wicker baskets. There were boxes and baskets of food and fruit scattered everywhere, here and there a white jar of *pulque*. A train butcher squatted in the aisle arranging his basket of cigars and candies, adding his voice to the music. There were smells of food and humanity accented by the terrific heat which poured through the open windows, and two or three babies were crying—quietly and apologetically, as Mexican babies cry.

Then, up toward the front of the car, Piper caught sight of the girl whom he had decided to confront, the fresh, impulsive girl in the yellow dress. She happened to be in close conversation with the blond youth in the beret, the boy whom Piper had seen enter the Pullman at Villaldama. "That girl surely gets around," the inspector said to himself.

He saw the young man rise, smiling broadly, and come swaying down the aisle. As they came face to face the youth stared at him appraisingly, then grinned. "Hello, Meester New York!" Then, as Piper grunted something, he passed on toward the diner.

The inspector leaped to some very interesting conclusions. If these two were mixed up together…

When in doubt, Oscar Piper had always said, plunge forward. He stepped around the train butcher, climbed over baggage and outstretched shoes, and finally planted himself firmly on the arm of the seat beside Miss Dulcie Prothero.

The girl rose to her feet suddenly, startled. But Piper held out thirty dollars, waving the money in her face like a flag. "You dashed off and forgot something," he reminded her. "Something of yours. Or is it?"

"I don't see…" She closed her mouth, accepted the money, and began to cram it automatically inside her handbag.

"Wait," said Oscar Piper. "You'd better count it." He reached suddenly forward with a clumsiness that was unusual for him, and somehow the bag, money and all, fell to the floor.

"Sorry!" he said, and they both knelt to pick up the scattered articles. The inspector noted that the bag, for all its capacity, was empty enough. It contained only a handkerchief, several pawn tickets, some small silver, a tarnished vanity case, and some tattered newspaper clippings. One was of a young man with large ears, wearing some sort of extremely unbecoming fancy dress. "That's funny," he observed conversationally. "I didn't know Clark Gable ever sang in *Carmen.*"

"It's not Clark Gable!" Dulcie told him, her voice trembling with anger. She hastily refolded the picture, tucked it away. "And now, if you don't mind…" She was waiting for him to go away, but he didn't go.

"Interesting country, Mexico," he observed, sitting down on the arm of the seat again.

"It was," Dulcie said. Some of the starch had gone out of her.

"Interesting customs," Piper went on. "Do you know that they don't have juries down here? Just a judge, and then afterward usually a firing squad." He shook his head. "It's a tough exit."

The forcefulness of his stirring period was somewhat marred by louder strains of music from up forward, as the trio broke into *"Rancho Grande."*

"Go on," Dulcie prompted him. The inspector frowned at her.

"Go on, make some more conversation," invited the girl. "You'll lead up to asking me to come back to dinner with you, and I'll say no." She looked at him appraisingly. "I even said no to the Gay Caballero in the beret, and his approach was much nicer than yours."

"I wasn't talking about dinner. I was talking about murder," the inspector corrected her bluntly.

She caught her breath.

"Murder of that customs man this afternoon," he went on. "Plus one or two more attempts. By the way, do you mind telling me what kind of perfume you use?"

"I don't use any right now!" she flared.

"Ever own any like this?" He showed her a glimpse.

"Oh, no! Never in my life!" gasped Dulcie Prothero, staring intently at the seat in front of her.

Piper nodded, stood up. "Funny you're so sure when I didn't show you the label," he said happily and stalked back through the car. Let her stew over that for a while. In the meantime…

Telegram from Inspector Oscar Piper to Miss Hildegarde Withers, 32 West Seventy-fourth Street, New York City, filed at Palo Blanco, province of Nuevo Leon, Republic of Mexico, at 7:40 CST:

NO FOOLING THIS LOOKS SERIOUS WIRE IMMEDIATELY INFORMATION DULCIE PROTHERO FORMERLY EMPLOYED SODA FOUNTAIN NEIGHBORHOOD AMSTERDAM 72ND STREET IF SODA FOUNTAIN IS IN DRUGSTORE DO THEY SELL POTASSIUM CYANIDE

OSCAR

Telegram from Miss Hildegarde Withers to Inspector Oscar Piper, Monterrey, Nuevo Leon, care Tren 40 Ferrocarriles Nacionales, filed New York City at 9:18 EST:

UPTOWN DRUGSTORE REPORTS PROTHERO GIRL QUIT WORK WEEK AGO WITHOUT NOTICE WAS GOOD AT HAM AND CHEESE SANDWICHES BUT HER BANANA SPLITS WERE TERRIBLE SHE SOUNDS LIKE NICE GIRL HAVE HEARD NAME SOMEWHERE YES DRUGSTORE KEEPS POTASSIUM CYANIDE BUT WOULDN'T SELL ME ANY THEIR POISON BOOK SHOWS NO SALES FOR FIVE MONTHS BUT THEY DO A GOOD BUSINESS IN ELIXIR DAMOUR AT FIFTY CENTS OR FREE WITH TWO DOLLAR JAR OF FRECKLE CREAM AM DYING OF CURIOSITY WHAT ARE YOU UP TO

HILDEGARDE

The train roared and rattled southward through a dusty desert. When Piper came into the diner he found that most of the tables were filled now. Hansen and the blue-chinned newspaperman were matching coins to see who would pay for their dinners and the ensuing beers. It was the little man in the cowboy hat who won, but it was a hollow victory. It developed that Rollo Lighton had left his money in the Pullman along with his coat and necktie.

They departed finally, and Oscar Piper leaned his elbows on the table in deep self-communion. Things were beginning to fit together. And Hildegarde Withers had always insisted that he could get nowhere without the machinery of Centre Street to help him! In his suitcase right now reposed her derisive going-away gifts to him—a magnifying glass and a set of false auburn whiskers. Well, they'd see who had the last laugh.

It was with a light heart that Oscar Piper beckoned to the waiter. And then he suddenly realized that, after all the efforts he had made to memorize the Spanish for ham and eggs, the words had slipped his mind.

He said it in English several times, in a loud voice. But the waiter only flinched. And then, just as it appeared that he would have either to send for the Pullman conductor or else go hungry, a pleasant voice spoke in his ear.

"May I service you, *señor*?

Without waiting for an answer, the tall blond youth sat down opposite him, bringing his cup of coffee. He told the waiter, in flowing Spanish, to produce instantly *huevos con jamón,* the *huevos fritos* on both sides. "Okay?"

"Thanks," said Piper grudgingly. "By the way"—he confronted his table mate—"how did you know I was from New York?"

The smile widened. "But your necktie!"

Piper stared down at the somewhat twisted and bedraggled cravat, genuinely pleased to think that there was something metropolitan about it. "The inside label, it says Epstein Kollege Klothes of Broadway," pointed out the younger man. So it did, but the inspector instantly doubted if it could have been seen in the one brief glance the youth had given him when they met in the coach ahead.

"Didn't doing so good with the *señorita*, eh?" his companion continued, as one man to another.

Piper stiffened, but the smile was an ingenuous one. "Only pretty girl on these train, hell-damn it," went on the youth, in tortured English which the inspector thought faintly reminiscent of some play he had once had to sit through, a play about a lovely Castilian girl and an American aviator and a bandit who was "the best damn caballero in all Meheeko."

"She didn't encouraging me so much neither," the youth went on. "But I know her name. Her name is Dulcie, and that means 'dessert' in my language."

The ham and eggs arrived. "You live here, then?" Piper asked.

"Allow me!" With a flourish the young man produced a narrow engraved card bearing the name *Señor* Julio Carlos Mendez S. "The initial is for Schley, my mother's name," he explained. "I use it to give a something at the end, you understand? From my German mother" I get my blondness. Everybody takes me for one American, I'll tell you. Because I speak such hell-damn good English. I pick that up in Tijuana when I used to go there for spending the money my papa make raising bulls for the bull ring. Me, I like very much Americans."

Piper introduced himself, without going into his official status. "¡*Mucho gusto, señor*!" They solemnly shook hands.

"I like girl Americans," Julio Carlos Mendez S. went on cheerily. "I like to learn slang from pretty *señoritas*. Not many pretty girls on these train, except Miss Dulcie and"—he added this most casually—

"the lady in our Pullman who make all the peddlers on the platform happy buying so many curios."

The inspector suddenly realized that the other was watching him covertly, waiting for an answer.

He nodded and went on eating.

Julio leaned confidentially closer. "I hear stories that there was this afternoon a misfortunate accident on this train. In that lady's room!"

The inspector cautiously admitted having heard a rumor or two.

"But you yourself were there, no? Or very soon afterward?"

"I was," admitted Piper. He wondered if this came under the head of idle curiosity, or if he was being cleverly pumped.

"What you think, eh? You think that poor Manuel Robles died by heart failure?"

So that was the customs man's name. Piper made a mental note. "I wouldn't know about that," he said.

Julio shrugged. "I happen to know the family of that poor young man. Very healthy family, that. They don't have heart failures. I never hear of one person in that family having heart failures."

"Then your idea is..." Piper broke out into the open.

Julio Mendez hesitated. Something was in his dark intent eyes, something hovered on the tip of his tongue. But he did not speak.

"You're not thinking of murder, are you?" the inspector pressed.

"I'm thinking," said Julio Mendez earnestly, "that it is sometimes better to let the police pulling their own irons out of the fire." And he rose and walked away.

"Funny his knowing the name of the customs man," Piper said to himself. Possibly either a dupe or an out-and-out accomplice. Because this seemed to be stacking up as a woman's murder. Poison, that was distinctly feminine. And all that roundabout stuff of the smashed tea glass. A man wouldn't have shot the air gun or whatever impelled that bullet at the glass. A man would have shot at the intended victim.

Well, the Mexican authorities could thresh that all out for themselves. No use trying to contact any of these jerkwater police chiefs along the way; Mexico City was the only place for a showdown. Thanks to Hildegarde, it was a pretty fair chain of circumstantial evidence that he had prepared to lay before them.

Oscar Piper counted off points, one, two, three, on his fingers. Not entirely complete as yet, but no bad holes in it. Not even Hildegarde Withers could knock holes in this setup. Though it was only fair, really, to let her in on the inside.

Taking some yellow blanks from the rack down the car, he returned to his table and settled down to the throes of composition. The next stop would be Saltillo in half an hour, and he could put it on the wire there. He began:

MURDER IS WHAT IT ADDS UP TO INNOCENT BY-STANDER DEAD THROUGH POISON PLANTED FOR ADELE MABIE IN PERFUME BOTTLE STOP YOUR IN-FORMATION SHOWS PERFUME STOCK OF DRUG-STORE WHERE PROTHERO GIRL WORKED BEFORE TAKING JOB WITH MABIES STOP AS DISCHARGED EMPLOYEE SHE HAD FAIR MOTIVE EXCELLENT OP-PORTUNITY STOP POLICE HERE HESITANT HAVE NO CHOICE BUT TO FORCE THEIR HANDS ON ARRIVAL MEXICO CITY THANKS

OSCAR

He read it over, frowned and shook his head. You never could tell when information would leak out. If there only were some possible code—but of course! He tore up the first message, dropped the scraps into his ashtray and began again, using a code that would be Greek to Mexicans and simplicity itself to a Manhattan schoolteacher.

URDERMAY...INNOCENT...YSTANDERBAY...OISONPAY

He wrote on and on, finishing as they drew into the station. It was only the work of a moment to cross the platform, file the message with the telegraph operator, and return to the train. As he walked back through the dining car he noticed with some surprise that while his ashtray still held the remains of his after-dinner cigar, the scraps of the first tele-gram he had written had completely disappeared.

IV

Things Over Mexico

A GREAT TIGER-STRIPED CAT welcomed Miss Hildegarde With-ers on the sidewalk outside the rooming house on Eighty-sixth Street, escorted her up the steps and waited patiently beside her while the schoolteacher rang the bell.

The cat obviously only wanted in, but Miss Withers considered its purring companionship as a good omen.

"Dulcie Prothero don't live here any more," the wrapper-clad land-lady advised her midnight caller. "She's gone to Mexico to seek her fortune."

"To do *what?*" Miss Withers blinked.

"To seek her fortune, I said," the woman repeated stoutly. The door was not very far open, but the tiger cat managed to parade through without any loss of dignity, and Miss Withers edged after it.

"I'm a sort of relative," she announced shamelessly. "I just wanted to find out some things about Dulcie."

The landlady pondered this. "An aunt from out of town, eh? Well, if you've come for her things I couldn't really let you have them with-out you pay me the two weeks rent she left owing," the woman con-tinued apologetically. "Left in a hurry, the child did. But she was al-ways in a hurry, always up to something. Such a one! And when I was her age I was such another, let me tell you!" The vast bosom sighed.

"So she rushed off to Mexico, eh? To make her fortune." Miss With-ers' equine visage wore a somewhat puzzled smile.

"She did that. Some sort of job came up overnight, and whist! she was gone. Says to me, 'Auntie Mac' (my name being Macafee) 'I'm going to Mexico, and I'm either coming back in such grand style that you won't know me or else I'm not coming back at all,' she says."

"It was sudden, then?"

"It was and it wasn't. Heaven knows she'd talked enough about Mexico and read all the books in the rental library. Being the kind of girl she was, a tomboy and a man-hater, I think foreign parts took the place in her mind that most girls give to being boy-crazy."

"She didn't leave because of a man, then?" Miss Withers wanted to know. "She wasn't running away?"

"Her?" Mrs. Macafee laughed. "She wouldn't run away from the divil himself if he stood in her way, and that's a fact. As soon slap your face as kiss you, and likely to do both in the space of five minutes. But I tell you, men were no more important in her life than—than nothing." Mrs. Macafee sighed again. "I wish I could say the same."

"I wonder if I could see her room?" the schoolteacher hinted. "I know it's late, but…"

"Her things are upstairs, two flights in front. I haven't even got around to packing them and putting them down cellar, with this hot weather and all. As I said, I shouldn't be turning them over to anybody until I get my two weeks' rent—eighteen dollars it is and fifty cents telephone—but if she wants them sent to her I would be the last person in the world to say no, having been young once and poor all my life..."

The cat escorted them up the stairs into a long narrow room which still held a trunk and other traces of its former occupant. There were no less than a dozen empty picture frames on the wall, a row of well-worn dresses in the closet, and one bureau drawer was full of recipes. "Not that the child ever cooked anything," Mrs. Macafee said. "But no magazine went out of this house without her bringing her little fingernail scissors—"

"You haven't a picture of her anywhere around?" Miss Withers asked.

"Only this!" The landlady laughed. "Isn't it a scream? Dulcie used to keep it around, she said, to keep from being vain."

It was a faded photograph of perhaps forty little boys and girls, none of them over ten or eleven. In the front row stood a plump and freckled child with fat legs. Mrs. Macafee indicated it with her thumb. "That's her, taken when she was in school. That's the schoolhouse steps they're on."

Miss Withers nodded, recognizing those steps. Mrs. Macafee was opening a shelf in the closet. "And here are her newspapers—subscribed she did to every sheet in Mexico. Not that she could read a word of the lingo, but she'd spend hours over them every time they arrived."

Miss Withers was slowly building up a picture of Dulcie Prothero, a picture composed of the drawer of recipes, the scent that clung to the top bureau drawers, the old class photograph...

Even the way the great tiger cat wandered purring happily through the place, as if a regular visitor there. Then there was the little bookshelf above the bed, with *His Monkey Wife, The Oxford Book of English Verse, Gulliver,* and *Modern Home Decor.*

Miss Withers took out her handbag. This sleuthing was getting to be an expensive avocation, what with fifty-word telegrams and back-rent bills to pay. Yet she felt a real and personal interest in this case.

"How much did you say was due you, Mrs. Macafee?"

The woman hesitated doubtfully. Then—"Now, did Dulcie really go and write you to send her things down there?"

Miss Withers had to admit that she had received no such message. "Then if you don't mind I'll keep them here for her," the landlady decided. "She'll pay me when she can, and if she came back and found her room changed or her things gone I know she'd feel bad. She'd probably skin me alive. She hasn't got red hair for nothing, that girl. I was just like her forty years ago," Mrs. Macafee added. "Only with less sense as regards men."

They were at the head of the stairs when Miss Withers remembered to ask one last question. "What sort of pictures did Dulcie have in those frames that are empty now? Of whom were they?"

Mrs. Macafee picked up the purring tiger cat, ruffled its broad striped face. "Oh yes, she did take those along. Moment I came into the room I knew that something was different."

"Were they movie stars?"

"You'd never guess," the landlady confided. "Not in a thousand years. No, they weren't movie stars nor painted pictures nor portraits of the boyfriends she had so little use for. They were pictures of cows!"

"Cows?" echoed Miss Hildegarde Withers weakly. "You said 'cows'?"

Mrs. Macafee nodded solemnly. "Cows, as God is my judge."

Train number forty of the Ferrocarriles Nacionales roared southward into the night, its cars darkened, its passengers presumably asleep. Inspector Oscar Piper had, in fact, seen most of them to bed.

The inspector was taking no chances in the interim before arriving at Mexico City and turning his Pandora's box of headaches over to the authorities there. He had been standing, smoking a good-night cigar, in the corridor, when the Mabies admitted the porter to make up the berths. "I'm so glad you're keeping an eye on things," Adele said. "I feel so safe now."

"Thanks," said the inspector. "But lock your door all the same."

He had watched from his vantage point in the corridor while the little world of Pullman car Elysian turned in. First to disappear behind the green curtains were the Ippwings. "Guess there's no chance of bandits or any more excitement tonight, Mother," the old man had decided. "Guess we'd better hit the hay. Tomorrow is another day."

Closely following had been the Mexican-American family with the children—a consul at New Orleans, somebody said, homeward bound for a vacation. Hansen and Lighton quit their checker game. Somewhere along the way the two broad-hipped and giggling *señoritas* had disembarked, but the Spanish gentleman with the handlebar mustaches was still in evidence, snoring thin patrician snores in his upper berth.

Julio Mendez S. (the S. to give a something at the end) was the last. He came into the Pullman shaking his head. "She won't do it," he told Piper.

"Who won't what?"

"Miss Prothero. She has damn small *dinero,* that charming one. I try to get her to take my berth. I tell her I don't mind sit up in the day coach. But she says she don't sleep anyway. So..." He shrugged and climbed into his berth along with the guitar and the two alligators.

The train roared and rattled, steadily climbing now, lurching in its rough roadbed. At length the weary inspector sought his berth, slipped off his coat, vest and shoes, and settled down to a night's vigil. He chewed on a dead cigar as insurance against sleep, stared out at the dark sky and darker hills, while little towns jerked by gray and ghostlike without the flicker of a single light.

Positive that he had not closed his eyes for a single moment, the inspector suddenly opened them very wide, sat up so suddenly that he banged his head against the upper berth. There was a hand reaching through the gap in the curtains, a brown clutching hand that moved toward his shoulder.

Oscar Piper seized it—and immediately found that he was holding the swarthy little porter in a grip of death. The little man blinked, squirmed and then produced a yellow envelope.

"Una mas telegrama, señor," he said, shaking his head wearily.

It was a telegram from New York City for the inspector, received at Carneros, province of Coahuila. It was a short and surprising telegram, which the recipient read three times with growing asperity.

OBVIOUSLY ON WRONG TRACK PLEASE DO NOTHING
UNTIL YOU HEAR FROM ME
                                        HILDEGARDE

And the train rolled interminably on, up the tilted narrowing plateau that lies between the two great mountain backbones of Mexico. It rolled on through the night, through the bright morning and the blazing white heat of the day.

Steadily the sun-bleached stations went by, the bare, crowded, identical railroad stations of Mexico.

At Jesus Maria, Rollo Lighton and Al Hansen got down from the train to purchase copies of the Mexico City newspapers, shook hands happily over the news therein displayed, and then spent most of the morning in deep conclave, making many figures on bits of paper.

As the train went through Villa Reyes Miss Dulcie Prothero, still in the yellow dress, came into the dining car. She pounced upon the newspapers which Lighton and Hansen had left on the table there. Unlike those two gentlemen, she was disturbed and disappointed at what she found in the Mexico City press, for she sipped unhappily at her cup of black coffee, refusing to chat with Mr. and Mrs. Marcus Ippwing across the aisle, although that cheery and birdlike old couple assured her that they had a daughter just her age back home in Peoria.

At Pena Prieta, fresh as a daisy, *Señor* Julio Carlos Mendez S. joined her without an invitation. Over the orange juice he told her the story of his life. Over his eggs *rancheros* they discovered that their favorite movie actor was Donald Duck. By the end of the last cup of coffee Dulcie Prothero laughed out loud.

At Rio Laja Mrs. Adele Mabie, wearing smoked goggles to protect her eyes from the bright blinding sun, was on the point of buying a magnificent green parrot when her husband cried warnings about psittacosis. She compromised by bringing back aboard the train a small round wicker basket containing, she announced with great éclat, a genuine baby spotted lizard. Inspector Oscar Piper, lurking watchfully in the background, refused to admire the lizard, saying that reptiles human and otherwise made him sick.

At Begona the Pullman conductor, mopping his pumpkin face, refused to hazard a suggestion as to what baby lizards should be fed.

At Escobedo Alderman Francis Mabie became a kibitzer at the Lighton-Hansen checker game, intimating that he was no longer able to remain in the drawing room and listen to Julio Mendez teach Adele the interminable words of the song "Adelita," to the accompaniment of his guitar.

At Queretaro Adele Mabie rushed out onto the platform to buy a garnet necklace, a riding whip, and a large gourd tray three feet across, painted in violent colors.

At Cambalache Julio Mendez bought ice-cream cones for Mr. and Mrs. Ippwing. There was no telegram from New York for the inspector.

At St. José de Atlan there was no telegram for the inspector.

At Teocalco there were three sets of musicians, a juggler, a fortune teller, and eight beggars on the platform, but there was no telegram for the inspector.

At Coyotepec Oscar Piper glanced at a crinkled newspaper in the dining car and saw there amid gray lines of unintelligible Spanish the strange face of a young man pictured on a hospital cot. Unacquainted with the gentle Mexican interest in the appearance of corpses in the day's news, it came as something of a shock to him to realize that this young man was dead. The name beneath the picture was "Manuel Robles."

"That settles it!" he said savagely.

At Lecheria he took the bull by the horns and sent a telegram to the *Jefe de Policía,* Mexico, D.F. It was a crisp and definite message, indicating that immediately upon arrival he wished to turn over to agents of the department of public safety proof that the death at Nuevo Laredo of customs examiner Manuel Robles yesterday was not a natural death, together with party indicated as responsible for same.

At Tacubaya, fifteen minutes out of the capital, five faintly harried-looking men in plain clothes boarded the train and were taken by the conductor to the seat wherein Inspector Oscar Piper waited. One of them, it appeared, could speak English.

They were, he announced, *agentes de la Seguridad Publica.* And what was all this about?

The inspector, a little regretfully, named Miss Dulcie Prothero as suspect number one. He mentioned the possible motive for her having attacked her former employer, a grudge motive. He touched upon the suspicious actions of Julio Mendez. And he produced the bottle of Elixir d'Amour.

At last the *agentes* showed real interest. They seemed to have no doubt at all of the identity of that faint bittersweet odor of almonds which the perfume had half concealed. They took the bottle, studied it gingerly and with great respect.

"One of your suspects is in the day coach," Piper said. "The other— and I'd give him a good going-over—must be up there with the girl, because he ducked out of this car as you came in."

They translated for each other, made copious notes. And then, as the train pulled into the Mexico City station, it was requested of the inspector that he produce his credentials.

"Gladly," he said. From his coat pocket he took a large envelope, well stuffed. But when he saw that it was stuffed with a folded railway time-table instead of his pink tourist card, instead of the splendid letter from the Mexican consul in New York which commended him to the civil and military authorities of the Republic, instead of his police identification card, his letter of introduction to the *jefe* from the commissioner of New York—when he saw that this sheaf of invaluable impedimenta was gone, the inspector murmured words and phrases quite untranslatable.

He felt in his vest pocket with anxious fingers, but there was no gold badge where it should have been. Billfold, American and Mexican money, silver, his watch—all were intact. But he had not the faintest proof of his identity. The train was coming to a stop now.

The *agentes* drew closer, conferring in liquid Spanish which he could not understand. They were suddenly very grave, very stiff and distant. Perhaps if the gentleman would accompany them… One motioned toward the front of the car.

Piper went up the aisle. And then his companions started down the steps toward the platform instead of going toward the girl in the day coach. They waited for him to advance.

He twisted his arm away. "What in hell…"

"A few minoots, *señor*, and no doubt everything can be explained," said the agente.

"What? Do you know what you're talking about?"

"But yes, *señor*. Possession of poison by an alien, concealment of evidence for twenty-four hours, lack of the required tourist card…"

Even then it might have been smoothed over somehow had not the inspector quite lost his temper and taken a poke at the nearest of the bland, anunderstanding faces. Before he could say "Jack Robinson," or anything more suitable to the occasion, Oscar Piper found himself whirling through the murky streets of Mexico City faster than even a taxi could have taken him, found himself whisked down the Calle Revillagigedo and put behind the bars of a large, dark, and extremely solid-looking cell.

He was still fuming there at eight o'clock next morning when he heard the sound of quick resolute footsteps in the corridor. Someone rapped sharply upon the cell bars, and the weary and disgusted inspector looked up to behold an apparition.

It was certainly a mirage, a fantasy born of his sickness of soul. There was no sense, no reason, in this sudden appearance of the visage of a plain, angular spinster, tinted a pale Nile green from the effects of twenty-four bumpy hours in the air.

Miss Hildegarde Withers peered at the three bedraggled and alcoholic *Indios* who were his cellmates. Then, as the inspector rose from his cot and came bewilderedly forward, she cleared her throat.

"Dr. Livingstone, I presume?"

V

Let the Buyer Beware

"I COULDN'T REMAIN in New York and let you railroad Dulcie Prothero into a Mexican jail," Miss Withers advised the inspector a few minutes later, thoughtfully poking her finger at a massive steel bar.

"Wait a minute!" gasped that gentleman. "Correct me if I'm wrong, but who's in this Mexican jail? I go to a lot of trouble to investigate a murder case, and these idiots turn the suspects loose and put the detective in the cell! Beat it while you can, Hildegarde, or they'll have you in here too. And we're crowded as it is."

"Don't be so subjective in your viewpoint," she chided him. "On the plane coming down here I got to thinking that the trouble with your theory is—"

"Hildegarde!" he broke in, speaking with a painful distinctness, "Hildegarde, please! Will you *do* something? For God's sake wire the commissioner in New York or get in touch with Washington or something. Haven't we got an ambassador in this country?"

Miss Withers smiled wryly. "From what I hear there are two schools of thought on that subject. It appears—"

"If I was a British subject they'd have a gunboat in the harbor inside of twenty-four hours," he declaimed.

But Miss Withers reminded him that Mexico City has no harbor. "I, Oscar, am your gunboat," she consoled him. "No remarks, please, about my superficial resemblance. But I have the matter well in hand. Unless I miss my guess this person coming down the corridor has the keys to your cell."

The jailer, a bowlegged man with sweeping mustachios, puttees and a denim jacket, unlocked the gate with much ceremony, stood back as the inspector stepped out, and then barred the way to the remaining prisoners.

"G'by, boys," the relieved Piper called back to them.

They responded with wide smiles and a united "*¡Adios, señor! Hasta luego!*"

"That means 'Until we meet again'," Miss Withers obligingly translated for him as they went on down the corridor.

"Yeah? Well, suppose you tell me what this means. Am I turned loose, or do they line me up against a brick wall?"

It turned out to be a little of both. A reception committee met them in the hall, just inside the main gate of the *Delegación*. The inspector found his hand shaken by a number of officials in business suits, by an officer or two in uniform. The spokesman, a worn, youngish man with a prematurely bald poll, introduced himself as no less than *Capitán* Raoul de Silva, aide and assistant to the lieutenant colonel of police. There were explanations and apologies.

"If we had but known, *señor!*" There was much shrugging of shoulders. "To know is to forgive, is it not? Never in the world would we have given the slightest inconvenience to a representative of the police force of Nueva York, a fellow warrior in the endless battle against the forces of the underworld. But how could our men know? By the way, it is that the *Señor* is feeling much better this morning, is it not?"

"Huh?" grunted Piper. "I wasn't..."

Miss Withers nudged him sharply in the back, as Captain de Silva sailed on. "I have the honor—we all have the honor—of extending to you the courtesy of the *ciudad!*" Piper found himself fingering a small card embossed with the red, white and green flag of the Republic. "If during his vacation in our midst the *Señor* finds his pleasures"—the spokesman cleared his throat—"finds his pleasures interfered with by overvigilant officers, he has only to display this card!"

"Thanks," Piper said. "But I don't see—"

"We also wish to extend to you, *señor*, the most cordial invitation to make the *jefatura* here your home-away-from-home while in our city. As we say in Spanish, my house is your house. The unfortunate episode of last night is forgotten." There was a chorus of smiles and nods from the other members of the committee.

"Forgotten, is it?" The inspector managed a faint, one-sided smile. "Thanks. And any time you boys come up to New York City we've got some things we can show you too. Make you right at home in the back room..." He winced again under Miss Withers' bony thumb.

Then, as a parting gift, Captain de Silva handed over a wad of papers which looked familiar to Piper. "All in order, *señor!*"

Oscar Piper ruffled them, then buttoned the identification papers carefully inside his coat. He was wearing a new, rather pleased expression. "So you did nab that girl, then? Found that I was right after all, didn't you? She *had* swiped my papers trying to avoid arrest? Get a confession yet?"

"A confession, *señor?*"

"You know," he insisted. "The girl I wanted picked up as a suspect in the murder case at Nuevo Laredo."

"That matter, *señor*, is being taken care of by the lieutenant colonel personally, who flew north yesterday to investigate. An arrest is expected at any moment."

Piper found himself being escorted to the street door. "Good morning to you, *señor*. Good morning, *señorita.*"

"Wait a minute," objected the inspector. "If they haven't picked up the Prothero girl, then how in blazes did they get my identification papers?"

"Shhh," Miss Withers counseled, hurrying him down the steps. "They got the papers from me."

"Now I know I'm nuts," said Oscar Piper, all resistance gone. "And that crack the guy made about my feeling better this morning? I suppose that was your work too?"

The schoolma'am nodded, led the way into a taxicab. "Yes, Oscar. Forgive me. But I thought they might be more apt to overlook your poking an officer in the eye if I insinuated that you were—er, just a teeny bit under the *influence* when you arrived on the train last night."

They rode on for some distance in comparative silence. Then the taxi came to a stop, remained there indefinitely.

"This isn't the Hotel Georges," Miss Withers accused the driver. "I distinctly told you to drive to the Hotel Georges!"

The *chofer* turned, said something about "*la huelga*," and shrugged. Then Miss Withers noticed that all other traffic was stopped. A parade came into view, several hundred extremely gay young men with bright placards and a few red flags. One group was doing its best to remember the words of the stirring "*Internacionale.*" Sellers of fruit juice and sliced pineapple were doing a rousing business by running along the sides of the marching ranks, and the general atmosphere was one of holiday.

"This can't be May Day!" the inspector ejaculated. "Oh, I know. It must be that strike they were talking about on the train. Looks more like a Boy Scout parade. Anyway, we might as well get out and walk."

There was no room to walk anywhere but in the street, and so it was that Miss Withers and Inspector Piper came marching into the heart of Mexico City on the fringe of a *Communista* demonstration.

Suddenly the street narrowed and changed its name, and Miss Withers peered into the doorway of a massive tile building. "It looks like a giftie shoppe combined with Grand Central," she observed, "but I smell coffee." They wandered through a silver shop, an art store, past counters filled with genuine "Made in Japan" Mexican curios, through a drugstore, a perfume shop, and a liquor counter, but finally they found themselves seated at a round table in the center of Pangborn's restaurant, the inspector mellowing a little under the prospect of eggs and coffee.

"Well, Hildegarde?" he faced her. "Glad you came. But why?"

"I," she said, "am Jack Dalton of the United States marines, galloping up at the last moment to save the day. Your telegram, Oscar! All about that little Prothero girl—fiddlesticks! I investigated farther than the drugstore. I went to her home. And any girl who can win the affections of a New York landlady—owing back rent too—has a noble nature. Besides—"

"Facts, Hildegarde, facts!" he demanded.

She still shook her head. "Besides, Oscar Piper, my real interest in the case is this. When I went to the Prothero girl's room I found a class photograph among her belongings—taken on the steps of Jefferson School. Shortly afterward I looked over my class records, and I find that Dulcie Prothero was for one year a pupil of mine—and an honor pupil too! So..."

He shook his head wonderingly. "So she couldn't do anything wrong ten or fifteen years later! But, anyway, now I see how you got her to hand over the papers she filched out of my pocket while I was sleeping in my berth."

"Correction, Oscar. Will you please get it out of your head that Dulcie Prothero stole your precious papers? I didn't get them from her. I haven't seen her. She isn't staying at the hotel, though almost everybody else is. Mr. Mabie, by the way, had your baggage sent there. But when I arrived from the airport this morning, looking for you, I came to the Georges. There was an envelope left at the desk in your name. Of course, everyone was talking about what had happened to you, so I immediately took the papers to the authorities."

"Left at the desk—for me?" Piper frowned. "But that could still have been the girl!"

"They were left by a man, a young and handsome man."

"Yeah? What was his name?"

"Heaven only knows," confessed Miss Withers. "I didn't see him, and the girl at the desk wouldn't tell me a thing when I tried to pump her. Only—"

"How do you know he was handsome, then?"

"Elementary, my dear Oscar. I knew that by the way the girl giggled when I asked her how he looked. But never mind that. If we want to solve this mystery it has to be done in some other way than by hounding a suspect. Why not concentrate on the intended victim? If this is really a plot to murder Mrs. Adele Mabie, why not watch her and nab the killer at the psychological moment?"

"Theories, Hildegarde!"

"Well, your much-vaunted facts and common sense didn't get you anywhere but in jail, did they? I tell you, the thing to do is to watch Adele Mabie like a hawk!"

Piper chuckled. "If you'll turn your hawk eye over your shoulder you'll see the lady in question coming in the door." It was Adele Mabie, carrying a small wicker basket hugged to her breast, and followed by her husband. They caught sight of the inspector, waved, and came threading their way through the maze of tables.

"Well, if it isn't the jailbird!" greeted Alderman Mabie.

"You poor man," said Adele. "What you must have gone through!"

The inspector invited them to sit down. "You've already met Miss Withers here, who has—"

"Been hearing the most exciting things about your weird adventures on the train!" the schoolteacher put in, neatly kicking the inspector under the table. You could trust him, she thought bitterly, to advertise her when she wanted to keep quiet, and to introduce her as his secretary when she wanted to appear in authority.

Alderman Francis Mabie picked up the menu, squinted at the long lists of American food with Spanish names. "What's good?"

"God knows," Piper said. "We haven't got a waitress yet." He snapped his fingers, but the impassive and bulging women with their huge trays went serenely by, like expresses past a local station.

There was a thin vinegar-blonde hostess leaning over a table near the door, practicing loud and inaccurate French with a customer who had finished his breakfast and opened his vest to display a bright blue silk shirt.

"Try the hostess," Miss Withers suggested. The inspector snapped his fingers again, but nothing happened. Miss Withers called out "Miss!" in a somewhat peremptory tone, and Adele Mabie, who had been around the world on the *Empress of Australia* and prided herself on Continental manners, clapped her hands.

The vinegar blonde looked up, smiled vaguely at them, and said

"Just a minute." Then she bent again over the man in the open vest.

"I don't care so much for myself," Adele said, "but I did want to ask her what I ought to order for a baby lizard." She pointed to the wicker basket. "I wonder if he would eat flies?"

There were plenty around, but much too lively to catch. "Why not try bread crumbs?" suggested Miss Withers helpfully, reaching to an adjoining table and purloining a plate of rolls.

Adele opened the basket gingerly, dropped in a little shower of bread crumbs. "He doesn't seem to care for them," she said. "I don't think he's doing at all well."

They all stared in the basket, watched a gaudy worm of a thing move sluggishly amid tattered and soggy banana leaves. The inspector made a wry face. "Hate all reptiles, and lizards are no exception. Not even cute sport-model lizards like that barber pole you've got."

"This lizard is exceptional, all the same," observed Miss Withers suddenly. She frowned, peered in the basket again. "Where're his legs?"

Adele could explain that. "It's a baby lizard—they don't grow legs until later."

Miss Withers' eyebrows went up. "You're thinking of tadpoles! Lizards are lizards—and that one has the wrong stripes!"

Adele Mabie tilted the basket, and suddenly her reptilian pet writhed up toward her face. She threw herself back, letting basket and all slide to the tiled floor. Her mouth opened to scream.

Out of the basket poured a thin streak of harsh bright colors no longer than a ruler and about as large around as a man's thumb. The thing writhed, twisted, slithered across the slippery tiles, its tiny evil head swaying from side to side with a satanic grace. They all watched, fascinated.

"Stand back!" cried a masculine voice behind them. "Look out!"

The table tipped over in the inspector's grasp, and he found Miss Withers clinging to him with a grip of death. From somewhere behind them Julio Mendez, the silly laughing youth in the blue beret, had materialized. He leaned down toward the thing on the floor, and the three shots from the immense pearl-handled automatic in his hand came so close together that they sounded like one.

The beautiful bright coils loosed, the colors began to fade. It was no wisp of incarnate evil now, but only a blasted, shredded bloody pulp. Julio put the gun carefully back into its holster. "Coral snake," he said. "Sorry for butting in, only coral snake very damn dangerous kinds of snakes!"

The restaurant was in something of an uproar. "Always knew I'd someday be glad for carrying these *pistola*," Julio Mendez said. "My friends they call me Tom Mix, but..."

And then the hostess appeared, out of breath and angry. "I'm coming, I'm coming!" she exploded. "I was on my way—no need to go causing such a fuss and shooting off guns and shouting!"

She fumbled for her pad and pencil, but at that moment she happened to look up and notice that Julio's bullets, ricocheting from the tile, had done considerable damage to a large mural painting of impossible peacocks on the farther wall. The young man cocked his eye at it. "Looks more better these way, I think," he told her frankly.

There was even something said about damages and calling the police, which made the inspector apprehensive as he foresaw another night in jail. But Julio gallantly took the arm of the vinegar-blonde hostess, led her away, and spoke soothingly in Spanish. A moment later he was back, smiling in triumph.

"Everything is okay," he announced. "But maybe we go now, eh?"

They came out to the street again. "Anyway, it's luck again for you, Mrs. Mabie," the inspector suggested. "The way it turned out."

"By the way," cut in Miss Hildegarde Withers, "just who was it that gave you the *baby lizard?*"

Adele, still a little white around the mouth, shook her head. "Nobody! I bought it at Rio Laja from a man on the platform."

"Oh yeah?" snapped the inspector. "Yeah?"

"Could be!" Julio Mendez came to her aid suddenly. He had seemingly taken the whole group under his protection. "Sometimes the *Indios* bring snakes up from the Gulf, from the swamps south of Tampico. They hope to sell to naturalists. But no *Indio* is going to mistaking a *culebra de coral* for a lizard, a harmless *lagartito*." Julio shook his head solemnly. "Not much!"

"But this one did!" Adele cried. "You must believe me!"

"Was it an Indian?" the schoolteacher asked.

"Why—why, I don't know! He had one of those dirty old blankets over his head. I didn't pay much attention to him. He just recited something about 'prettee leezard ten pesos.' "

"Then you couldn't swear that he wasn't an educated Mexican or an American playing a part?" Piper shot at her. Adele shook her head blankly, unable to swear to anything.

"My wife buys almost everything in sight," the alderman put in. "It's pretty obvious that somebody took a clever way of striking at her through the snake, either by dressing up in a serape or by hiring some Indian to lie about his wares."

Miss Withers nodded. "And your wife was supposed to get familiar with the thing, perhaps take it out of its basket, and..."

Adele seized her husband's arm. "I—I think I'll go back to the hotel room and lie down for a little."

"When you go to your room," Miss Withers said seriously, "don't forget to look under the bed. And if you take my advice you'll cut this visit to Mexico as short as you can. They have planes to New York in twenty-four hours, you know."

Adele Mabie nodded, murmuring, "Yes, but—"

She started to cross the street, left her husband for a moment to come back and say fervent words of thanks to young Julio Mendez. "You've saved my life," she told him.

Then Julio nodded, touched his beret, and said: "See you all some more, eh?" And he strode off down the street.

Miss Withers and the inspector stood alone on the sidewalk, alone except for half a hundred itinerant vendors of lottery tickets, blankets, carved boxes, handkerchiefs, and shoeshines. They spoke to each other in small shouts, due to the fact that the Avenue Madero was packed with taxicabs from sidewalk to sidewalk. No Mexican *chofer* has ever succeeded in making a red light turn green by hooting his horn at it, but it is not for want of trying.

"Well," said the inspector, "this means we can eliminate Julio, anyway. If he'd planted that snake he wouldn't have appeared and shot it."

"No? Don't be too quick in absolving that mysterious young man. Why was he hanging around anyway? Besides, he didn't appear until the snake had failed of its purpose and was running wild. It might be that the gay youth with the comic-opera accent didn't want *another* murder by accident!" Miss Withers shook her head. "On the other hand, wouldn't this seem to clear Dulcie Prothero? Because she couldn't disguise herself as an Indian, nor could she deal with the Indian snake seller. I learned from her landlady that Dulcie doesn't know a word of the language!"

They started to cross the street during a lull in traffic and then were suddenly cut off in midstream, dodging among the fenders of the massed cars. They had one intimate glimpse of a taxicab containing a pretty, obviously American girl. She was looking up into the eyes of a tall man, a man who had a beautiful tan face and above it a thick head of waved gray hair.

As the taxicab started to move away Miss Withers heard the girl's voice ring out during a second's hush in the din, heard her saying "… *pájaro en mano que ciento volando…*"

Oscar Piper stared after the slowly moving taxicab, on his face a most peculiar expression. Miss Withers had to half drag him to the safety of the curb. "Oscar! What is the matter?"

He turned, grinning from ear to ear. "Nothing, Hildegarde. Nothing at all. Only that pretty girl in the taxi, the one that was rattling off Spanish a mile a minute…"

"Well, what about her?"

"That," he said, "is your former pupil, Dulcie Prothero."

The schoolteacher's eyes widened. "She? As pretty as that, eh?" She nodded. "Dulcie would turn out just like that!" she said. "She'd be good at languages. She was good at everything except deportment."

"Anyway…" began the inspector. But Miss Withers was out of earshot.

VI

The Mountain That Smokes

"MAIL ISN'T IN YET!" snapped the woman behind the desk at the American consulate. She was a plump woman with streaked white hair, and looked rather like a character actress made up for a mother role, in costume and shoes that fit too tightly.

"I'm not expecting any mail," said Dulcie Prothero. "Can you tell me please how to find somebody? Somebody that's down in Mexico?"

"Look in the book," said the woman. She pointed with her pen toward a register on a table near the door. "All Americans are supposed to sign their names, but some don't."

Dulcie had already looked in the book in vain. "You see, I really must find this person …" she began again.

"Mail isn't in yet!" snapped the woman at a newcomer. It was a man, an exceptionally pleasant and well-dressed man with a beautiful tan and grayish wavy hair. He smiled down at Dulcie, small and lost looking, as she turned to go.

"Perhaps," said Mr. Michael Fitz pleasantly, "perhaps I'm the person you're looking for."

Dulcie looked at him, shook her head.

The Fitz smile was engaging. "Then perhaps I can be of help to you. It's a cinch that Old-Mother-East Wind won't. Here's my card—I'm something of a fixture down here in the American colony. Always finding apartments for somebody, or getting them out of a traffic ticket."

"My problem is more serious," said Dulcie politely. "Thank you, Mr. Fitz, but I'm afraid—"

"Wait," he said. "Do I look like the Big Bad Wolf?"

"N-no," she admitted.

"Well, then! We Americans must stick together. If you go running around the town, especially without knowing Spanish, you'll get into all sorts of trouble. I know everybody in the city, and all the angles and all the shortcuts. And I'm at your service."

"Well," Dulcie admitted, "I'm looking for a man."

"That ought to be easy—for you," he said jovially.

"A certain special man," she told him. "It's a long story..."

Mike Fitz offered his arm. "We have a proverb down here that says 'Long stories need long drinks!' Or at least a good lunch. I know a place not far from here, about five minutes in a taxi..."

He was very nice in the taxi, Dulcie found. Didn't even sit close to her, but chatted gaily and impersonally. "Teach me the Spanish for that proverb about the long stories," she begged him. He taught her that and several more. "A bird in the hand is worth a hundred flying," she repeated a moment later. "That's much nicer than the other way, about birds in the bushes!"

"It's true too," Michael Fitz said. But he didn't leer, not the slightest.

They inched down Madero in the midst of the late morning traffic, turned south for half a block, left the taxi.

"Oh, for goodness sake!" Dulcie said. Inside the door she was staring at the walls of the long darkish place, walls covered with anemic Harlequins and Pierrots and Pantaloons who seemed to be making merry with some very buxom and lightly clad ladies. "Are you sure this is a restaurant?" Dulcie said to her companion. "Looks like a bar..."

Fitz pouted. "Of course," he told her, "you can eat here if you insist. But I don't advise it. Always bad to eat on an empty stomach." He waved at the waiter, who ushered them into a red-leather booth. *"Dos* champagne cocktails." He gave her a long and interesting black cigarette which tasted, Dulcie thought, like the odor of burning leaves. Then he leaned upon his elbows, studying her white skin as if he wished to commit every soft brown freckle to memory. "Now then, drink your medicine and then tell your Uncle Mike all about it. You're looking for a man. *A young* man?"

"Yes," she answered quickly. "Younger than I. You see..." Mike Fitz listened, now and then ordering more cocktails.

"Waiter!" Fitz cried. The waiter was at the moment having his troubles in the next booth with an angular lady tourist who had obviously wandered into the Harlequin bar under the impression that it was a soda fountain, and who was demanding lemonade. "Lemonade with lemon, and not those nasty little green limes!"

Dulcie was talking, her eyes fixed across the shoulder of her companion on one of the disquieting frescoes. "Obviously, Grandfather found those four emeralds while he was on the sketching trip down here," she said dreamily. "They were all he left when he died—besides the pictures nobody would buy. And then on one of the sketches my—my brother and I found a title, *'El Cañon de las Esmeraldas'*!"

"The canyon of the emeralds, eh?"

"It was just a sort of smeary study of a rocky gorge with a few pine trees at the top, but in the background there was a mountain with snow on it."

"Not much to go by," Fitz pointed out. "Mexico has dozens."

"Yes, but this mountain had a wisp of smoke coming out of it! There aren't many volcanoes, are there? Anyway, my brother Bob thought he might be lucky enough to discover the place. He came down here—and when I'd sold all the emeralds but this little one"—Dulcie's eyes dropped to the clear green oblong set in the clip on her shoulder—"I decided to come down and look for him."

"You're afraid he didn't have any luck and couldn't face—"

"Oh no," she said. "I'm afraid he did find the canyon—and stayed. You see, Bobsie isn't to be trusted when there are women around. And that," concluded Dulcie Prothero, "is why I need help."

In spite of its white softness, Fitz's hand was surprisingly firm as he gripped hers across the table. "Count on me, all the way."

Dulcie noticed that he didn't let go of her hand, and that he was frowning a little, staring toward the entrance. "Someone I don't want you to meet," he explained quickly. "Couple of fourflushers I used to know. You can't trust all your countrymen down here, you know." He leaned farther into the booth and bent over Dulcie in an attitude indicative of deep absorption.

But she shook her head, and her lips noiselessly formed the word "Jiggers!"

Fitz turned and saw that two men had come up to the booth and were standing motionless. One was tall and gaunt and blue-chinned, the other was short and bulging beneath a big black Stetson. It was wonderful to see the expression of amazed and delighted surprise which came over the face of Mr. Michael Fitz. "Well, I'll be a horned toad!" he cried, waving hospitably toward the opposite seat. "Sit down, sit down! We'll drink to this. Meet a charming compatriot. The more the merrier, I always say."

There was a silence. "We've already met on the train," Dulcie said. "Mr. Hansen and Mr. Lighton, isn't it?"

They both said hello. "We've been looking for you, Mike," Hansen continued.

"In the Papillon and Mac's and the Cucaracha," Lighton added hoarsely.

"We're not drinking," Hansen said. He motioned.

Mike Fitz nodded. "Excuse me a *momentito,*" he asked Dulcie. "I'll be back in a second or two." He rose, slipped his hands companionably through the elbows of the two men, and they all walked back through the bar toward the *excusado,* disappearing around a corner.

Dulcie Prothero took out a powder puff, dabbed at the faint brown-gold specks along her nose. Then a shadow loomed beside her, a soft voice spoke in her ear.

"Am I protruding?"

It was no less than *Señor* Julio Mendez, sporting a malacca stick. He insinuated himself into the opposite seat, grinned amiably.

"Are you going to buy me a drink?" Dulcie demanded.

Julio edged toward her around the circular seat. Then he stopped suddenly. "I am not," said he. "Because you've been ditching 'em behind this cushion," he accused her. "It's all damp. And with cocktails at four *pesos* is that a nice kind of trick to play on an old friend of the family?"

"Mr. Fitz is not an old friend of the family!" Dulcie said.

Julio looked surprised. "I thought that that *caballero* is always an old friend of the family, any family."

"And if I want to ditch my drinks—"

"It's hokey-doke on me," he assured her. "Anyway, I have find you. Last night you slip away from the train without giving me your address in Mexico City."

Dulcie's smile denoted innocence. "It seemed to me that it was you who slipped away, about the time the police came on the train!"

"Well..." he began. Then suddenly, "How about ditching this Mr. Fitz and going places with me?"

"I—I can't. He's a very important man in the city, and he's going to help me. Maybe he'll give me a job to carry me until—until I can go back."

Julio Mendez almost choked.

"Well, he is! A very nice person, and he owns a brewery and a plantation and a gold mine! And he's got a beautiful apartment in the ritzy Principe building on the Paseo that he wants to show me!"

Julio was silent for a moment. "I would take you to Xochimilco," he said softly. "We'll ride in boats on the canal through the floating gardens of flowers, with *mariachis* following us playing old tunes. It is very, very romantic."

"I didn't come down here for— Sometimes I *hate* romance!" she said. Then she softened a little. "Tomorrow's Sunday," she hinted. "And if you wanted to pick me up at the Hotel Milano and take me to the bullfights..."

Mike Fitz walked past them, obliviously. He went to the door with the newspaperman and Hansen. He nodded very many times as the departing Hansen said "Tomorrow night, then—at the latest!"

Julio hadn't answered. Dulcie looked hurt. "But why the *Toreo?*" he finally asked. "There is so much of my country that is beautiful—the villages, and the road that runs to the craters of the Nevada de Toluca, and the *charros* in their gay costumes on fine 'Arab horses, and—"

"I think that bullfighting must be the most beautiful and thrilling spectacle in the world, and if you won't take me I'm sure Mr. Fitz will be glad to!"

"He certainly will!" cried that gentleman, as he came back into the booth. His glance at Julio was not especially warm.

"An old friend from the train," Dulcie said. After introductions there were perfunctory invitations to have a last drink and refusals of the same. Julio rose, yawned politely.

"One o'clock—*siesta* time," he observed. "See you some more."

Fitz and the girl moved after him, walking more slowly. The door closed behind them, and then suddenly it opened and they were back. The spinster in the next booth, having put aside the Spanish-Made-Easy with which she had been struggling, was about to leave. Her curiosity, however, got the better of her as she saw the girl and man pawing among the red-leather cushions of their booth, looking under the table...

"Lose something?" inquired Miss Hildegarde Withers. "Anything valuable?"

"Only an emerald pin!" cried Michael Fitz, red-faced from groping on hands and knees. "That's all!"

The lobby of the Hotel Georges is decorated in the prevailing fashion of the *ciudad* of Mexico, which denotes furniture of extreme geometrical angles, with much glass and metal. In the midst of this somewhat unreal grandeur sat Oscar Piper, his nose buried in a four-day-old copy of the New York *Times.* A small brown man was shining his shoes, in a fury of noise and effort.

"Getting prettied up, Oscar?" inquired Miss Hildegarde Withers as she approached from the dripping outdoors.

"Third time today," he confessed. "No sales resistance, and I don't know the Spanish for 'scram.' How's tricks with you?"

"Well, I—"

"Knew you wouldn't get anywhere dashing off after that taxi," he jeered. They both looked up as someone approached—a birdlike little old man closely followed by a birdlike little old lady.

"Oh, Inspector!"

Piper tried to stand up, to the discomfiture of the shoeshine expert. He introduced Miss Withers to Mr. and Mrs. Ippwing. "Of Peoria."

"Great place to come from," said Ippwing with a twinkle.

"And a great place to go back to," his wife added loyally.

"We were just at the desk, to mail a letter," Ippwing went on. "Had to write our invalid daughter back home all about the excitement on the train. We had a *murder* on the train!" he confided to Miss Withers.

The schoolteacher said fervently that she wished she had been there. "And it's not over and done with yet, if you ask me!" Mrs. Ippwing went on. "Because our room is near the Mabies' suite, and we heard them having a nice family argument over something. And just now—"

"Just now at the desk we heard the girl at the switchboard—lovely girl, speaks English just as good as you or me—and she was asking about plane reservations for Mr. and Mrs. Mabie!" Ippwing added.

"Running away!" was the little old lady's parting shot. And they went blithely out into the inevitable rain of a summer afternoon in Mexico.

"Looks like the Mabies are taking your advice," Piper said to the schoolteacher. She was playing an imaginary tune on the edge of the table.

"Oscar," she demanded, "what sort of a man is Alderman Mabie?"

"Francis?" Piper blinked. "Age about forty-five, fond of thick steaks and thin wheat cakes, a good district leader, but not any ball of fire. Thought he'd help himself by marrying money, but hurt himself because the boys think he's playing society. Plays a fair game of poker but overbets his hand and always stays in no matter what he is dealt."

"His mind, his emotions?"

"Reads Eddie Guest. Cheers when the band plays 'Dixie.' Wears a carnation on Mother's Day."

"Women?" pressed the schoolma'am.

"Not especially. Why should he? Married to a good-looking, not too smart woman with a million or so?" Piper shrugged. "He would inherit, of course, if anything happened. But he was frank about it."

"Which we could have found out for ourselves easily enough, so don't give him too much credit for frankness! You know, Oscar, once in a blue moon a murder *is* actually committed by the person who has the most to gain by it. Although I admit that poison in a perfume bottle, to say nothing of the fantastic business of the smashed tea glass and the snake, sounds like someone other than Mabie."

"Sounds like that merry redhead, though you're so set on the idea she's lily pure."

"I didn't say that," Miss Withers told him. "But I'll still give her high marks in composition. And I'll admit that Dulcie Prothero is not to be ignored in this case."

"You're telling me!" Piper sat up straight. "I wish to heaven I knew why Mabie slipped her that thirty dollars on the train."

"Well, why not ask him?"

Oscar Piper snorted. "I did! About half an hour ago, right here in the lobby. I covered it so he wouldn't know I saw him give it to her. Said something about her saying that he'd given her a loan. And what do you think he said?"

"No guessing games, please !"

"He said she was a liar and stalked out into the street!"

Night fell upon the ancient capital of the Huastecas, a swift gray twilight which swept over mountaintop and tower, skyscraper and park. The city faded away, merged into obscurity like an overexposed photograph. There were no lights, no lights anywhere except the feeble electric torches in the hands of the traffic policemen, the glaring eyes of the taxicabs. Even these lazy howling nuisances seemed abashed, swiftly decimated, as if frightened into their lairs by the grip of the all-pervading darkness.

"When they have a strike in Mexico, they have a strike!" said Miss Hildegarde Withers to herself as she stared down from the tiny balcony of her hotel room into the murky cavern that was Madero. She lighted the feeble taper which an apologetic hotel clerk had proffered her. Then she lifted the telephone and asked to be connected with the room of *Señor* Piper. There was no answer. "Please let me know the moment he comes in," she insisted.

She sat down with a book, but she could not read. Suddenly Miss Withers went out into the darkened hall and went up the stairs to 307, the room almost exactly above her own. Her knock was commanding.

"Yes?" said the surprised voice of Adele Mabie. She opened the door cautiously.

"I want to talk to you," began Miss Withers.

"Come in, come in—I'm all alone. Francis had a business appointment…"

The schoolteacher accepted a chair. "I hope you don't mind my interfering?"

"It's high time somebody interfered!" said Adele. "But why are you—What's happened?"

"Nothing," Miss Withers told her. "Nothing must. You remember my suggesting a while ago that you take a plane out of here as quickly as you could?"

Adele nodded. "My husband is trying to book passage on the next plane—"

"Don't do it! You mustn't take that plane. For your own safety you ought to stay here!"

For a long, long time Miss Withers was to remember the look which came over Adele's smooth, pretty face. It was a look of amazement, of shock, and of desperate relief.

"Thank you for the advice," she said.

"Then you're not going?"

Adele shook her head slowly. "I don't care what Francis or anybody says," she announced. "I'm not going. I never had the slightest intention of going. I'd die first!"

"We'll try to see that you don't," said Miss Hildegarde Withers. She started for the door, paused. "By the way—the question is a delicate one. But is there—has there been any friction in your family? Any difference of opinion?"

Adele looked amazed. "But of course not!"

"Positive? There was something said about it this afternoon."

A bewildered, hurt smile crossed Adele's face. "Why—why, of course, Francis *was* a little grumpy because I didn't want him to get those plane reservations. He is too sweet to stay angry, though. He went out and walked literally miles to get me some of the French liqueur chocolates I like, as a peace offering!" She indicated a neatly wrapped box on the writing desk. "Does that look as though there's anything wrong between my Francis and me?"

Miss Withers was forced to admit that it did not. And then the door suddenly opened, and Alderman Francis Mabie plunged into the room, dripping wet. His voice boomed out, "Adele, it seems that the whole deal has blown sky-high!" He was angry.

Then he saw Miss Withers. "Oh, hello."

"Still raining outside, I see?" she remarked conversationally. "Well, I must be running along."

Husband and wife were exchanging a wordless message, she noticed. Under cover of the comparative darkness of the candlelight she made a hasty exit, one hand concealing a small package against her side. Miss Hildegarde Withers was rather pleased with herself.

She was still pleased when, some time later, the inspector knocked at her door and entered, with his usual disregard for the stricter proprieties.

"Well, Oscar?"

He sank wearily into an easy chair. "No results. Hansen and Lighton spent the evening in a *cantina* down the street. The alderman joined them for a little while, but they're all back here and in their little beds by now."

"And Dulcie Prothero?" inquired the schoolteacher. She bustled around the room, lighting more candles and trying to make the place look as if it were inhabited.

"She went off somewhere with a man in a taxi—he fits your description of this Fitz," Piper admitted.

"She was dressed up."

"And that's the total of your evening's sleuthing?"

He nodded. "Except that twice I thought I saw that Mendez boy dodging around corners. Hasn't he got a home to go to? I don't shee why thash comish-opera idiot—"

"Oscar, will you please take your cigar out of your mouth when you speak?" she scolded from across the room.

"Cigarsh?" He swallowed. "I'm not smoking. It's this candy in the box. Not bad, not bad at all." He groped again on the table.

Miss Withers crossed the room in two strides, her face a mask of mingled horror and amusement. "Oscar Piper! That's not my candy. It's what Mabie brought to his wife. I stole it, to have it analyzed for poison!"

"Wha-what?" Oscar Piper choked, went pale around the lips. "It's certainly a hell of a time to tell a fellow!" And he went hastily out of the room.

It was hours later when Miss Withers finally locked her door, gave her hair its requisite hundred strokes with the brush, and snuffed the candles. There was no real reason to feel despondent, not yet. She was planning to follow her timeworn and time-tested practice of throwing a monkey wrench into the machinery and waiting for something to happen. "Catalytic agent" the inspector had called her, because she caused a chemical combination to form, usually an explosion. "Clear all wires— Catalytic Agent Five reporting," she murmured dreamily and went to sleep smiling.

She awoke with a start as something bumped against her bed, woke instantly and in full possession of her faculties.

"Stop where you are," she challenged the Stygian darkness, "or I'll blow you to smithereens!"

The schoolteacher fumbled for the bedside lamp, remembered suddenly that the electricity was off, and finally found a match.

She lighted it, and then let the menacing hairbrush fall from her hand. It was no longer necessary to pretend to be armed. The only intruder in her room was an inkwell, a heavy glass inkwell. Affixed to it by means of a rubber band was an oblong pamphlet which, Miss Hildegarde Withers soon ascertained, was a timetable of the *Ferrocarriles Nacionales.*

Frowning in honest bewilderment, she went swiftly to the open window, peered down at the dark and deserted street. Then, lighting another match, she noticed that on the timetable all northbound trains had been marked with suggestive red crayon.

VII

Miss Withers Sees Red

INSPECTOR OSCAR PIPER awoke suddenly from the troubled sleep which was always his lot in a strange bed. He yawned, scratched his neck, and blinked at the glorious sunshine which flooded his hotel room. The windows were twin pictures, watercolors of incredible blue sky, soft moist clouds, and a fine gray-yellow stone church tower in the distance.

Unfortunately it was not the mellow clang of the ancient church bells of Santa Veracruz which had awakened the grizzled police veteran but the overshrill screaming of a telephone placed on a table some few inches from his left ear. Wearily he picked it up, said "Hello?"

"Not dead yet?" came a brisk feminine voice.

"Huh?"

"The candy, you know," explained Miss Hildegarde Withers. "Any bad results?"

"Certainly not!" Then, with a rising wrath, "Did you have to go and wake me up just to ask foolish questions?"

"I thought it best, Oscar. The early bird, you know."

The inspector said petulantly that he didn't care for worms and never had. "But since there's no chance of any rest with you in town, I suppose I might as well get up. Meet you in the lobby in half an hour."

"Good!" said Miss Withers. "And I'll have something to open your eyes." Hanging up the receiver on this cryptic remark, she hurried out of her room, climbed one flight of stairs, and knocked at the door of 307.

Within all was silence, and she knocked again. And then the door was opened, but not by Adele Mabie.

She found herself staring closely into the face—much too closely, the thought struck her—of Alderman Francis Mabie. He was clothed in a greenish-yellow dressing gown, beneath which showed well-wrinkled lavender pajamas. Having as yet neither combed his sparse hair nor shaved, the alderman looked as villainous as a man can look. In one hand he gripped a tall highball.

Miss Withers sniffed disapprovingly. "Oh, I didn't mean to interrupt your *breakfast*." She looked past him. "I'd like to see your wife for a moment."

"Adele's gone out."

"Out? Out where—with whom?"

"She didn't say," Mabie admitted. "Shopping, I guess. She just got up early and went." Suddenly his eyes fell on the two-kilo box of Larin chocolates which Miss Withers held in her hand. "Oh, so *that's* where they went!"

She nodded, held it out to him. "Just my old kleptomania coming back on me," the schoolteacher told him. "I always repent afterward."

Mabie stepped backward, eying her dubiously. "Take it," Miss Withers said. He accepted it automatically, placed it on the little glass-topped writing desk across the room.

"Do you want to know why I really borrowed it last night?" She went on. "Or can you guess?"

It was evident that Mabie could guess.

"The police," Miss Withers said, "are only interested in murders after they happen. I would rather prevent one murder than solve a dozen." She walked toward the desk. "Do you mind if I leave a note for your wife, now I'm here?"

"Go ahead," he invited and sank into a modernistic armchair to nurse his drink.

The schoolteacher crossed the room, sat down at the tiny desk. There was a rack of hotel stationery, a long wooden pen with a rusty steel point. "No ink?" she asked casually.

"In the drawer," he suggested. There was a heavy glass inkwell in the desk drawer, half full. It was of a type, Miss Withers thought, which she had seen before. Concealing her disappointment as best she could, she scribbled rapidly.

"Just giving your wife some good advice," she explained, as she put the message in an envelope and sealed it.

"My wife needs some advice," Mabie said, with sudden feeling.

Miss Withers looked at him sideways. "Oh yes—a little family argument, wasn't it? Over whether it was best to stay and face this situation or take a plane?"

He was in a mood to talk. "Not at all! The argument was just the usual thing that married couples quarrel about."

Miss Withers leaped to the conclusion that she understood everything. She knew all about triangles and green-eyed monsters.

"The little Prothero girl?"

He shook his head blankly. "Only one thing worth quarreling over." He drained his drink, even smiled. "Know what it is? It's money!"

And now Miss Hildegarde Withers was surprised. "I thought—"

"You thought my wife had all the money in the world, almost? Well, she has. But the more you have the more you think about it. I've always looked on money just as—well, as chips in a game. She thinks it's the end and the beginning. And just because I take a little flyer—"

"By any chance did you fall for one of Mr. Hansen's schemes to sell baskets to the Indians or ship coal to Newcastle?" The alderman winced a little at this thrust.

"Nothing like that!" he retorted, beginning to freeze up. "Adele wouldn't have said anything if she wasn't upset over this being a human target all the time. It's enough to get on anyone's nerves. Ordinarily Adele is the most levelheaded person I know, and the shrewdest. But now..."

He crossed the room, took up a bottle and siphon. "This Mexican brandy isn't so bad with soda," he suggested. "Join me?"

"Not this early in the morning," Miss Withers declined, and then, both intrigued and disappointed at the results of her call, she took her departure.

Out in the hall she hesitated, put her eye shamelessly to the keyhole of the door she had just passed through. She could see nothing but a square of window. But her ears were excellent, and she had no difficulty whatever in hearing Francis Mabie as he tore open the sealed envelope—the envelope containing an extremely unimportant and improvised message—that Miss Withers had left for his wife.

Down in the lobby she found no trace of the inspector as yet, so she invested fifteen *centavos* in a copy of *Universal* and settled down with her pocket dictionary to translate the headlines.

But it developed that the lobby of the Hotel Georges was this morning no place for lounging. Trucks were backed up under the front canopy, several workmen in faded denim marched in and out bearing wrenches, bits of board, and measuring tape. New as she was to Mexico, the schoolteacher realized that it must have taken an earthquake or some similar cataclysm to bring out workmen on a Sunday morning.

The inspector finally joined her, his face well whittled from the combination of a razor with cold water. "This strike is getting on my nerves," he began. But the hotel manager approached, full of apologies. He was a bouncing, bulging man in a wing collar and looked, Miss Withers thought, like a cross between Wally Beery and Ramon Navarro.

"Ah, we have good news!" he announced, with a wide and toothy smile. "No more candles! No more cold water! Even if this strike goes on a week more, the Hotel Georges will from today have its own generator, its own lighting plant, at great expense. Tonight I promise lights, and hot water from seven until nine. Hotel Georges service!" And he hurried away to supervise the entrance of a large and unwieldy gasoline engine.

"Oscar!" began Miss Withers. "Has it occurred to you..."

He took her arm. "Breakfast first, clues afterward." They went out into the sun-flooded street. "We'll need our strength today."

Enjoying their breakfasts, this oddly assorted pair of detectives found, was easier said than done. In the first place it took even longer than usual to attract the attention of the vinegar blonde in Pangborn's and secure menus. The breakfasts, when they came, were sketchy and cold. The waitress mumbled, when complaints were made, that everything had to be carried down four flights of stairs from charcoal ovens improvised on the roof. "¡*La huelga, señor!*"

Then too, they saw where the bullet holes in the farther wall were visible, two staring black eyes. There seemed also to be a smeary stain on the tile floor where only yesterday a horrible blotch of color had died. The gaudy worm, the writhing snake with its rings of yellow and red and black...

As dessert Miss Withers handed to the inspector a railway timetable marked in commanding red crayon. "First blood, Oscar! Results!"

"I don't get it," he said.

"Well, I do. A delicate little hint to mind my own business and catch a train out of town. Which must mean that we are getting warm."

Piper conceded that. "But who do you suppose..."

"If we knew that, this case would be washed up," she told him. They came out into the street again. The sun was gone, and the Hotel Georges loomed against the sky, a sky now more slaty gray than blue. Great dark thunderheads massed from the south.

Miss Withers pointed up. "There's my window, the one where the curtain is blowing."

He squinted. "It proves one thing, anyway. You were right all along in eliminating the Prothero girl."

"Was I? Why?"

"No dame in God's world could throw hard enough and straight enough to toss a weight in that window from here," he pointed out. "That's two stories up."

Miss Withers agreed. "We can now eliminate everybody but Hansen and the alderman and Lighton and Mr. Ippwing and Julio Mendez and-and yourself."

Somewhere in the direction of the Alameda a crowd was gathering and a band was playing under the great elms. But Miss Withers at the moment felt no interest in civic affairs.

"One moment," she told the inspector. There was some building in progress on the corner of San Juan de Letran, and a pile of bricks stood invitingly near by alongside the boardings. "I'd like to make a harmless little experiment."

Before he could stop her the good lady seized a brickbat and poised herself beneath that high distant oblong which was her window. "I wonder, Oscar…"

But the experiment was nipped in the bud as a voice behind them spoke sharply. "No, lady!" They both turned to see a policeman, a very military and dapper policeman. Upon his right sleeve he wore tiny American, German and French flags as a sign that he was an accomplished linguist and thus received three *pesos* extra pay a day for his ability to speak to tourists in their own tongues.

"No, lady!" he repeated earnestly, taking the brickbat from her and tossing it back on the pile. "You ought to be ashamed of yourself, a fine lady like you—at this hour of the morning!"

His voice was thick with that persuasive, buttery tone which people save for naughty children, the insane, and alcoholics. But Miss Withers faced him, snapped: "I am not a typical American tourist, young man. And I am not under the influence of liquor."

Piper put in: "You ought to see that this lady isn't a night owl."

Swift comprehension dawned upon the face of the policeman. He looked from Miss Withers to the scene of the excitement in the Alameda, saw the red banners tossing against the green of the trees, heard the music of the "*Internacionale.*" "But of course," he said. "It is only a little demonstration, a protest against capitalist greed? The lady, she is sympathetic to Labor? A thousand pardons." With a wary and apologetic smile the officer withdrew, faded around the corner.

Miss Hildegarde Withers, whose mind was something of a single track, looked longingly at the pile of bricks, but the inspector took her arm firmly. "Come on, Emma Goldman," he advised her. "Let's get inside out of the Revolution."

They ascertained, by the simple expedient of inquiring of the pleasant young lady at the switchboard, that Adele Mabie had not yet returned.

"Oscar, I'm a little worried," Miss Withers announced. "I promised myself that I wasn't going to let that woman out of my sight if I could help it, and now she's running around the city alone."

"As long as she's alone," Piper pointed out dryly, "she'll be all right."

"You know what I mean," the schoolteacher said. "Anyway, I'm going to sit right down here and wait until she comes in. I have a very strong hunch that something is about to happen, and a stronger one that

I'm going—that we're going—to miss out on it.''

They sat down and busied themselves with ineffectual efforts to snub the swarms of shoeshine boys with their little boxes and their wide hopeful smiles.

"You know," Piper said ruefully, "at thirty *centavos* per shine this is running into money."

They waited and watched. At eleven o'clock the *chofer* of a taxicab entered, loaded down with parcels, boxes, an armful of bulky Tolucan baskets painted with *peones*, horses, cockfight scenes, cactus, and Mexican flags—all in bright yellows and reds and greens on a loud purple ground. He dumped them at the desk, mentioned a name, and departed.

"Adele is busy somewhere, we know that," Miss Withers pointed out.

At noon two small urchins appeared, bearing armfuls of red carnations, lilies, gladioli and water lilies. They also carried earthen pots, bright green pottery ware and glassware, and several *serapes* much brighter than anything seen heretofore.

"Adele Mabie has discovered the markets," Miss Withers deduced.

This interlude ended, the manager approached. "More Hotel Georges service," he told them gaily.

"We have tickets in the *primera filia* for the *Toreo*—first-row tickets. Better get yours while they last."

"Tickets?" Piper demanded. "For what?"

"Ah, for the bullfight, *señor*! Everybody goes to the *Toreo* on Sunday afternoon in Mexico."

"Everybody but us," Miss Withers told the man firmly.

Then she caught sight of a familiar gaunt figure at a writing desk across the lobby. She waved invitingly, and after a moment Rollo Lighton came cheerfully toward them, stuffing hotel stationery into his coat pocket.

"Didn't know you were living here too," Piper greeted him.

"I'm not," Lighton said. "You must come and see my little apartment sometime. Nothing grand, but furnished in some antiques that I've picked up here and there. I use it as my office too—where I do all my publicity work."

"Oh, you don't confine yourself to corresponding for newspapers?" Miss Withers asked him.

He shrugged. "I'm only hooked up with the New York *World,* the Chicago *Tribune,* the *Christian Science Monitor,* the Seattle *P.I.* and the Los Angeles *Examiner,"* he explained, with a wave of his thin arm.

"Doesn't keep me busy, not me. So I do booklets and ads and publicity. Just got a swell order too," he confided, sinking comfortably into a chair. "A rush order from the government!"

"Really!" said Miss Withers.

Lighton nodded. "Have to turn out a hundred publicity stories by ten o'clock tonight, all about the Laredo highway. For the news broadcasts that the government sends to American newspapers. Ought to bring tourists down, eh?" He looked inquiringly from Piper to Miss Withers. "Don't suppose either of you has a typewriter I could borrow? Mine is just temporarily out of service."

"I haven't a typewriter," Miss Withers assured him, "but I could lend you a fountain pen."

Much to her surprise Mr. Lighton took the pen. He lingered a moment. "I happen to know a wonderful little bar around the corner," he hinted hopefully. "Their brandy cocktails are famous all over the world. It's chock-full of atmosphere too—a place you really ought to see."

Nobody took him up on the suggestion, and he finally faded away. "You know, Oscar," Miss Withers said, "I don't like that man."

The inspector laughed and said that newspaper men were a funny lot.

"Yes," she agreed. "Particularly correspondents for the New York *World*. You wouldn't remember, but the *World* died four or five years ago—just about the time we were mixed up in that aquarium affair."

At that moment another *chofer* entered the lobby, bending under the weight of two wicker chairs and a card table with a leather top painted with *mescal* plant designs around the yellow circle of the Aztec calendar stone. "Adele is still going strong," Piper said.

This time there seemed to be a certain amount due on the purchases, and as the clerk seemed dubious about laying out the money, the alderman had to be telephoned. He came weaving down the stairs, walking with the exaggerated dignity of the half swozzled. Without protest Mabie paid for the C.O.D. He also paid for two bullfight tickets, leaving one encased in an envelope to be placed in the letter box in Adele's name.

"Tell Mrs. Mabie that I'm out doing a little shopping of my own," he said in a loud and petulant voice. "I'll meet her at the bull ring."

He went out of the hotel, with only a surly nod at the two watchers. "Ten to one he'll do his shopping at the Papillon bar," Piper said.

Miss Withers nodded, "Oscar, there's a man with something on his mind."

"Huh?" said Piper. "Guilty conscience, eh?"

She shook her head slowly. "I don't know. But *somebody* must have!" As she was about to continue, the Ippwings suddenly hove in sight, dressed in their Sunday best.

"Oh, I do hope it doesn't go and rain!" cried the little old lady, peering dubiously at the somewhat murky exterior. "I'll be so disappointed if they call off the bullfight. I know our daughter is counting on my writing a long, long letter all about it."

"Mr. Hemingway is our daughter's favorite author," Ippwing confessed. "Myself, I like biographies better."

"We have only five days in the city," Mrs. Ippwing continued. "These tours, you know!" She smiled at Miss Withers. "We've got to get through two frescoes and a church somehow this afternoon, besides the bullfight!" They trotted out.

It was true, the afternoon was drawing on. Suddenly Miss Withers arose. "Oscar, we must up and away."

He nodded. "If everybody's going to the bullfight, we might as well—"

"We might as well do nothing of the kind!" the schoolteacher snapped. "Don't you see—with everybody accounted for at the bullfight, this is a wonderful chance to do a little quiet research?"

"A little breaking and entering, you mean?" Oscar Piper brightened at the prospect of action.

Miss Withers was already hailing a *libre.* And she amazed the inspector by the address she gave.

"I thought you'd eliminated Dulcie!" he complained. "What use is it…" But they went to the Hotel Milano all the same.

It turned out to be a small hotel, an old and sad and dingy hotel stuck off and forgotten on a side street not far from where a great unfinished Arch of Triumph stood as a monument to the incurable optimism of some previous political administration.

The lobby was narrow and dark, and deserted besides. Piper rang the bell on the desk and finally a callow youth appeared, with a bottle of beer in one hand and a tortilla in the other.

They learned, after much travail with language difficulties, that the *Señorita* Prothero was registered in Room 23 but was out.

"Never mind," Miss Withers said confidently. "Have you any vacancies on that floor?" The youth gaped at her, open-mouthed. She tried again, calling upon her Spanish dictionary, and finally succeeded in making the lad understand that she wanted a single room.

Borrowing five *pesos* from the inspector, since lack of baggage indicated that payment in advance was required, she received a massive iron key at least four inches long. The number on it was twenty-eight.

"See you later, Oscar!" said Miss Withers meaningfully. The youth led her up one flight of stairs, indicated a door, and departed clutching his *tostón* tip.

Five minutes later the inspector, feeling a little foolish, came stealthily up the stairs and caught Miss Hildegarde Withers in the act of picking the lock of Room 23, making use of a hairpin. The door finally yielded, and they entered a small cubbyhole whose only window was a square of glass opening onto an airshaft.

"I still don't see why we're going to all this trouble," Piper complained. "I told you I'd come around to your idea that this Prothero girl is innocent."

"I'm just contrary enough," Miss Withers told him, "to keep on the opposite side from you. It will, I think, improve my average. Besides..." She put on her most cryptic expression.

"Besides what?"

"Besides, the real reason we're here is the geological fact that there are no emeralds in Mexico. Gold, yes. Silver, yes. Rubies of a sort, garnets and aquamarines—but no emeralds!"

With a deftness born of long experience the inspector took the lead in searching the little room. It was simple enough, for the place held only a bed, a dressing table, a chair, and a wardrobe. In one corner stood Dulcie's suitcase, empty.

The inspector worked slowly from corner to corner, from one piece of furniture to another, Miss Withers following closely after him. "Well, Oscar? What do you make of it? What story does this place tell to the trained observer?"

He frowned in his best professional manner. "The girl is broke, certainly, or she wouldn't have come to a hotel like this, where there isn't even a private bath. She's neat, because what clothes she has are all laid out nice and straight in the drawers. She's clean..." He pointed to an improvised clothesline stretched from bedpost to window, upon which depended four pairs of silk stockings plus other more intimate articles of feminine wear.

Miss Withers nodded. "Please go on!"

"Only one thing strikes me as out of place," he said. "That!" And he pointed to a grisly object which hung by a bright red ribbon from the top of the mirror frame. It was a dried, mummified triangle, oddly curved, and covered with bleached reddish hair. "Looks like an animal's ear," he concluded.

"Doesn't it! And I suppose that there's a dried toad plus some foul-smelling herbs and a wax image of Adele with a pin stuck through it, if we only can find them." The schoolteacher shook her head. "Dulcie will have to explain her quaint keepsake later. But right now, isn't there anything else?"

The inspector said he didn't see anything.

"On the dressing table, perhaps?" she hinted.

He still shook his head blankly, shook it even when the schoolteacher pointed to a half-empty jar of cream.

"You don't mean you think there's poison in that?" Piper demanded.

"Poison? Oh no. Just freckle cream. Elixir anti-freckle cream, sold in Longacre Square drugstores for two dollars…"

Suddenly he remembered her telegram. "With a fifty-cent bottle of Elixir d'Amour thrown in!" The inspector smacked one fist into his other palm. "Then the poison bottle *was* hers!"

Miss Hildegarde Withers looked very thoughtful. "This changes everything," she said. "Perhaps we'd better drop in at the bullfight after all."

"I told you so!" Oscar Piper insisted.

VIII

The Moment of Truth

THE Plaza de Toros was a great black pillbox against the sky, against a low, confining sky that shut away the usual view of the pure snowy peaks of Popocatepetl and Ixtaccihuatl. Yet to mountains who have looked down upon black obsidian knives exposing the blood and entrails of a thousand Aztec captives on one of Moctezuma's gala afternoons, it could have been no hardship to miss the death of six bulls.

A moist, malicious little wind, promising rain, whipped at Miss Withers' skirts as she followed the inspector through the outer gate. From inside the pillbox came the roar of the crowd, a vast and muffled yapping. Then suddenly, over everything, the piercing crystal-pure notes of a trumpet.

Ahead of them was the short flight of steps leading to one of the *sombra* entrances, but first they must run a long tawdry gauntlet—a gauntlet of screaming children offering long green strips of lottery tickets, vendors of blood-darkened souvenirs of other bullfights in the shape of darts and strips of torn cape and polished, mounted horn. There were flower sellers, grimacing beggars who waved their horrible deformities in the air, naked babies with outstretched palms, dogs that were only snarling hairy skeletons...

"Oh dear!" cried Miss Hildegarde Withers, gripping the inspector's arm irresolutely. But they went on, on to meet a man who was running down the steps toward them at a ridiculous sort of trot. It was Francis Mabie, his plumpness somehow deflated, and his face—usually a smooth expanse of pink flesh—now a sickly green tint. He was cold sober.

"Surely it's not over?" Miss Withers demanded of him. He paused for a moment, smiled feebly with pale gray lips.

"For me it is," said Mabie, and he plunged on past them. The man looked, Miss Withers thought, as if he had just seen an exceptionally grisly ghost. They both stared after him curiously for a moment and then went on. Through a gate, and then suddenly they found themselves standing on a ledge of concrete halfway up a curving slope of tiers, somewhat like two ants on the inner side of half an orange peel. Over the heads of the crowd they looked down upon a circular arena of bright smooth sand, a circular stage upon which two actors played.

There was a small roan bull and there was a boy in a bright-spangled gold jacket, and they faced each other in the exact center of the arena. The boy held a wisp of scarlet serge and a long thin sliver of curved steel, but the bull was watching only the rag.

There was no usher, and the numbers on the gray concrete seats were hard to find. "Let's just sit anywhere," the inspector said, putting his tissue-paper stubs away in his pocket.

Miss Withers glared at him. "We're not here to sit! We're here for a purpose!"

"To find the Prothero girl?" Piper said, with a sidelong glance.

"Something like that."

But they found almost everyone else first. The Ippwings were most easily located, the birdlike old couple vociferously applauding the young matador as he lured the bull into a series of charges, lifting the cloth at the last moment so that the animal slapped its horns vainly against air.

The old couple moved over hospitably. "Sit down, folks," cried Mr. Ippwing, "and Mother will read out of the guidebook so we'll know what it's all about."

"Not just now," Miss Withers regretted. The things she had to know weren't printed in the guidebooks. "Is anybody else here—anybody we know?" she asked.

"Why, let me see! Mr. Hansen is in the front row down there—right next to those two Mexican hussies that made eyes at Father when they came in. Oh yes, they did too, Marcus Ippwing. And we saw that red-headed Prothero girl a moment ago, going down the aisle with a man. And..." Mrs. Ippwing rose suddenly to her feet, screeched "Look out, son!" and subsided. "I thought the bull had him that time," she confessed. "Where was I?"

"We ran into that newspaperman, Lighton, or whatever his name is, outside the gate," Ippwing reminded her. "As we came in."

"Oh yes, and he said he'd left his billfold and all his money at home. He wanted to know if Father would buy a ticket for him, but—"

"But I've seen smooth talkers like him at the state fair," said Marcus Ippwing. "Mother thought I was impolite—"

"Many thanks," Miss Withers cut in. "You haven't seen Mrs. Mabie anywhere, then?"

Nobody had seen Adele Mabie. They moved on along the aisle, the inspector tripping from time to time as he turned to watch the events in the arena. Out there the atmosphere grew tenser, the bull flinging himself more furiously at the rag but slowing in the speed of his rushes. The boy grew more daring. Once he raised the sword to his eye level, but the crowd across the ring in the cheap *sol* seats cried "No" with one voice.

Protesting feebly, the inspector was dragged up and down the tiers of seats, through the crowd. They found many a familiar face as they climbed higher toward the roofed boxes and balcony which lined the upper rim of the pillbox. There was the manager of the Georges, the vinegar blonde from the restaurant, the pumpkin-faced Pullman conductor with his family. The inspector recognized, with a start, two *agentes de policía*. They were the two who had formed part of his reception committee at the train. One of them wore a fine purple eye.

Most surprising of all, the *agentes* were bending over a young man who sat alone in the last row under the shadow of the empty boxes overhead. They were speaking in excited Spanish accents to *Señor* Julio Mendez, who was equipped with the blue beret and the bright malacca stick but was without his accustomed air of jauntiness.

"*Sí, señores,*" Miss Withers heard him say. "*Sí.*"

Then suddenly Julio looked up with a bright welcoming smile. "My

American friends!" He rose, pushing aside the officers, and came toward the two intruders as if more than happy to be interrupted in his conference. The *agentes* looked at him queerly and then finally moved away.

Shaking hands with Miss Withers, young Julio looked over his shoulder, murmuring "Dumbsbells!" At her raised eyebrows he smiled widely and said, "Such police we are having in my country. Such meddlesome idiots! They can ask more questions than two men can answer."

Piper said, "Uh huh," a bit dubiously.

"But never mind them. Sit with me and I tell you about bullfights, eh? From up here we get a fine view, we see the fiesta complete with crowd and everything."

"That's what we came for—to see everything," Miss Withers admitted. They sat.

Far below them the spectacle in the arena was coming to its climax. The silver-jacketed subordinates with the cerise capes had been deploying the bull, but now the matador came forth again, jaunty as a fighting cock.

"We see how this one can kill," Julio explained. "All these boys today, they are *novilleros,* beginners."

"Amateur Hour, eh?" said the inspector. "An amateur fighter against a little bull, to make it even."

Julio laughed scornfully at that. "Even? Nothing, my friends, is even, is sporting, in all this. The bullfight is the assassination of a bull in the most possible of beautiful and dangerous methods. This young Perez has done well with cape and cloth, but it is the sword that counts."

Down in the arena the bull had stopped charging and now stood with head down, feet apart, eyes on the *muleta* which Perez held with his left hand, flicking it gently from side to side. As it moved the bull's head followed it—the entire scene in the slowest of slow motion.

Perez, the crowd hushed and waiting for him now, drew the thin sliver of sword again. Suddenly he poised himself like a ballet dancer and then ran toward the bull as it charged.

They seemed to meet head on, and Miss Withers wanted to close her eyes but could not. Then somehow the bull's horn swept past under the boy's spangled shoulder, the bull's head was buried in the folds of the *muleta*, and the sword began to disappear.

Inch by inch, as the young matador rose on slippered toes, the sword went into the humped shoulder just in front of the gay fluttering darts which hung there. The sword disappeared, down to the hilt.

For an instant bull and man stood linked in a strange embrace, as if a film had suddenly been stopped.

"'The Moment of Truth,' so the Spanish call it," Julio explained.

The bull plunged on, turned suddenly. Men ran out with pink capes, but the young matador waved them back, dancing like a madman in front of the bull. *Toro* braced himself to charge, shaking his head and planning just where to place the horn now that his tormentor was within reach. He lowered his head...

Then suddenly, wearily, he lay down on the sand and was still.

The crowd arose and cheered. There was a frantic snowstorm of handkerchiefs waving in the opposite stands. "They want the matador to have the ear of the bull as a reward," Julio explained, his voice suddenly gone dull.

"You're not applauding," Piper said, looking curious.

Julio shook his head. "One outgrows all this," he confessed. "My country will outgrow it soon. You see, my father raises bulls on a big *rancho* in Sonora. They are very brave and very stupid, no antagonists for a man."

"Then why," pressed Miss Withers, "are you here?"

He hesitated for a moment. "What else is there to do on Sunday afternoons?"

Down in the front row, far below them, they could see Al Hansen's great Stetson hat waving in the air.

A broad-beamed lady in purple, presumably one of the sirens who had smiled so fruitlessly upon Mr. Ippwing, stood beside him with her hand on his shoulder. As the jubilant matador trotted past on his circuit of the arena to receive the applause and bouquets and offerings of straw hats which came skimming down, the lady in purple screamed vociferous Spanish words of adoration and then tossed down a large long-heeled purple evening slipper.

As with the hats, it was picked up and tossed back by the ring followers. "Odd how women can worship bullfighters," Miss Withers remarked disapprovingly.

"Yeah, even the Prothero girl, it looks like," said Piper, pointing.

Away to the right in the very first row, almost against the high iron barrier dividing the *sombra* from the *sol*, stood Miss Dulcie Prothero, a small and at the moment a very noisy person.

"Yoo hoo!" she was crying.

The man who sat beside her, a tall, faintly amused man with beautiful gray temples, patted her shoulder. But it seemed that Dulcie would not sit down, in spite of what Mr. Michael Fitz said to her.

The matador looked up, smiled genially through the sweat that dripped from his low forehead, but she looked past him.

A dozen or so ring servants in blue uniforms with bright red jackets were running about in the arena, smoothing and spreading sand over the hoof marks and the bloodstains in preparation for the next bull. A trio of trotting mules came in, and their chain was hooked around the horns of the dead champion. *Toro* was dragged ingloriously across the ring.

"Wait!" Dulcie Prothero cried, but they did not wait. She sank slowly to her seat. Everyone else was sitting down, and the band broke into an old heartstirring tune.

"Listen," Julio said. "They play '*El Novillero*'—the song of the young bullfighter who goes out not knowing if as the price of his glory he pays with his life."

The last of the ring servants was running out with the brooms and shovels, and from high overhead a trumpet sounded its pure sweet summons to the next bull to come out and be killed. And then the crowd rose to its feet again.

Dulcie Prothero was stealing the show.

"She's jumped!" gasped Julio Mendez. "The crazy one!"

Suddenly the red head of Dulcie Prothero appeared down in the *callejón,* the narrow runway below the seats. She was waving, crying out something lost in the roar of the crowd. Across the ring, in a gateway next to where the dead bull had been dragged, a door was being unlatched.

The girl was leaning on the barrier itself, seeming about to mount it and dash out on the sands of the arena, armed only with a handbag and a scarf.

The bull, a great plunging beast, came flashing across the sand, but even as his eyes caught sight of the girl she was rudely snatched from his horizon. A swarm of gold-spangled *picadors*, silver-clad *peones*, sword carriers and water boys had seized ruthlessly upon Miss Dulcie Prothero and borne her out of sight.

Julio rose to his feet, as suddenly sat down. "They won't arrest her, probably," he said, half to himself. "And if they do—"

"And if they do I suppose you'll use your influence and have her set loose?" the inspector asked, with a touch of sarcasm.

Julio nodded. "One way or another," he said slowly.

"I don't see why she would want to do that," Piper went on.

"In this country," Julio explained, "we have what we call 'The Madness of the Bull Ring.' Every so often some spectator leaps the barrier and tries to play *torero*. It looks so easy."

"Fiddlesticks!" Miss Withers put in. "That girl wasn't trying to play bullfighter."

Julio didn't answer. "Anyway, since her escort sits there calmly and lets her get into troubles, we may as well do the same, no? For the time being, anyway. Watch this bull."

It was a bull to watch. He stood half again as high as the preceding sacrifice, this *toro*—a red-grayish beast with fine wide horns, deep chest, and a neck and shoulder humped high with power.

"A good bull," Julio Mendez said. "Maybe too good."

Already the impetuous *gringa* girl was forgotten, and all eyes were on the bull, who raced around the arena hooking at the capes which were being fluttered along the barrier.

"Perhaps it's just as well having Dulcie Prothero out of the way for a while," Miss Withers whispered to Piper. "I'd feel safer if several other people were locked up too."

A *peon* ran out suddenly, dodged as the bull charged him, and then dashed across the ring, trailing his wide cape slowly from side to side in front of the pursuing beast. Julio pointed to a pale young face above the farther barrier, a face beneath the odd flat cap of the matador. "That Nicanor, he is to kill this bull. He watches now to see which horn the bull favors—the one he must dodge."

The imminence of death rested so heavily upon the place that Miss Withers imagined she could smell and taste it. She had to keep reminding herself why they had come. "Oscar, do you see Mrs. Mabie anywhere?"

He grunted. "Bother that woman! Let her wait and get murdered after this is over."

She understood, somehow, how he felt. There was something atavistic in the appeal of this spectacle older than Rome or Byzantium. It was something which reached down into dark uncharted corners of the human soul, took command of the emotions.

Perspectives were all out of focus, murder and the possibilities of murder became dwarfed in importance. At any moment one expected to see the ring cleared for a battle royal between unicorns and lions, or to watch a row of oil-soaked Christians blazing merrily.

Nicanor, he of the glittering gold jacket and the white face, was in the arena now, for the preliminary work with the *capeta*. Feet together he stood, moving the cape with wrists and fingers so that it seemed to float in front of that charging mountain of flesh. Again…

There was a rumbling of thunder and the strong scent of moisture in the air. But the skies held off, as if waiting for the death of this bull among bulls. "I should think the bull would have sense enough to forget the cloth and go for the man!" Miss Withers said.

Julio Mendez smiled. "You think, lady, that they don't? The man tries to keep the bull's eye fixed, but there comes a day—and a bull…" He shrugged. "Bullfighters do not die in bed."

There was a trumpet call, and the bull, his wind back after a moment's rest, saw two more enemies come forth, in the shape of gaunt and ridiculous horses mounted by tremendous fat men with cockades on their hats and lances in their hands.

"*Los Rocinantes!*" howled the crowd delightedly.

"I—I think I'll go and look for Mrs. Mabie somewhere else," Miss Withers suggested, her voice strained, after the first charge of the bull against a horse.

There was thunder, and a few thick fat drops of rain came down. Instantly a surge of spectators rushed back to the shelter of the boxes and gallery; others, hardier, went forward to take their places.

And then suddenly there was Adele Mabie in the entrance gate, her arms loaded with a bundle.

"Mrs. Mabie!" shrieked Miss Withers.

The woman looked up, waved. "Have you seen my husband?" she cried.

"He went home—won't you sit with us?" the schoolteacher invited. "It's dry here."

Adele hesitated, shook her head. "I want to see!" she called. She signaled frantically to one of the umbrella vendors who were passing up and down crying "¡*Paraguas! Paraguas se vende!*"

They watched from their high but dry seats as Adele Mabie took an umbrella. Like all the others it was painted gaily to insure its being left behind at the end of the day. It was a bright umbrella, with white and red concentric circles around the top. She raised it jauntily and went forward, taking advantage of the departure of a large party of tourists from one of the front rows. They saw her plump herself down, saw the gay umbrella settle snugly over her shoulders.

"Good heavens!" gasped Miss Withers. "Do you see what I see?"

The inspector looked blank, but Julio slowly nodded. "That umbrella, it looks like a thing that you hit with the bow and arrow, eh? How do you say?"

" 'Target' is the word," Miss Withers told him. The bugle had just blown to signify that the affair of the horses was over, the bull having borne three times the punishment of the *picador*. The gaunt mounts were being hurried, limping, through the gates.

"Once *toro* has wet his horn, let the matador take care," Julio said.

Miss Withers was silent, being busy with the mental composition of a letter to the S.P.C.A., an organization of which she had for many years been a loyal and active member. She saw without any special attention that Al Hansen, hat and all, was hurrying up the steps and through the exit, leaving his newly acquired lady friend behind.

"And another *turista* bit the dust!" announced Julio, as if it gave him pleasure. "Sometimes we have as many as a dozen fainting in their seats."

Piper was counting on his fingers. "You ought to relax, Hildegarde," he said. "Our party of suspects is thinning out. First Mabie has a weak stomach, then the Prothero girl gets locked up or chucked out on her ear, now Al Hansen sneaks away—"

"And Mr. Lighton didn't seem to be able to get in at all, as far as we know," the schoolteacher added. "There's nobody left but the Ippwings—and us."

Julio cocked his head thoughtfully and said that they'd have to be watching each other, then. Which, Miss Withers thought, showed an odd perception on the part of the Gay Caballero.

For a moment the bull stood alone, master of the arena. And then his enemies returned.

A man in a silver jacket ran out onto the sand, holding a long slender *banderilla* in either hand, darts covered with twisted paper frills of black and gold. Bull and man converged, the one in silver swinging sidewise as they met, posing for an instant like a high diver or a fencer.

As they separated the man sprinted away, while the bull paused to hook fruitlessly at two stinging barbs that had entered his humped shoulder muscles. "*Mucho!*" roared the crowd, indicating approval.

Another man, another charge, and this time a pair of mauve and green darts dangled in the bull's hide. And a third man, who failed to plant one of his blue-gold darts, and who flung himself over the barrier only a split second before a half ton of infuriated beast struck head on against the heavy planking.

"Aw, he got away," said Piper, who was strictly rooting for the bull.

And now the trumpet sounded for the *faena,* the last act of the tragedy. "Nicanor has got to kill this bull now," Julio said.

The youth in the gold-embroidered jacket seemed in no hurry. He deliberated over swords, discarding one because it was too whippy and another because it was too stiff. He found fault with the *muletas* of soft scarlet serge, and when he finally decided upon one insisted that it be wetted so that it would hang more heavily against the breeze.

"Poor old bossy looks sort of peaceful now," the inspector said.

"He is tired from lifting horses, from chasing capes, and from the pikes and darts in his back," Julio admitted. "But now he is most dangerous, for the last affair has taught him defeat. He knows that this is to be fighting to the finish."

In spite of the breeze and the drizzle of rain there was a heavy thickish smell in the air, an ammoniacal smell mingled of blood and sweat and fear.

Julio consulted his watch. For some time, Miss Withers had noticed, he had been fidgeting like a schoolboy kept in at recess. Now he stood up. "Sorry I must tearing myself off," he explained. "But I have— I have a date with a *señorita.*"

He hurried off down the steps. "To keep a date with the *señorita,* eh?" said Miss Withers thoughtfully. "You know, that young lady of his needs a shave." She pointed.

On the exit platform below Julio Mendez was listening to questions from one of the *agentes*. He seemed to protest at something and then gave in with a shrug and went through the exit.

The inspector and Miss Withers looked at each other wonderingly. "Are the Mexican police investigating this case after all?" she mused. "Have they got something on the Gay Caballero?"

"Probably parked against a fireplug," Piper decided. Another spatter of rain swept over the place, heavy enough so that they watched the ensuing scene above a sea of umbrellas. The crowd was damp, uneasy and impatient, and across the ring in the ranks of the cheap *sol* seats some wag loudly inquired if the matador was waiting for the bull to drown in the rain.

The big clock over the Glaxo sign showed that three minutes of the allotted twelve were gone. But it was young Nicanor's sense of humor and not his nervousness which kept him back. The other novices, in fact, all the hangers-on in the runway, were still laughing at the spectacle of the young lady from *yanquilandia* who had leaped down from the front seats—with a display of silk stockings which was not bad, either—leaving her escort alone, high if not very dry.

Hence the point of Nicanor's joke. The crowd would appreciate it, the newspaper critics would certainly mention it among the bright spots of the afternoon. It was the sort of whimsy which makes a crowd follow an ambitious young bullfighter, gives him color.

Young Nicanor marched along the barrier, passed into the arena, and then, with a wary eye out for the bull in the distance, looked up at the front row of the audience.

"*Señor!*" cried the novice matador, waving to a handsome man who sat glumly in the front row, wrapped in a gabardine coat. Mr. Michael Fitz blinked as he was startled out of his apathy.

"To you, *señor!*" And Nicanor whipped off his funny little pancake of a hat, tossed it neatly up into the American's lap. "To you I dedicate this bull!" he cried in Spanish. "As solace for the loss of your *querida!*"

There was a pause, and then a ripple of half-friendly, half-jeering applause. Mike Fitz had no choice but to stand up, wave the hat. He was caught, he knew he was caught, for, according to the ancient tradition of the bull ring, that hat had to be thrown back to the triumphant matador full of bank notes when the bull was dead.

Now Nicanor left the barrier and ran stiff-legged across the damp sand of the arena. There was a faint "Ah" from the crowd, a shared sense that the curtain was going up on the last act. They had come to smell, to taste, the presence of death. Death was the invisible companion of every spectator, death mingled chummily with the young *toreros* in the runway, and death hovered over that loneliest of all, the red-gray bull.

Until today that bull had had no practice in fighting dismounted men. According to the theory of the bull ring he was to achieve that knowledge as he died.

He charged, and charged again, that *muleta*. He charged like an express train along a track, in the manner which offers the matador the finest opportunities in the world for stunting. Again and again Nicanor drew the bull, working now on his knees, now in sharp quick *pases naturales* which made the bull swing around himself in a quarter circle.

The crowd howled with delight, howled louder as young Nicanor, drunk with success, set out to emulate not only Belmonte but also Chaplin. He jeered at the bull, he hung a straw hat on one horn as it whirled past him.

"Disgusting," said Mrs. Ippwing. "To sit in the rain and watch clowning!" And she and her husband rose and departed. "We'll come back to Mexico in the wintertime when they have real Spanish fighters," she insisted.

Nicanor made two brilliant *pases de la muerte,* snatching the scarlet rag up and over the bull's back so that the great beast tried valiantly to do a back somersault. *Toro* was tiring now, head low enough so that the vital spot between his shoulders was exposed.

It was time, Nicanor knew, for the swift and beautiful thrust of the steel. He profiled himself, sighted along the sword held at eye level. His left arm made a cross under his right, shaking the scarlet rag enticingly alongside his knee where the bull's head must go by.

The photographers, perched in their tiny nests around the lip of the stands, had their lenses trained on him now, he knew. As the bull prepared for a last charge Nicanor saw nothing but those photographs.

He raised himself on his right tiptoe so that he could fall sidewise, gypsy fashion, against the bull. It was a stunt that one dared try only with a brave and stupid bull who charged *carril* fashion along a track. He took a short step backward, flapped the cloth.

The bull raised his tail and, faster than a horse can run, his head held beautifully low, came dashing to meet the thirsty blade. It was a work of art, as perfect as a Brancusi statue, as a demonstration in Euclid, as swift and sure and easy as Astaire in dancing shoes or Perry with a racquet. Perfect, only...

Only *Toro* raised his head.

Taunted, goaded, tortured, his tremendous strength and courage at naught, the bull had still progressed one step farther in his education than a wise matador would have permitted. He knew what the *muleta* was for and resisted the impulse of his kind to hook at the brilliant color. He tore his gaze from the cloth and came in at the man who mocked him with his head held high.

Nicanor went a dozen feet in the air, seemed to hang there as if suspended with wires. Without sword, without dignity.

When he came down there was the bull, in spite of those who plunged forward with capes. *Toro*, enjoying the fiesta for the first time, would not be drawn away. He caught Nicanor neatly on his other horn, wore him for a moment as he had been forced to wear the straw hat.

Then suddenly the bull was blinded by a cape and two men were running with the *novillero* in their arms, sprinting for the barrier.

"Definitely the bull's round," said Inspector Oscar Piper a little shakily. "By a technical K.O."

Miss Withers did not answer, being busy phrasing a fifty-word straight telegram to the S.P.C.A.

Adele Mabie came up the aisle below them, minus the umbrella. "I've had plenty!" she called up to them. Miss Withers and the inspector, by mutual agreement, left their sheltered seats and came down to her. Piper gallantly took her bulging shopping bag.

"There are two or three more bulls, but enough is enough," he said. "We'll share a taxi, eh?"

"What a place!" said Adele Mabie. "What people! I've had to change my seat three times because of gentlemen who wanted to keep me company. I'm sick of being rained on and pawed, and I don't care if it takes them all afternoon to kill that bull; I'm going home!"

Miss Withers suddenly halted, looked back. "You mean, the bull hasn't won? Don't they let him go?"

Adele said she'd always read that if one matador was hurt another had to take his place. Indeed, a boy even now was advancing cautiously out with *muleta* and sword to finish the gray-red bull, who had taken a last desperate stand, back to the wall, and refused to charge.

"The authorities ought to stop this!" Miss Withers insisted. And the authorities did—the very highest authorities. There was a burst of wind, a clap of thunder, and at last the long-impending rain came down like a solid curtain of water. And the bull went out of the ring alive, as one bull in a thousand goes, without stigma.

"This bag is getting heavy," the inspector said plaintively.

They moved painfully out in the rush of the hurrying crowd. "I know," Adele said. "It's got vases, and two sets of dishes, and a riding crop, and some bookends, and things."

Through the gauntlet of beggars and peddlers they went. "Just one second," Adele cried breathlessly and paid a *peso* for a pair of bright black and gold *banderillas*, their tips black with drying blood.

"Aren't they grisly things, though!" she said, as she tucked them into the shopping bag.

The crowd rushed past them, hurrying to get out of the downpour. Tourists with the inevitable cameras, barefooted *Indios*, grand *señoras* with french heels and daring, painted eyes, whole families of half-blooded *mestizos*...

The crowd rushed out of the pillbox. All but one man, that is. One man who sat with an umbrella over his shoulders, leaning on the railing where it met the high grille between *sol* and *sombra*, staring down dully at the empty arena as if still waiting for something to happen

It was the boy who kept Nicanor's swords and accouterments who finally remembered and came back along the passageway, stopping to look up at the lone remaining spectator. He held out his hand, a little shamefacedly. "¡*El sombrero, por favor*!" He called again, and then his voice died away to a whisper.

The bull dedicated to Mr. Michael Fitz had gone out of the arena alive, but Fitz himself had remained behind. He was no longer worrying about the necessity of filling the matador's hat with money. He was no longer worrying about anything, for from between the shoulders of his raincoat protruded the shaft of a pretty blue-gold *banderilla*.

IX

Who Lies Down with Dogs

"THAT ISN'T A WHIP, it's a club," Miss Withers observed absently, as she tried the whippiness of the heavy alligator-hide riding crop. She was helping Adele Mabie unpack her shopping bag back in the hotel suite, after a long taxi ride home from the bullfight, broken by a brief stop for supper at *La Cabana,* where the three of them had ventured upon enchiladas drenched with green-pepper sauce and goat's cheese, washed down with thick hot chocolate. (The inspector had gone out in search of sodium bicarbonate.)

"I think these blue-glass bowls are the best buy of the day," Adele said brightly. "I had so much fun at the markets that I almost missed the bullfight entirely. And do you know, the man asked ten *pesos*, and I know they're worth that, but I chiseled him down to three!"

To make room for the blue bowls she pushed aside a litter of other curios from the table. "I don't know what I'd do without the fun of shopping," Adele went on. "It makes me forget."

"You'd better not forget to be on your toes," Miss Withers warned her. "No more baby lizards, mind!"

"I won't buy so much as a kitten that's alive!" she promised.

"Even kittens," Miss Withers mused, "have been used as murder weapons. Their claws dipped in poison, so that the first time the new owner played with them he received a dozen tiny hypodermic injections—"

"Please!" Adele Mabie said, flushing. "Let's not talk any more about such things, not tonight. I'm getting so nervous, so awfully jumpy. Though there's probably no real cause for it now."

Miss Withers sniffed indignantly. "No cause! Perhaps my hunch about something happening this afternoon was wrong, but you mark my words…"

And at that moment there came Alderman Francis Mabie through the door, waving a newspaper. "An extra is out!" he announced, in a frightened, almost whinnying voice. "There's a—it seems to me—"

"I know, I know," Miss Withers said calmly. "A revolution in Spain, a heat wave in New York, President Roosevelt has been prevailed upon to make a speech on the radio, and…"

Her voice died to an amazed whisper as she translated the headlines of the extra edition *of El Grafico,* looked at the grisly photographs spread all over the front page.

"And—and the man who sat in front of you at the bullfight this afternoon has been murdered!" she concluded, facing Adele. There was a brittle silence, and then two blue bowls, worth ten *pesos* and bought for three, crashed to the floor and became worthless blue chips.

"A man named Michael Fitz —American citizen—mining and railway interests—member of American Club and Mexican Country Club—resident of Mexico City for the past eleven years—leaves a wife and one child in Cuernavaca."

"A wife!" Adele Mabie echoed. "Oh, how awful for her!" She stood above the wreckage of the bowls. "He—he didn't look like a man with a wife and a child."

"You saw him, then?" Miss Withers demanded.

"Of course! He was the man who came with the Prothero girl! I saw them in the row in front of me, and very good friends they seemed to be, until she jumped over the railing and deserted him."

"Listen here," the alderman broke in. "You don't think that this could have anything to do with what happened on the train and all? You don't mean that the mysterious murderer you've been talking about struck at Adele again—"

"And missed again?" Miss Withers nodded. "It looks exactly like that. The police won't see the connection, but I see it. Of course, every other possibility must be eliminated. Have you a telephone book?"

"What do you want a telephone book for?" began the alderman suspiciously, but Adele was already leading the schoolteacher into the bedroom. There, in a drawer of the bare little desk which stood before the window, was a telephone book. The address given for Mr. Michael Fitz (of Ericcson 4419) was on the Avenue Juarez, number sixty-two.

"I'll be seeing you later," Miss Withers told the two of them hastily and headed for the door. There she paused, shaking her finger warningly at Francis Mabie. "Mind, don't let your wife get out of your sight until I return—and don't let her stand in front of any windows!"

She paused in the hall before the inspector's door, her hand raised to knock. Then she thought better of it. After all, this was the sort of scouting expedition with which he had the least sympathy or approval. She hurried on down the stairs, out through the lobby, and soon was whirling through dark and dismal streets in a taxi.

It was only a *tostón* fare to number sixty-two on the Avenue Juarez, but since number sixty-two turned out to be a large and gaping building excavation, that was of little help. "Back to the hotel, lady?"

She nodded—and then remembered something she had overheard. It was the name of an apartment house—Principe! that was it.

"Somewhere on the Paseo Reforma," she said. "A new building."

"Yes, lady!" The driver nodded. "It is but three statues and a monument down the street. One *momentito* and we are there."

They turned left under the statue of a vast and well-fed horse bearing on its back the inevitable posing general, and then raced southwestward along what Miss Withers thought might well have been the most beautiful boulevard in the world if there had been any street lights to see it by. One statue, two, three statues—and a monument.

They drew up before the Edificio Principe, a small high building built in the style usually blamed upon the modern Germans, being all of concrete and glass and sharp angles. There was a red canopy over the door painted in geometric angles, and beneath that canopy, to strike the necessary note of contrast, sat an *Indio* doorman in filthy overalls. He was engaged with a mouth organ and a milk bottle full of something which did not smell to Miss Withers like milk. He put the bottle hastily behind him as she approached, but gave no other recognition of the fact that a visitor was passing the portals.

There was, of course, no directory of tenants in the lower hall, but Miss Withers climbed resolutely up the dark stairs, relying upon the help of the flashlight in the shape of a fountain pen which she always carried in her handbag. To her pleased surprise she found on the second floor landing that an engraved card had been pinned to a door by means of a thumbtack. "Michael D. Fitz—*experto en minerales y aciete.*"

In a flash she had whipped out her faithful hairpin, thanking heaven that Yale locks had not formed part of the modern influence in Mexico—and in a moment she was inside. The place smelled of stale tobacco, alcohol and old clothes. Then the ray of her flash outlined a squarish white room with one narrow window onto a court. To make up for the lack of windows, however, there were no less than four doors.

It would be hard, the schoolteacher decided, to get any real impression of the occupant of this room from its appearance. For pictures there were only two raffish framed drawings in red conté crayon clipped from *Esquire,* for furniture there was a day bed, a settee, a love seat, a glass-topped metal-legged table, and a chest of drawers bearing an American radio and a vase of roses whose petals had rained over everything. There was no chair, only one lamp, and not a book in the place. But there was a little commode which, judging by its stains, was used as a liquor cabinet.

Tiptoeing softly as she went—for Miss Withers had no intentions of arousing neighbors who might ask embarrassing questions—she tried the first door. It was a bath; new, gleaming and competent. The shelves of the cabinet, she noticed, held several lotions for restoring the color of hair, for waxing mustaches, various pills for the improvement of digestion, and every known preparation sold to conquer the morning-after feeling.

The cakes of soap were scented, the towels were unclean. There was a box of bobby pins on the edge of the bathtub and a tiny round container of blue eye shadow on the window ledge, over which Miss Withers puzzled somewhat.

She tried the next door and found it to be a closet, containing a goodly collection of masculine shoes, suits and the like. There was a set of muddy golf clubs in the corner, well rusted.

The next door brought her into a kitchenette, which was about as untidy and uninteresting as a man's kitchenette usually is. There was a half-plucked, scrawny-looking chicken lying on the table, a pot and knife beside it. The icebox held nothing but beer and charged water.

She looked at the chicken again, telling herself that it would have made a poor supper even had Michael Fitz lived to eat it. Then, more than a little uneasy in the glare of those blue-lidded, faintly reptilian eyes, she closed the kitchen door.

Now the fourth and last door—her last hope if she were to discover anything which might throw a light on the personality of the mysterious Don Juan with the gray temples who had lunched so cheerfully with Dulcie Prothero. Lunched on cocktails, if Miss Withers remembered correctly.

She opened the door and stopped as if she had been turned to marble. The room was dark, except for one flickering candle.

Sitting on the floor in front of an open bureau drawer, his arms full of framed and unframed photographs of women, was young Julio Mendez, wearing his beret and smoking a cigarette. He looked up, dropped the photographs, and then—it was something of a feat under the circumstances—he smiled his bright and cheerful smile.

"Well!" he cried. "Mees Withers, as I breathe and live!"

Her hand was in her handbag. "Don't you dare reach for your field-piece, young man! I am armed—and besides, the inspector is waiting for me down in the street." She faced him menacingly. "Just what are you doing here?"

"Me, I am waiting for a streets-car," said Julio sweetly. "And you?"

"I am snooping," Miss Withers informed him acidly. "I'm trying to find out if there is any connection between what happened on the Laredo train and what happened at the bullfight this afternoon. I forced my way into this place, I admit."

Julio arose. "You weren't afraid that maybe police would come sometime to search the rooms of the dead man?"

Miss Withers sniffed. "Not if they're as leisurely as everybody else in this country."

Julio grinned and nodded appreciatively. "Just what I'm thinking myself. You know," he continued thoughtfully, "it begins to look like we better lay our chips on the table, you and me. We are both after the same things—"

"Are we?"

He nodded. "You are one amateur detective, no? Trying to trap the murderer? Me—I am the same."

"You?" Miss Withers gasped. "You a detective?"

He shrugged. "Can I help it if I look like your Harold Teen in the fonny papers? I tell you, for this once I am trying to be a so-smart detective. Believe me, I don't come to Mexico City for fun. I don't take that train because I like to be with Americans. Not me. I take that train because I want to find the murderer of my friend. In this case everybody talk about poor Mrs. Mabie, nobody think about Manuel Robles, the young customs man. He don't die from heart trouble, not him. We both know there was poison in that perfume bottle, like your inspector is saying. So now—"

"So now you deduce that there is a connection between the two cases?" Miss Withers sat down on the edge of the bed somewhat warily.

Julio shrugged. "I am not to the point of deducing. It is all one puzzle. Only—both my friend Robles and this Fitz have one things in common, just one. They die in different places, different times, different weapons. Nothing to connect them—nothing but one thing. When they both kick the pail, as you say in your so-wonderful slang, they both happen by accident—maybe on purpose—to be very close to one charming lady."

"Go on," Miss Withers prompted. "Meaning?"

"Meaning nothing—except that you can bet you my life that being next to Mrs. Adele Mabie these days is one plenty unhealthy place to be!"

Miss Withers digested that and nodded. "I suppose," she suggested, "that you are about ready to denounce her to your friends in the police?"

The young Mexican looked up sharply. "Friends? In the police?" He laughed bitterly. "I have not one friend, not in the police. I tell you true. They are—how shall I say?—very dumb. They are also afraid of these case, because everybody have orders not to offend visitors to our country and scare other tourists away. No, what we do we do privately— about Mrs. Mabie or anybody else? What you think?"

"I think you're going great," the schoolteacher told him. "For a beginner, that is. And what conclusions did you draw from the photographs?" She pointed at the heap on the floor.

"I think maybe these Mike Fitz was a lady's man, a grand caballero," Julio said thoughtfully. "A what-you-call chaser."

Miss Withers murmured something about calling the kettle black.

"Oh—you mean me?" He shrugged. "Me, I chase one at a time. When I find the right one, then I stop chasing. But I think these man, he chases many, and afterward he likes to sit and look at the pictures, no?"

Miss Withers looked over the pile. "Recognize any of these?" But Julio shook his head.

"You didn't discover anything at all? If you're going to play detective, you must try to use your powers of observation. Think, now!"

Julio thought. "Maybe this might have somethings to do with something, you don't think?"

From his pocket he produced a folded sheet of notepaper. "I found this when I came in—somebody tucked it under the door, maybe."

Miss Withers took it, read the penciled scrawl out loud: *"Say, Mike, who do you think your kidding, the boys won't give a buck on this they say it's lousy glass, so here it is back, yours sincerely, Benny.' "*

"Folded up in the note when I pick it up," said Julio, "was this!"

And he showed the schoolteacher a smallish flat green stone which shimmered in the candlelight. It was a stone which she had seen before, seen when she peered over the top of a booth at a cocktail emporium on the preceding day. Then it had been part of a shoulder clip on a red-headed girl's dress.

"It's Dulcie Prothero's lost emerald!" the schoolteacher gasped. "She said—I heard her say—that her grandfather discovered a whole mine of the things somewhere down here near a smoking mountain."

Julio's expression changed at the name. "Dulcie Prothero!" he repeated. "What a girl! The sweetest and the prettiest and the fieriest and the—"

"The biggest liar in the Federal District," Miss Withers concluded sharply. "Because I happen to remember from my geology books that there aren't any emeralds produced in Mexico."

"I remember too," Julio said. "But *Señor* Fitz, he didn't."

"And he died without knowing," the schoolteacher went on. "He stole that girl's emerald—not knowing it was a glass heirloom—and he tried to have some friend of his get it turned into cash for him…"

Suddenly Miss Withers snapped her fingers. "Wait! Suppose the girl didn't *know* that her emerald was false? Suppose that she thought it was real, treasured it highly, and then found that a man she thought her friend had stolen it? Would she—could she…"

Julio shook his head. "Couldn't be. Miss Dulcie is not our man. I mean," he corrected, "she is not the one we look for."

For a beginner, Miss Withers thought, this young man was very opinionated. "Still coming back to Mrs. Mabie herself?" she asked.

Again the head shook. "No lady kills Michael Fitz, I know that. To stick a *banderilla* through a man's back, into his heart—to kill him instantly like that was done? She is not strong enough, a woman. I read all about it in what the police say to the newspapers."

"That is a big help …" began Miss Withers. Then she stopped speaking, put her hand warningly on the young man's arm. "Listen!" she gasped. "It may be the police!"

There was a loud pounding on the outer door, a hoarse masculine voice. "Come on, open up in there!"

"Not police," Julio whispered. "Too early for them, and they don't speaking English much."

More pounding on the door. "Open up, I tell you! You've had time enough."

"Maybe we better open, eh?" Julio said. "You don't break an egg without making any omelettes, yes?" And he opened the door.

Rollo Lighton blundered into the room. He blinked at the unexpected couple he saw before him. His tone softened. "Mike Fitz here?"

"Why, Mr. Lighton!" Miss Withers greeted him cordially. "I didn't expect to see you out. I thought you said that you'd be busy until all hours doing those hundred publicity stories for the government press bureau?"

Lighton stood there, swaying perceptibly, and blinked. "Oh, that was nothing," he bragged, almost giggling as he contemplated his own cleverness. "Easy enough to fool these greasers—just scribbled out ten stories and sent 'em to a stenographer. Told her to make ten copies of each story and shuffled 'em good! They'll never know the difference!"

He paused, sensing that there was disapproval in the faces of the two who were before him. "Well, it's all the time I can afford to give for such lousy pay! I had to put up the dough for my own expenses going up to Laredo and back, and now they only give me five *centavos* a word for news stories!" He sniffed. "Five lousy *centavos!*"

He stopped short, the mention of money bringing him back to the reason which had impelled him here. "Say, is Mike Fitz here, or has—has—"

"He's gone," Miss Withers said gently. "Can we be of any help?"

"Gone!" Lighton said miserably. He looked past them into the bedroom, shaking his head. "Gone…"

Slowly he sank onto the day bed, his gaunt frame suddenly boneless. There were tears in the corner of his bleary eyes. "It's just the luck I always had," he complained. "The others won't miss the money, but to me—"

"What others?" snapped Julio Mendez, trying his hand. But his eagerness was too evident. Lighton stared at him warily, shook his head.

"It doesn't matter now," he said dully. "I'll never get back to East Orange. I was going home with this money we were going to make. I was going to show them back home that I was a big shot."

"Why did Mr. Fitz take your money?" Miss Withers tried again.

But that was all there was, there wasn't any more. Rollo Lighton stood up painfully. "I'm going—going out and get crocked to the gills, do you hear me?" The tears were rolling down his gaunt blue cheeks. "That's all that's left to do."

He turned and went out through the door, and they heard his heavy uncertain tread going down the stairs.

Julio nodded sagely. "That one, he didn't know Fitz was dead."

"Yes? It looked like a pretty good performance, if you ask me," Miss Withers pronounced.

But the Gay Caballero was serious. "If that one had killed *Señor*

Fitz, he wouldn't have come here. Because usually the *agentes*, they search the rooms of a murdered man. Sometimes they even—how you say?—ambush the place? And when they find someone comes there, they ask plenty questions."

"In which case," said Miss Withers, "we had better be getting away while we can." Then she stopped. She led Julio to the kitchenette door, showed him the half-picked skinny fowl on the table. "If you're going to play detective, draw me a deduction from that!"

He frowned, so seriously that he was again comic. "It's only—only a fight rooster, what we use in cockfights in this country. I can tell that by his spurs."

Miss Withers nodded dubiously. "Is it a Mexican custom to kill and eat fighting cocks?"

Julio Mendez, hand on his heart, swore that in all his life he had never eaten a fighting rooster and never wanted to try.

And that was that. "You run on ahead," the schoolteacher told him, "and if you see any police hanging around downstairs whistle three times. I'm going to use this telephone to make a call to Mr. Piper."

Julio's eyes took on a wicked glint. "But I thought you said that that gentleman, he is waiting for you downstairs?"

She sniffed. "Never you mind, young man. How was I to know that you were a fellow sleuth and not—something else? Besides, I've been around liars so much lately that I'm beginning to catch the habit, to my shame and sorrow."

"In this country," Julio admired her dreamily, "we have some very fine proverbs. We have one that goes 'He who lies down with dogs gets up with fleas!' " He waved his hand blithely, went out of the door.

Miss Hildegarde Withers stared after him, sniffed, and then made certain that he was really gone and not lurking in the hallway. She returned to the telephone and dialed a number. Finally she was connected with the clerk at the Hotel Georges.

"I wish to speak to Mr. Piper, please," she said. "Right away, it's very important."

"The *Señor* Piper, he has gone away with the police," the operator advised her.

"Really? Then please connect me with Mrs. Mabie."

"The *Señora* Mabie, she has gone to the hospital, the Methodist Hospital!"

X

Perchance to Dream

MISS HILDEGARDE WITHERS had never seen a Mexican hospital. Nor had she ever seen a hospital lighted with candles and farm lanterns. The general effect was distinctly weird.

The smell was reassuring, however—being that mingled odor of iodoform, ether and soap which clings to every hospital in the world. Shapes in white moved vaguely up and down on mysterious errands of their own.

She had great difficulty in finding anyone who could understand a word of English, even though this was supposed to be an American hospital. She had greater difficulty in getting directions.

"But you have a patient named Mabie here, I know you have!" she insisted.

And finally an orderly was dispatched to lead her up the flights of stairs, deposit her before a door. "*Aquí!*" he said and left.

Gingerly Miss Withers opened the door of the hospital room. One faint candle flickered on a bureau, and there was the inevitable high iron bed, like a catafalque, with its motionless white burden.

The schoolteacher tiptoed into the room. And then a voice spoke in her ear, making her jump half out of her skin. "Oh, thank you for coming!" It was Adele Mabie.

Moreover, it was Adele Mabie sitting in a rocking chair and smoking a cigarette, the glow of health on her cheek.

Miss Withers shook her head. "But I understood…" She stopped. "Who is that on the bed, then?"

"Have a look." Adele lifted the candle, and the schoolteacher looked down at the marble white face of Dulcie Prothero.

"Why—the child looks dead!"

Adele smiled. "She's still unconscious. But it's only a mild concussion, the doctors said." She put back the candle. "It's all right to talk if we keep our voices low," she said.

"But how—what happened? Was she attacked, or did she attempt suicide, or…"

Adele shook her head. "She just walked in front of a taxi half an hour ago—up on Violetta Street, in the very worst part of town."

"Hit-and-run driver?" Miss Withers hazarded, looking grim

"No, lucky for her. The man picked her up and rushed her here. Said it wasn't his fault, that she just stepped off the curb from behind a parked car, as if she were walking in a dream. They found her tourist card, giving my name as employer, and traced me from that. So I came— at a time like this there's nothing else one can do, is there?"

"Don't apologize, don't apologize," Miss Withers told her. "What can we do?"

"Just wait," Adele said. "They are short of nurses, and I said I'd stay until they found one. She may come to any minute—lucky that the child has such a thick head of hair. She'll have a headache tomorrow, that's all."

She went to the bed, lifted the limp wrist, and felt the pulse. "This isn't much different from beauty parlor operating," Adele said. "Which is where I got my start, you know."

The girl on the bed moaned a little. "I feel rather responsible for this girl," Adele went on. "She was so desperately anxious to get down here to Mexico City, and everything seems to have gone so terribly wrong for her."

The girl on the bed was moaning, muttering. There were a few words that were intelligible.

"Perhaps we ought to call the doctor," Miss Withers suggested. But when he came, the black-haired dapper young man expressed himself as completely satisfied with the patient's condition. Miss Withers found that he had taken his medical degree at Harvard, and she relaxed part of her vigilance.

"She's all right," said the *médico*. "If she hadn't been brought in here by the scared *chofer* she could have gone home. She'll come out of it slowly."

"But this babbling, Doctor?" Adele said worriedly.

"It's just like coming out of ether," he told them. "It means nothing except that she's comatose from shock. Somebody ought to be with her when she wakes, as she may be frightened. I'm still trying to find a nurse—"

"I'm bearing the expense, Doctor," Adele advised him hastily, "and I'll wait until you can find the nurse."

Miss Withers said that they would both wait. The two women, allied in a common cause, stood on either side of the bed and watched.

Suddenly Dulcie spoke faintly but clearly, "Auntie Mac! Auntie

Mac, don't punish Tige! It was my fault, for leaving the salmon where he could get his claws on it!"

Miss Withers relaxed. She had been hoping for revelations and received news of Dulcie's landlady's cat.

"Delirious, I guess," Adele Mabie suggested.

"No!" came the clear voice from the bed. "Not in the slightest. Why I'm clear as a bell, clear as a big bell ringing…" She babbled on.

"She hears and understands," Miss Withers whispered. "It's a coma. You know, it's the same sort of coma produced by twilight sleep, or scopolamine. I've been reading all about it—they call it the Truth Drug, you know. Suppose I ask her some questions?"

"Oh no!" Adele gasped. "Why—"

"I don't see how it could hurt her, as long as she's bound to talk her head off anyway!" Miss Withers was burning with curiosity to explore this mind—the same mind that she had once helped to cram with knowledge. "In her condition she simply cannot lie!"

"All right," Adele said slowly. "What shall we ask?"

"Listen to me, Dulcie," said the schoolteacher. "This is Miss Withers, your old teacher. You remember me?"

There was a pause. "Snoopy, snoopy Withers!" sang out the girl. "No more lessons, no more school, no more teacher, darned old fool."

The schoolteacher did not bat an eye. "Inhibitions are removed," she said dryly. Then: "Tell us, Dulcie, what really happened? Was it an accident?"

"He did it on purpose," the girl said, her voice lower. "He did it on purpose, he did it—"

"What? He ran into you on purpose?"

"No," Dulcie corrected. "He broke—he broke my heart, the bum."

"Who did?"

" 'Hearts don't break, it isn't true; but they ache, ah yes, they do…' " sang the girl almost cheerfully.

Miss Withers looked at Adele Mabie and hardened her heart. "Was it Francis Mabie?"

"What are you saying!" burst in Adele, but the schoolteacher hushed her.

"Go on, tell me! Was it Mr. Mabie?"

"Not—not him, that fat old toad with the wet hands…"

"But he gave you money, didn't he?"

Adele broke in to say that that was a lie. "My husband was never involved with this girl or anyone else in his life!"

"Answer the question, Dulcie. Did Mr. Mabie give you money?"

"Y-es," admitted the half-unconscious girl. "Money—"

"Why did he give you money?" The whole process seemed to Miss Withers like the senseless seances that once or twice in her life she had been forced to sit through, with spirit raps for no and yes.

"My money!" said Dulcie. "Week's wages—as a maid, oh, a very funny, funny maid, Maid Marian in the moated grange…"

"Of course," Adele cut in happily. "Don't you see? Francis was so softhearted that when he found the girl broke on the train he gave her a week's pay because I fired her without notice!"

Miss Withers paused, momentarily baffled.

"Now it's my turn," Adele cried. "After all, if anybody has a reason for getting to the bottom of this mystery, I do." She leaned over the girl. "Who was the man?" she insisted. "The man you loved so terribly? Was it Mr. Fitz?"

"Poor—poor Fitz," Dulcie murmured. "Poor little Fitzy." Her voice sounded stronger, more natural now.

"Perhaps we ought to stop this," Miss Withers suggested, having a few tardy compunctions. But Adele Mabie shook her head.

"Listen!"

Dulcie Prothero was off to a good start, needing no prompting. "Poor Fitzy thought he was fooling people, and he wasn't fooling anybody at all, not anybody. A bird in the hand is worth a hundred flying, is it? You ought to take love where you find it, and we're only young once…"

"It sounds," Adele said softly, "as if the girl had fallen into the hands of one of those wolves who hang around hotel lobbies all over the world and try to pick up girls."

Miss Withers nodded. "But Dulcie didn't want to look at his etchings."

The girl on the bed cried: "Bobsie! Get Bobsie!"

They both leaned closer. "Where is he? Who is he?" Adele begged.

"Handbag, please," moaned the girl. "In the handbag…"

"Now she's rambling," Miss Withers decided. But Adele suddenly crossed the room, returned with a worn brown purse.

"The taxi driver brought this along," she whispered. "Here is your handbag, dear."

"Open it," commanded the weak voice. "Open the handbag and take Bobsie out and tear him up."

The bag was well filled, but instead of money the two curious women found a folded wad of newspaper clippings. She held them to the candle.

"But of course!" she ejaculated. "They're the pictures of Mrs. Macafee's cows—bullfight scenes, in other words."

She held out to Adele one picture, showing a pleasant-faced young man with big ears under a funny hat, a man who wore with obvious pride the gold-spangled costume of a *matador de toros*. She read the caption out loud: " '*El Yonkers Matador, un Nuevo Torero de Yanquilandia.*' "

"An American bullfighter, eh?" mused the schoolteacher.

Dulcie took that remark up too. "American bullfighter gone native," said she. "Bobsie broke my heart, almost ..."

"She's coming out of it," Miss Withers whispered.

Adele nodded. "But we've gone this far—please let me ask just one more question." She bent over the girl. "Did you ever own a bottle of Elixir d'Amour perfume, Dulcie? You did, didn't you?"

The girl whispered a doubtful "Yes" and then, more loudly, "But it wasn't any good. I threw it away!"

"Where?" put in Miss Withers eagerly.

The girl moved restlessly beneath the covers, turned her face to one side. The marble pallor was gone.

"Where did you throw it?" There was a moment's wait, and then…

"Here's the nurse," Adele Mabie broke in suddenly. There were footsteps in the hall, and the nurse arrived, starched, crisp, and competent looking. The doctor was close behind her.

"Why, our patient is practically well!" he announced cheerfully. "Pulse slowed down, respiration normal—she'll be able to go out of here tomorrow." Adele Mabie drew him aside, took out her handbag.

Miss Hildegarde Withers bent over the bed, saw a pair of clear brown eyes staring up at her.

"Why—I know you!" cried Dulcie.

"Yes, dear. Don't talk. You've already done quite enough talking for one night."

The lips trembled into an uncertain smile. Dulcie Prothero was no fool. "Did I give the right answers?" she asked.

But Miss Withers was being paged. Adele Mabie drew her into the hall.

"Can you imagine!" Adele gasped. "I was telling the doctor here that I would be responsible for the hospital bill and everything. And what do you think he said?"

Miss Withers refused to guess.

"Dulcie has loads and loads of money!" Adele went on.

The doctor nodded. "When the nurses undressed this young lady, down in the emergency ward, they found this pinned to her slip!"

He produced a small cloth bag, a bag containing a sheaf of United States currency.

"Something over sixteen hundred dollars!" gasped Adele Mabie.

"A lovely nest egg, isn't it?" Miss Withers admitted. "I suggest that you arrange, Doctor, to have this put back under the girl's pillow tonight."

"But sixteen hundred dollars!" Mrs. Mabie repeated. "What is she doing with all that money? What if it should be lost?"

"Miss Dulcie Prothero," the schoolteacher said, "won't lose anything she doesn't want to lose."

In the lobby of the Hotel Georges that night—actually it had been Monday morning for some hours now—Miss Withers found a solitary figure stretched out in the easiest of the modernistic chairs, sound asleep. It was the inspector, with cigar ashes all over the front of his vest.

"Well!" she said sharply. Oscar Piper's feet came off the edge of the opposite settee, and he stiffened to attention.

"Ugh!" he greeted her. "You back?"

"Asleep at the switch, Oscar?" she inquired unkindly. "I'm glad that one of us can get some rest, anyhow. I've been hard at work." She told him, briefly, the results of the evening.

"Yeah? That money looks phony, eh? But it doesn't seem to fit into this muddle of a murder." He considered her results and found them small. "You don't care how you work, either, do you? Quizzing a hospital patient while she's half unconscious, and then you talk to me about the third degree! Anyway, you needn't crow. I've been busy too."

"Solved the mystery of the two murders, Oscar?"

"I'm getting closer," he insisted. "While you were running around in circles I was called in as a consulting expert by nobody else than Captain de Silva of the Mexico City Police!"

Miss Withers remembered him. "Oh yes—the worried young man with the high forehead, who loves so to make speeches! The one who helped me get you out of the police station lockup!"

"Yeah," said Piper. "Anyway, all that is forgotten. We're buddies now. What happened at the bullfight has blown the lid off everything. De Silva is fronting for the lieutenant colonel in charge. Seems that whenever anything happens down here the, big shots take a powder out of town and let somebody else sweat. Naturally de Silva wanted to get the inside. We compared notes—"

"You mean, he questioned you?" she asked shrewdly.

"We compared notes!" Piper repeated a little stiffly. "De Silva was very friendly. I told him everything that I noticed at the bullfight. That is—everything that could have any bearing on the case…"

He stopped short. "What are you smiling at?"

"You must have been a big help, considering that we both sat there and let a murder be committed under our very noses!"

"Yes," admitted the inspector. "That's what de Silva intimated. But like everybody else, we were watching the show in the arena. There's no use crying over spilt milk."

"Something worse than milk was spilled," the schoolteacher told him sharply. "It may have slipped your mind, but somebody sneaked up on that poor man and stabbed him in the back. Our job is to find out who!"

Piper smiled weakly. "De Silva thinks he knows. And I had hell's own time keeping him from making an arrest last night."

"What? Who?" Miss Withers went off like a string of firecrackers.

"Francis Mabie is suspect number one," the inspector admitted. "But they make it sound logical. You see, we didn't know that, like most young Mexicans of good family, this Robles chap was educated abroad—in Paris, in fact."

"The customs man? Paris—that's very incriminating."

"Wait, will you? Adele Mabie is a damn pretty woman, and she took a cruise around the world on one of the *Empress* liners a couple of years ago. What happens to a pretty woman gadding around alone, eh?"

"Don't ask me, Oscar Piper!"

"Well, anyway—she could have met a handsome young Mexican in Paris and had a red-hot affair."

"Please, Oscar! Leave the Latin Quarter out of this. Are you trying to say that Adele came back to New York, married, and then two years later on a trip to Mexico the phlegmatic alderman is so burning with jealousy that he leaves poisoned perfume where the boyfriend, now a respectable customs examiner, might smell it? The longest long arm of coincidence I ever saw in my life."

"Wait," Piper said. "That's not all. Leave it to these romantically minded Mexicans. They go farther than that—after Mabie got rid of the young man he is supposed to have started brooding over his wife. Maybe she flirted with somebody else—anyway, the alderman sneaks out of the bullfight saying that he can't stand the sight of blood, sneaks in again with a dart under his coat, and then slides along the seat until he is just behind the fancy umbrella that his wife has hired to keep dry under. Then"—the inspector made a gesture—"boppo!"

"Whoa!" Miss Withers interrupted. "Aren't you confused, Oscar? At last reports Adele Mabie was alive and well."

"Sure! Because when she left her seat she dropped the rented umbrella, and Fitz, in the row ahead, picked it up to keep himself snug. So he got killed by accident."

"It's building a house of cards without straw," Miss Withers declared. "Just guesswork."

"Not all guesswork," Piper corrected. "It doesn't show in the newspaper photographs of the stiff, but when they found Mike Fitz he had that striped umbrella over his shoulders!"

The schoolteacher wasn't saying anything, but she had an extremely thoughtful look in her cool blue eyes.

"But of course it's full of holes," the inspector continued. "Mabie has a good alibi. He says that after he left the bullfight he came back downtown to the Papillon bar and stayed there."

"That I can believe without straining myself," Miss Withers admitted. "It sounds more than reasonable."

"Sure does. And I got de Silva to send one of his *agentes* over to check it. The manager of the Papillon bar says he distinctly remembers a man of the alderman's description being there from four-thirty to sometime around seven."

"And the murder was at five?"

"Within a few minutes, anyway. De Silva figures it happened just as the deluge came down, with everybody rushing to get out of the place."

"When you and I and Adele Mabie were standing in the exit, perhaps? And all our suspects out of the place. Dear me, it's most provoking! But, at any rate, doesn't that alibi clear your friend Mr. Mabie?"

Oscar Piper said he hoped it would. "All the same, I wish I had a better setup to spring on de Silva tomorrow morning, something that would tie up the two murders."

Miss Withers said that offhand she could think of three possibilities, all better than the fairy tale he had just suggested to her. "Involving the Ippwings, the Gay Caballero, Dulcie, or any combination of the three."

But as he looked hopeful she shook her head. "Not tonight, Oscar. The guidebooks all mention the difficulty of sleeping in this high altitude, but not even you are going to prevent me from trying."

She gave her hair the requisite hundred strokes in record time, blew out her candle. Then she slept, so soundly that not even the messenger which floated in her window disturbed her slumbers.

XI

Guess Who!

ALL THAT NIGHT strike committees in the Palacio Nacional dictated terms to the secretary of the luckily absent *presidente*, while owl cabarets closed their doors in dismal candlelight, milk soured in the suburbs, scalpels went unsterilized in the hospitals, and American tourists grumbled even in their sleep. But the sun rose over the mile and a half high capital of Mexico, strike or no strike, strictly on schedule.

With it rose Miss Hildegarde Withers. The good lady girded her loins for battle in a prim blue serge suit that was in its third summer. She descended the hotel stairs and much to her surprise caught the inspector buying his day's rations of cigars in the hotel lobby.

"Have you changed your mind about early birds and worms?" she greeted him. "Stealing a march on me, Oscar?"

They found a hole-in-the-wall place where black Mexican coffee, smelling vilely of chicory, could be obtained. She was afire with excitement but would not talk until they had broken their fast and the inspector had lovingly lighted that first wonderful cigar of the new day.

"I've got just ten minutes," he said. "So shoot!"

Then he leaped out of his chair as she suited the action to the word and from a newspaper parcel produced, almost in his face, one of the most vicious weapons he had ever seen.

It was a round slender shaft a little more than two feet long, wrapped in frills of blue and gold tissue paper, with a harpoon-shaped point of blood-darkened steel.

"The murder weapon, Oscar!"

He stared in wonder. "The police let *you* have it?"

"Well, perhaps not *the* murder weapon. But a *banderilla* is a *banderilla*, except for the difference in color of the paper they glue on them. After the bullfights they take the things out of the dead bulls and sell them as souvenirs."

"Yeah, but you didn't buy any..." Piper stopped. "Did you get that from Mrs. Mabie?"

Smiling, Miss Withers shook her head. "The souvenirs that Adele bought were of black and gold. This particular little toy was sticking into my floor this morning when I woke. It must have come sailing in the window during the night." She sniffed. "A difficult country for a lover of fresh air, Oscar. I've half a mind to keep my window closed."

"Good Lord, yes! Why, that thing might have struck you."

"Not much chance of that. It's just another warning to mind my own business."

Piper took the thing, hefted it. "Why, it's only a wooden stick with a sort of straightened-out fishhook at the end!"

She nodded. "The point is fearfully sharp, Oscar. But, all the same, I think it would take quite a bit of doing, as the English say, to drive this thing through cloth and flesh into a man's heart, from behind!"

Oscar Piper agreed to that. "Which is why de Silva thinks it must have been a man who killed Fitz."

"Even a man must have had his work cut out for him," said the schoolteacher. "There must have been some commotion—a gasp or a moan. You'd think that in all that crowd of a thousand or two people we could have one eyewitness!"

The inspector shrugged. "Everyone was doing just what we were doing, looking at the bullfight as the rain stopped the fun. Anybody could have moved up behind Fitz, and biff!"

"Easy as that, eh?" Miss Withers looked a bit dubious. "Oscar, I have an idea. Do you suppose that Captain de Silva would like two visiting experts instead of one?"

"What?" Piper drew back.

"I'd like a talk with that young man, because I have a theory—"

"Now look here, Hildegarde, I don't think that the authorities here will be anxious to take theories from a foreigner—and a woman at that. You work your theory out and tell it to me, and I'll suggest it to the captain." He looked at his watch. "Say, I've got to run if I'm going to see him at his office. You amuse yourself this morning."

He rushed jauntily away, leaving a ruffled spinster staring after him.

"Amuse myself!" said Hildegarde Withers. She went out into the street, then suddenly stopped, nodded and hailed a taxicab. "I'll just see how little Dulcie is this morning."

Dulcie was fine.

She was sitting up in bed with a tray of breakfast, the nurse already gone. But the two women met with a certain strained note in their voices.

"I can't look at you without thinking that I'm playing hooky," Dulcie admitted after a while.

"You mustn't feel that way," said the schoolteacher gently. "I believe in you, Dulcie. And I'm sure that you have some excellent explanation for the money they found pinned to your underwear when you were brought in here last night."

She waited hopefully. But Dulcie was through answering questions. "No," said the girl, "I haven't any explanation at all."

"But my dear child! Don't you see—"

"It isn't mine," Dulcie admitted. "It belongs to somebody else." And that was that.

There was a large and exquisite bouquet of roses on the table beside the bed. Miss Withers bent to sniff them. "Ah," she observed brightly, "are these from your friend Bobsie?"

The girl on the bed did not speak. She looked down at the coverlet, pleated it carefully, and then smoothed it out again. She shook her head soberly.

"From Julio—I mean, Mr. Mendez," she confessed finally. "I don't know how he heard that I—that I'd had an accident, but they just arrived. And he sent a note saying that he'd be over a little later."

"Then I must be running along so that you can comb your hair and make yourself beautiful," Miss Withers said. She stopped in the doorway. "Oh, by the way—I know that was an accident you had, but take my advice and don't go wandering around Violetta Street after dark any more."

Dulcie's eyes widened. "Oh! Why, of course not! Why should— Oh well, I'm coming back to work for Mrs. Mabie, anyway."

At Miss Withers' honest amazement the girl flushed. "Oh, not as a maid this time. That was an awful flop. But Mrs. Mabie says she has forgotten all that. She says that she wants to make up to me for being so short-tempered when she fired me in Laredo. I'm to be a big help to her with her curios. She wants to start a curio shop when she gets back to New York, you see. And I can help in buying and packing and checking."

"The two of you ought to be able to buy out half Mexico," said the schoolteacher thoughtfully.

"So I'm moving over to your hotel today," Dulcie went on. "Do you think I'm doing the right thing?"

Miss Withers told her that she would hesitate to say that about anybody's doing anything.

"Mrs. Mabie said that it would be a real favor, that she would like to have someone with her all the time," Dulcie went on explaining.

The schoolteacher nodded. "Perhaps it's not such a bad idea at that, if you keep your eyes and ears open."

Dulcie looked shocked. "You mean I ought to spy on Mrs. Mabie?"

"On Mrs. Mabie, and on Mr. Mabie, and on everybody else within spying distance," Miss Hildegarde Withers went on solemnly. "And that includes the Gay Caballero too." With that parting shot she hurried out of the room.

She had several other errands to accomplish this morning, errands of the greatest importance. One of them took her to Cook's Travel Bureau, where she spent some time in thumbing through booklets. Then on down the street.

"I hope Oscar and the captain are having better hunting than I am!" she said to herself in the high spirit of sportsmanship.

There were worried lines on the high forehead of Captain de Silva of the Mexico City Police that morning. Nor did the checking of alibis serve to smooth his troubled brow. Indeed, inside of half an hour he and the inspector were up to their ears in alibis.

Mr. and Mrs. Marcus Ippwing were trapped in their room at the Hotel Georges, trapped in the very act of writing a joint letter to their daughter back home in Peoria. "Our invalid daughter, you know. Poor girl, she does love hearing everything. She was badly burned in an accident some years ago, but thank heavens we finally got a good cash settlement out of the lawsuit, and Ella has every comfort."

Captain de Silva cut in to say that all he wanted to know was how they had spent their time from four to six o'clock yesterday. The Ippwings stared at each other. "You don't mean—he doesn't mean—"

"It's only a formality, folks," Piper hastily put in. "Just a matter of elimination. You see, we've all been rather mixed up in this thing."

"Yes, of course," said Marcus Ippwing dubiously. "Why, Mother and I walked out of the bullfight because we didn't like the way it was going—"

"I didn't mind their killing the bulls, but it didn't seem right to make fun of them," Mrs. Ippwing finished for him.

"And after you left?" prodded the captain, notebook in hand.

The birdlike old couple looked at each other again, each spoke at once. "Why, we came home—home to the hotel!"

De Silva nodded amiably. "The clerk says that you arrived here about seven o'clock or after, yes?"

"That's right! We walked home, and we didn't know how far it was—and then, coming through the square they call the Zocalo, Mother wanted to stop and have a look at the cathedral…"

Captain de Silva wrote down solemnly that the Ippwings had walked from the bull ring to Madero Avenue by way of the Zocalo, which amounted to going twice around Robin Hood's barn.

"Sure, come on in!" welcomed Mr. Al Hansen. He sat at the desk in his hotel room, the radio going full blast, and was dressed informally in his underwear. Before him a number of sheets of hotel writing paper were covered with neat pencil sketches.

"Just trying out some designs for sweepstakes tickets," he admitted. "You know, a lot depends on how you impress the buyer with a ticket. And I just got the idea that if I could get the Mexican National Lottery to authorize me to run a sweep on the Santa Anita Handicap, there'd be millions in it—millions!"

"There'd be a million headaches trying to get those tickets across the border," the inspector told him. "But that's not why we came."

"Sure, I was wondering when somebody would be along to ask me questions about Mike Fitz, poor guy," Hansen told the officers. "I've known him for years, and we've made a few dollars for each other now and then. I used to handle the San Francisco end, because I wasn't popular down here south of the border with the old regime. Mike was a great promoter, but he had one weakness—dames. If you want my opinion, it was a dame who did him in yesterday."

Captain de Silva nodded, and his voice came smooth as satin. "We only want to know where you went when you left the bullfight, Mr. Hansen."

"Yeah," agreed Piper. "Not that it cuts any ice, but just as a formality."

Hansen nodded, but his pink face was reddening a little. He went over to the wardrobe, fumbled in his black suit. "Here's my alibi," he said, producing a small photograph of a large woman, a large and slightly leering woman. She was photographed as only a Mexico City photographer could have pictured her, and looked somewhat like a madame on parade.

"Her name's Consuela," he admitted. "But the telephone number I'm keeping to myself. I met her at the bullfight, and is she one hot number! Crazy about bullfights too, and that's how we got to talking."

"Yeah," interrupted the inspector, "but what we want—"

"Sure, sure," Hansen agreed. "You saw me walk out of the place while young Nicanor was monkeying with that light-colored bull? Well, it's simple enough. I wanted to make a hit with the dame, so I went out to get some flowers."

"What in blazes for?" demanded the inspector. "Why not later, if you had to give her posies?"

"Women like to throw down roses to the matador," Al Hansen said. "When he's killed his bull. Only I had hell's own time finding a flower place open on Sunday, and, as it worked out, the lady wouldn't have tossed them down anyway on account of the bull didn't get killed. I didn't get back to the bullfight in time to beat the rain, so I missed her."

"Then how the picture?"

Hansen smiled. "She had my card. And in the mail this morning she sent me the photo—and her phone number."

Captain de Silva wrote steadily in his notebook. He looked up, shook his head sadly. "It is unfortunate, *señor*, that you have not better witnesses to say where you were. Because of your known ill will toward the deceased Mr. Fitz."

"My what?" Hansen was amazed. "Why, Mike and I were like that!" He held up two pudgy fingers.

Captain de Silva looked toward the inspector, and his left eye folded in a wink. They started for the doorway, turned.

"It is too bad then that my *agentes* lie. They say, *señor*, that you appeared before *a juez municipal* on Saturday and asked for a writ of attachment against the property, real or personal, of Mr. Michael Fitz. I shall personally see to it that the men responsible—"

"Wait!" cried Hansen. "Take it easy, will you? That writ was only to scare Mike with if he still held out. He had until Sunday night to come through on a little business deal. You see, from the train we wired him—I mean, I wired him—some money—"

"*We?*" said Captain de Silva pleasantly.

Hansen shook his head. "Not at liberty to talk about that, I'm afraid. It was just a business deal." His mouth closed like a trap.

"You just wanted to put a little scare into him, eh?" prompted the inspector.

"That's right," Hansen admitted.

"But first somebody put five inches of steel into him, no? Good morning, *señor*." And Captain de Silva led the way out into the hall. The door closed firmly behind them.

"Listen," said Oscar Piper, "I realize I'm only butting in, but I'd have beaten that guy's ears down. He knows something."

The captain smiled and shrugged. "Perhaps he does. But we try to use the French methods here. Psychological crime investigation dictates that the course to follow is to let Mr. Hansen worry—how do you say it?—let him stew for a while. Then he talks without having his ears beaten down, no?"

The inspector murmured impolite things under his breath, but Captain de Silva wrote happily away in his notebook.

"About the *Señorita* Prothero," the captain explained a few minutes later, "we do not need to bother ourselves now. It is quite obvious that a woman could not possess the strength to commit this murder, and, besides, she is, I understand, ill."

"All right, skip her," Piper agreed. "But the boy I want to talk to is this Julio Mendez. I want to ask him—"

"We have already talked to that gentleman, *señor*."

"Yeah?" Piper nodded, grinned. "So he's known to the police, eh? A record?"

"A police record of a sort, oh yes."

"You got ways of bearing down on him so he'll talk, I guess."

The captain nodded. "I'm afraid that we must eliminate him as a suspect. At the time of the murder, which certainly took place between the time of Nicanor's injury in the bull ring and the fall of heavy rain, Mendez was in the bullfight offices beneath the stands."

"Another alibi, eh? And he said he had a date! What was he doing there?"

"Getting the *Señorita* Prothero out," explained the captain. "There have been recently so many accidents with spectators jumping into the bull ring that they are now usually held and given thirty days to cool off."

"He was getting Miss Prothero out, eh?" Piper nodded. "The guy has pull!"

The captain admitted that such things were possible.

"And where did Mendez take the girl then?" Piper pressed.

"Ah, nowhere, *señor*. It seems that—according to Mendez' story— they went out to the street and he left her to secure a taxicab. But when he came back with the taxi the young lady was gone."

Piper nodded. "Gone to keep a date with another taxicab in Violetta Street, eh?"

Rollo Lighton, picked up on the street by two *agentes* and brought before Captain de Silva, announced that he had spent all of Sunday at home, in the preparation of one hundred publicity stories for the government press bureau.

"I did run over to the bullfight, but all of the best seats were sold out so I went back home, and—"

"Yeah?" cut in Piper from the captain's elbow. "What about your telling Miss Withers that you'd written ten stories and had them shuffled to look like a hundred? Leaving your afternoon free?"

Lighton backtracked. "I went home and found that I was out of liquor, so I went downtown to the Papillon, figuring I'd find somebody there who'd buy me a drink." This was defiant.

"Too bad, *Señor* Lighton, that you have nobody to come forward and bear witness to your being there." Captain de Silva smiled icily.

"But I have!" he insisted. "Mr. Mabie, he bought me a drink!"

The inspector, jubilant, whispered something to his confrere. Captain de Silva nodded. He beckoned, to an *agente*. "Will you ask the *Señor* Mabie if he will do us the kindness of his company?"

Alderman Francis Mabie was delighted, he said, to take part in an identification parade. He wanted that alibi established. There was nothing he would rather do, he said, than accompany the inspector, Captain de Silva, Mr. Lighton, and several of the captain's men down to the Papillon bar.

Everything went off as planned, everything moved with the smoothness of clockwork. As they came up the steps and past the swinging doors, the fat little cock robin of a manager rushed toward them with a happy smile. He had been warned over the telephone of what was coming, and he seemed to know exactly what was expected of him.

"Ah yes, *señor*!" he cried. "Delighted to have you come back. And delighted to say again, as I said to the gendarmes yesterday, how you come here, how you buy drinks for people, how you enjoy our special, wonderful Pancho Villa cocktails—yes, from four o'clock to maybe seven or eight…"

His voice died away as he saw the expression of the faces confronting him.

It had all been as perfect as clockwork, this establishing of a perfect and ironclad alibi for Alderman Francis Mabie. Only it had not been to the alderman—nor yet to blue-chinned Rollo Lighton—that the

little cock robin had been addressing his fervid greetings. He was pointing, with the dogged assurance of a man who thinks he never forgets a
face, to no one else but the disgusted Inspector Oscar Piper.

The strained silence that followed was broken by the ringing of a
telephone. The bartender stepped into a booth, came out to announce
that it was a call from headquarters for "*El Capitán* de Silva."

The captain took it, emerged from the booth with his Latin suavity
almost gone.

"Someone reports a dead body at the Puertasol Market," he told the
inspector. "¡*Vamonos*!

XII

A Pig—and a Poke

THE BIG PACKARD SEDAN roared through the sunny streets of
Mexico City with a great screaming of sirens. The impassive little brown
monkey at the wheel ignored stop lights, went the wrong way on one-
way streets, dodged around parkways, and once, when traffic jammed
the way, he flipped the wheel and sent the big machine up on the sidewalk, down again with a bump.

They were at the Puertasol in three minutes flat. Three minutes
more, Piper insisted, and his hair would have been snowy white.

The market was closed for the noon *siesta*, iron door drawn down.
But there was an excited clerk in a white apron waving them to a side
door. In answer to questions he only pointed.

"¡*Allí, señores, allí*!"

Through the market, into the *carnicería.*

"Well, where's this dead body?" the inspector demanded, as Captain de Silva paused at the door of a long dark room, chill and odorous.

"It is here," said a familiar voice. There was Miss Hildegarde Withers, sitting patiently upon a chopping block. As the little group of officers stared unbelievingly at her she indicated a grisly and exceedingly
anatomical-looking specimen which hung head down from hooks stuck
through the tendons of its heels.

"A dead body," she went on. "Not, I admit, a human one. It was the
only way I knew to bring you here, Captain de Silva."

There was a rising murmur among the *agentes*, a rustling of indig-
nation like wind in distant trees. Captain de Silva's forehead wore two

new wrinkles, but he did not trust himself to speak.

"Good Lord, Hildegarde! If this is your idea of a joke—bringing us here to look at a dead pig!" Piper was almost burbling.

"It isn't my idea at all," she insisted. "It's from Sherlock Holmes. 'The Adventure of Black Peter' or something like that. Anyway, in the story Holmes takes up a case where a man is pinned to the wall with a harpoon, so to prove how it was done he got a similar harpoon…"

As she spoke, an exceedingly strange expression had begun to come over the worn and harried face of Captain de Silva. Suddenly he snapped his fingers.

"Allardyce's!" he sang out delightedly. There was a new respect in his voice. "I remember, of course! It was Allardyce's back shop, and there was something about a dead pig swinging from a hook in the ceiling!"

Now it was Miss Withers' turn to look flabbergasted.

"I forgive all!" Captain de Silva insisted. "You have quoted the highest authority, madame. And why are you surprised? Conan Doyle, he is not English or American property. Why should we not read him in Spanish? I, myself, happen to be a corresponding member of the Baker Street Irregulars!" He shook hands with the schoolteacher.

"Now we're getting somewhere," Miss Withers announced. "Here!" And she handed to the captain the *banderilla* which she had pulled from her own bedroom floor that morning. "The whole idea is a bit gruesome, I admit," she confessed. "But as you say, the precedent is of the best. Suppose you see who can stick the thing farthest into the carcass?"

They tried. First Captain de Silva, fired with a new gaiety, poised like a fencer. Then the inspector, bayonet fashion, then the *agentes* and the huskiest of the gendarmes.

A slow, satisfied smile crept across the face of Miss Hildegarde Withers—for not one of these gentlemen, try how he might, was able to make the dart penetrate farther than an inch or two into the carcass of the dangling pig.

"I see what you're driving at!" admitted the inspector. "It must take a special knack to sink this thing—which means that our murderer must be a trained and expert bullfighter!"

"Wait!" cried Captain de Silva. "Wait just one minute. *Banderilleros* study for years to learn how to use these darts—but they study not to sink them in deeply but to place them just below the skin. They are not weapons of death—they are only ornaments!"

"Then our murderer must be a gorilla," Piper growled. "I've got as good a punch as the next man—that *agente* of yours with the black eye will testify to that—but I can barely make the thing stick into the pig at all!"

Miss Withers nodded. "Has any of you gentlemen a bullet?" she inquired.

"You mean a cartridge?" Piper corrected.

She meant a bullet. Finally, at her insistence, a leaden slug was twisted out of its casing. "Now how far could any of you push the bullet into that carcass?"

"Not at all, of course!" said Captain de Silva.

"I get it!" Piper cut in. "But we could stand a block away and shoot this slug of lead halfway through anything!"

"Of course," said the captain seriously. "It's just a matter of initial velocity. A whirlwind can blow straws through a tree."

"If all this applies to a bullet, then why not to a *banderilla?*" the schoolteacher demanded.

"Now listen, Hildegarde," the inspector complained, "you can't get a dart this size into the barrel of a pistol."

"I'm not saying that was how it was done. I'm saying that was how it could have been done!" she retorted.

But it was Captain de Silva who liked the new idea best. "An air gun!" he cried. "Why, this murderer needn't have been down in the ring seats at the bullfight! He might have been up in the boxes, which are almost empty in the summer season. Or even on the little platform which runs around the top—for it's uncovered, and when it rains no spectators climb away up there."

The inspector was forced to fall into line. "Anyway, now it doesn't matter who we saw leaving the place during the bullfight, because any one of them could have gone to the outside stairs and up to the boxes or higher."

Miss Withers gave him an odd look. "You like my theory?"

Both officers were delighted with it, they said. She shook her head slowly. "I'm not," admitted the schoolteacher. "I think it is as full of holes as a sieve."

She would have continued, but there was the roar of a motorcycle outside, and then a brisk young gendarme in puttees came hurrying in, saluted the captain, and spoke in swift Spanish.

"Tell the lieutenant colonel I'll be there at once," commanded de Silva. He turned to Piper, and there was a look of new triumph on his face. "You'll excuse me, please?"

"Yeah? What's up?"

The captain rubbed his hands together. "What's up? Ah, my friend, the power of the psychological method of dealing with crime! Mr. Al Hansen, whose ears you were so anxious to beat down, has appeared at the *jefatura* and wishes to make a statement!" De Silva lowered his voice. "In fact, a *confession!*"

Captain de Silva hurried complacently out of the market, and his sedan screamed away.

"Any confession made by Mr. Al Hansen leaves me in a state of indifference bordering upon the supernatural," Miss Withers was saying.

It was an extraordinarily glum luncheon which she was sharing with the inspector, in spite of her modest triumph in the *carnicería*.

Oscar Piper said he wished that he could get his hands on the person who kept tossing things in at her window.

"Who wouldn't, Oscar!" she told him. "When we get him we'll have our murderer. Because don't think for a moment that any innocent bystander has been going to the trouble of warning me to keep out of the affair."

Piper nodded slowly. "But I don't see what help your new theory is to poor Mabie," he went on. "After all, the alderman is entitled to everything I can do—everything we can do—"

"Hew to the line, Oscar, let the chips fall where they may. Of course, if Mr. Mabie had been planning a long and involved series of crimes, or even one big one, he would hardly have been foolish enough to provide for carting along his own detective on the trip. And, besides, he doesn't strike me as a crack shot with an air gun or anything else."

Piper agreed. "Mabie can't even shoot pool," he declared. "Says his hands tremble too much. But, all the same, that theory of de Silva's involving him ís the only one that holds together."

"Nonsense, Oscar!" Miss Withers gave a hearty sniff. "I'll give you a better one. Mr. and Mrs. Ippwing—"

"What?"

"I said Mr. and Mrs. Ippwing! They have an invalid daughter, Oscar, the apple of their eye. She was injured some years ago by a permanent wave machine in one of Adele's beauty shops, burned so that she is a helpless cripple. They read in the paper that Mrs. Mabie, now married and retired, is to accompany her politician husband to Mexico. Determined on revenge, they take some potassium cyanide from Mr. Ippwing's drugstore and set out—"

"Now wait a minute, wait a minute!" the inspector broke in.

"Quiet, Oscar. They place the poisoned perfume in Mrs. Mabie's bag but get the customs man by mistake. Again they try, with a snake, and again they miss. A third time they shoot a *banderilla* from a box that they have sneaked back into at the bullfight, taking aim at the bright umbrella which Adele has dropped and an innocent bystander has picked up. How's that, Oscar?"

He scowled dubiously. "But how—how in blazes did you find out that?"

She shook her head. "I didn't. As a matter of fact, I doubt if a word of it is true. I made up the parts about the beauty parlor and the family drugstore and the rest of it. But it's as good as the police theory, isn't it?"

The inspector subsided mournfully.

Miss Withers tapped her teeth with a pencil. "Here's another suggestion," she continued brightly. "Let's suppose, just for fun, that Fitz wasn't killed by accident. Suppose that *he* was the murderer of Manuel Robles, the customs man—motive as yet undisclosed. Suppose he thought of the clever indirect method of putting a bottle of poisoned perfume in the baggage of some passenger on the train, then waiting for his victim, making a routine inspection, to find it? Then Mr. Fitz catches a plane, arrives here before the rest of you, and thinks he has gotten away with it. But he does not know that Julio Mendez, a friend of the dead Robles, is on his trail. Julio lays his plans, gets Dulcie Prothero—innocently, of course—to put the victim on the spot, and then pops him off with the air gun and banderilla?"

"That leaves out the snake," Piper complained.

"And it leaves out most of the facts too," Miss Withers retorted. "Come on back to the hotel. I'm going to take a nap and see if I'll dream a solution."

But there was to be no nap for her today. As she went up the stairs an apparition descended upon her in the shape of Rollo Lighton. She hardly knew the man, for he was shaved, dressed in clean linen and a not too badly fitting Palm Beach suit. In his outstretched hand was the fountain pen that she had never expected to see again.

"Thanks a lot for trusting me with it," he told her. Then, as she smiled and started to continue up the stair, he held out his hand. "I wonder if I could talk to you," he said. "I've got something to confess."

"Something to what?" she demanded blankly.

"To confess—conscience and all that, you know. It's been working on my mind all day. I got ready to go to the police, but I don't know if they would listen. I thought maybe you—"

"Come on, come on," she said and led him to her room. Lighton sank heavily into the easy chair.

"I know who killed Mike Fitz," he said.

Miss Withers waited in silence.

"If I tell, do you think they'll protect me—or get me out of town? Because my life won't be safe a minute."

"Go on," the schoolteacher told him. "As things are now, nobody's life is safe a minute."

He nodded, looking at the floor. "Well?" prompted Miss Withers.

"It's Hansen," he said, his voice barely audible.

"What?" Of all the names Miss Withers had been expecting to hear, this was the last.

He nodded. "We were in together on a deal," he said. "A deal to corner all the generators in the city, and coin dough on renting them during the strike. It was Al's idea. One of the things I did in Laredo was to cash my bonus bonds, so I had quite a bit of money. Anyway, we sent it by telegraph down to Mike Fitz. And when we got here we found he'd crossed us. I wanted to go to court, and I actually did get Al Hansen to go with me and try for a writ. But the law in this town is slow and involved. We gave Fitz until Sunday night to dig up the money, but we both knew he wouldn't. So I went out and got drunk, but I know that Al Hansen—well, he's a tough customer. I begged him not to do anything crazy, but—"

"You don't know anything more definite than just the motive?" Miss Withers demanded impatiently.

Rollo Lighton stared at her. "I know that Hansen has been a bull-fight fan for years—that in his house in Frisco he's got a dozen swords and half-a-hundred *banderillas*."

"Is he a good shot?" the schoolteacher asked thoughtfully.

Lighton nodded. "When he was with Villa, running guns, he could outshoot anybody in the crowd. He's got medals for marksmanship—but what has that got to do—"

"Plenty," said Miss Withers. "Don't go away." She went to the telephone, gave excited instructions to the girl downstairs at the switchboard. A moment later she was speaking to Captain de Silva. She spoke, listened and finally put the receiver softly down.

"You may be interested to know," she told Rollo Lighton, "that Al

Hansen is in the office of the *jefe* right now, making a confession."

"Yes?" Lighton gaped, showing his snags of teeth.

The schoolteacher nodded. "A confession that *you* were the one who killed Michael Fitz! You two gentlemen ought to get together…"

But Rollo Lighton was going out fast through the door, and he did not turn when she called after him.

"It's clear enough," the inspector insisted later. "The two of them are in it up to here. And now each one is trying to pin it on the other, just like in the Snyder-Gray thing. Fitz tried to hold out the dough that Hansen and Lighton had sent him to work a deal with…"

Miss Withers shook her head. "If he'd had the money he would have given it back, Oscar. Especially if he thought he was in any danger, and he must have known that Lighton was once in the army and could shoot—and that Al Hansen used to be a gunrunner. Besides, if he had had money cached away he wouldn't have snitched Dulcie's glass emerald and tried to raise cash on it."

The inspector stuck to his guns. "Anyway, I'm satisfied," he declared. "I think de Silva is too, but he won't arrest those two guys. He just passes the buck. Says he has to have the authority of the *jefe* or of this figurehead of a lieutenant colonel. They do everything roundabout in this country."

"Anyway," Miss Withers demanded, "there's no more talk of arresting the poor alderman, alibi or no alibi?"

"Not until they wash up this Lighton-Hansen mess one way or the other. But why?"

She told him, displaying a sheaf of travel folders. "I spiked that theory of de Silva's, anyway. At Cook's I checked on the itinerary of the Empress round-the-world tours. They have all the dope in the local office, because once in a while passengers leave the ships at Acapulco on the Pacific, make the trip across Mexico, and catch them again at Havana. Anyway, I know this. No Empress liner makes a stop at any port not flying the Union Jack if they can help it. Gibraltar and Egypt and Bombay and Sydney—but not Havre nor Naples. 'Buy Empire' is the motto. Therefore, Adele Mabie was never in Paris, she did not meet Manuel Robles there, and the whole case against her husband is just so much applesauce."

"Great work, Hildegarde!"

But she took no pleasure in the praise. "Oscar, there's a key to this whole thing that we're missing," she insisted. "We're shooting in the dark…" Suddenly she stopped. "Speaking of shooting, Oscar Piper, I have an idea!"

"Yeah? Go ahead."

Miss Withers hastily consulted her watch. "Yes, the stores are open again. Where's the nearest place to get curios, Oscar?"

He grinned. "Up in Adele's room."

But the schoolteacher told him that this was one curio Adele Mabie did not possess. Completely mystified, the inspector followed her out of the hotel, waited in the taxi while she made a tour of the shops on Juarez Avenue. At length she returned with a parcel almost as tall as herself. With the greatest of difficulty the thing was dragged inside the taxicab, and then she told the driver "¡A la plaza de toros!"

Her accent was poor, but he understood, broke into English surprisingly. "No bullfight today, lady—only on Sunday!"

"Never you mind," Miss Hildegarde Withers told him sharply. And they rolled away. At last they came into view of the great dark pillbox against the sky. "There ought to be a caretaker somewhere, Oscar," she said. "You'll have to bribe him, because we've got to get inside."

"Okay, but how about leaving the doohickey in the taxi?"

"You bring the doohickey along," she told him. "We'll need it inside."

There was no caretaker at the gate, but for some reason or other it turned out to be unlocked. They entered, walked stealthily along the muddy path where yesterday had been ranked the peddlers and beggars, up the first short flight of stairs…

From somewhere in the pens and corrals underneath came a fierce bawling and the crash of horns against wood, but otherwise they seemed very alone in the vast place.

It was dark on the stairs that led to the topmost tier, darker even than the gray clouds overhead would seem to warrant. "Looks like we'll get our daily rainstorm in a little while," the inspector observed, as the wind tugged at his hat, swished at the paper wrapping of the tall bundle he held.

And then they heard footsteps coming down the stairs above them. Swiftly Miss Withers drew the inspector into a cubbyhole under the steps, and they peered warily forth.

They saw a man come into view, a young jaunty man carrying a package almost identical to the one which the inspector was complaining about. This young man wore a blue beret and was softly whistling "El Novillero."

"Julio!" gasped Miss Withers. "Julio Mendez!"

He stopped short, and for an instant an expression emphatically not of welcome flickered across his face. Then the wide smile returned.

"Hello!" said Julio. "What's bringing you here? The murderers revisiting the scene of the crime, yes?"

Miss Withers, who had been about to make the same remark, sniffed as meaningfully as she could.

Julio looked at his watch. "Sorry I must running along," he told them. "But I have a date to take Miss Prothero for a boat ride—if it doesn't raining. At beautiful, *romántico* Xochimilco!" And he went blithely down the steps.

"What in blazes is this all about?" Piper demanded. But the schoolteacher shook her head.

"It can't be!" she insisted. "It can't be! And yet I wondered how the murder weapon could have been taken away from here without someone seeing. I never thought that it might have been left to be picked up later!" She pulled at the inspector's arm. "Come on, Oscar."

Up they went, coming out at last on the very topmost tip of the pillbox, in the shape of a narrow railed platform running completely around the place. Below them was the roof of the boxes, then the circular rows and rows of benches, and down in the center the faintly flattened yellow circle of the arena, still bright with pools of rain water.

"You might open the package, Oscar," suggested Miss Withers.

He tore at the paper. "Good Lord, woman! I'm not playing cowboys and Indians at my time of life!"

He was holding a great six-foot bow of ash, wound with brilliantly colored cord and beads. There was a bowstring of gut, and under the schoolteacher's direction Piper painfully strung it so that it twanged musically.

She handed him a sheaf of bright *banderillas*. "Take your pocketknife and notch the ends a little," Miss Withers suggested. "Then let's see if you can shoot one—aim at that end seat in the farthest row, which is where Fitz was sitting. Somebody has left a newspaper to mark the place."

At last he took the bow, tried awkwardly. "Say, this dart isn't long enough to make a good arrow!" he complained.

"Try it anyway!" demanded the schoolteacher. "Why, I've had boys in my classes at Jefferson School who could shoot bigger bows than that!"

The inspector bent the bow, aiming down as best he could at that distant spot in the front row of the *barrera* seats. Then he let it go.

There was a sharp z-z-zing, and then a flash of color in the air, a flash of color that curved slowly and at last struck and remained in a mammoth sign advertising Glaxo, almost at right angles to the direction of the inspector's aim.

"Try again, and aim carefully!" Miss Withers demanded, producing another dart.

But as the inspector started to bend the bow again he suddenly stopped, pointed.

"What's the use, Hildegarde?"

She noticed now that theirs was not the only *banderilla* hanging where no *banderilla* should be. There was another in the Glaxo sign, there was one dangling from a smashed flood lamp in the center of the arena, and several more were stuck into the roof of the boxes to their left and right, others lying in the rows of the seats.

There was only one point in common between all of the scattered missiles. Not one of them had come to rest within two hundred feet of the newspaper which marked the spot where Michael Fitz had been found dead.

XIII

But Don't Go Near the Water

THE room was filled with boxes and baggage, and there was the strong pleasant odor of leather and varnish and excelsior. "Sorry to intrude," Miss Withers said, "but I haven't any use for this thing after all, and I thought you might like to add it to your collection of Mexican curios." She held out the great six-foot bow of ash, with its beads and colored windings in the ancient formal fashions of the Toltecs.

"Why—why how nice!" Adele Mabie accepted the offering, looking pleased and a little bewildered. "Oh, Dulcie"—she raised her voice—"when you finish wrapping those cups, please come here a moment." There was a murmur from the bedroom.

Miss Withers was honestly surprised. "But I thought the little Prothero girl was going to the Floating Gardens this afternoon!"

Adele Mabie lowered her voice to an intimate whisper. "So did she! But, after all, she's working for me now. And if she is well enough to go off excursioning with a young man, she's well enough to help pack my curios!"

The schoolteacher didn't say anything.

Adele went on: "I feel responsible for her, you see—and I'm not going to let her go off with a young man nobody knows for a boat ride—until all hours! He seems to be always hanging around, this Julio, but what does anybody know about him?"

"What indeed?" agreed Miss Withers.

"After all, we don't know that it wasn't he who…" Adele broke off as Dulcie Prothero came into the room. "Take this thing and see if it won't fit into the big packing case, will you?"

Dulcie, looking rather pale, and with a small bandage half concealed by her red mop of hair, greeted Miss Withers with a smile and nod. Then she accepted the unwieldy weapon and departed, closing the bedroom door behind her.

"About Julio," Miss Withers took up again, as if the subject interested her. "Of course, he carries a cane, but outside of Chicago and the Midwest that isn't definite proof of anything wrong with his morals. The most interesting thing about him is the way that—under moments of strain and excitement—he lapses into perfectly good English!"

Adele had noticed that too. "Tell me something," she demanded in a voice which showed that there was strain beneath her layer of composure. "Are the police any closer to finding out who—"

"If you ask me, the problem before the police isn't so much *who* as *how*," the schoolteacher declared. "No, I don't think they are closer to anything, even though they have two confessions. Mr. Hansen confesses that Mr. Lighton did it, and Mr. Lighton confesses that Mr. Hansen is the guilty party."

Adele ran her fingers through her hair. "What a lot of silly nonsense! Those two couldn't have killed Mr. Fitz. Not just because he misused some money of theirs. You might as well say that it was Francis, just because he lent some money to Mr. Hansen on the train to put into this ridiculous shoestring proposition!"

"Oh!" said Miss Withers.

"Have I given something away? Well, you'd be bound to find that out sooner or later, so it doesn't really matter. You know and I know that my husband wouldn't kill a flea."

"He will if he stays long in this country," Miss Hildegarde Withers pronounced grimly, having had her first experience with the smaller fauna of Mexico a short time previous. "But I think I know what you mean, and I'm somewhat inclined at the moment to agree. You see, the motives are all wrong for your husband. Besides, he is a rather poor shot, I understand."

Adele's eyes widened. "A shot? Oh—I see." She smiled a faint smile. "Anyway, we're getting out of the country on Wednesday's boat—leaving tomorrow for the port of Vera Cruz."

"Bag and baggage, eh?" Miss Withers surveyed the impedimenta which littered the room, the gaping suitcases, trunks half open, boxes, and the rows upon rows of curios arranged straight and neat against the wall and upon every flat surface of furniture. Her gaze lingered on the two matched *banderillas* with their black-gold decoration. Then she looked up. "When you say 'we' of course you mean your husband and yourself?"

Adele looked blank. "Why—Francis is of the opinion that it might look odd for him to leave now, until this is all settled. So I'm taking Dulcie Prothero to help with the tickets and the baggage and the customs fuss—she's really awfully competent at that sort of thing."

"Competent is hardly the word," Miss Withers said. "She is certainly a good one at keeping secrets. And why she would do almost menial labor rather than dip into the wealth pinned to her underwear..." The schoolteacher shook her head. "And for all her desire to get to Mexico, Dulcie is perfectly willing to leave with you?"

"Willing and anxious!" Adele insisted. "Whatever was her errand in coming to Mexico, it is finished. I'm not going to pry and question her any more, and I hope you won't."

Miss Withers shook her head.

"Dulcie is just as glad to get out of here as I, and of course Francis will follow as soon as the mystery is cleared up."

The schoolteacher thought that the alderman might be wearing a long white beard by that time, but she held her tongue. She looked down admiringly at the long row of riding crops which lay, neatly arranged according to length, on the desk ready for packing.

"Every one of my friends has started to go horsy!" Adele explained. "Long Island and Connecticut—everywhere people are taking up riding. So these will be real novelties when I get them back to New York."

There were riding crops of polished horn joined painfully together by the convicts on the Islas Marias. There were crops of whalebone covered with the skin of pigs, crops of braided brown calf, of brilliantly painted wood, of inlay, and even of cane with crudely carved horses' heads for handles. There were whips of every conceivable variety except one.

"Oh yes," Adele said. "The alligator one. Nicest of the lot, and it's gone."

"As if we hadn't mystery enough already," Miss Withers remarked, thinking of something else.

"I wouldn't be surprised if one of the maids in the hotel..." Adele went on sadly.

Miss Hildegarde Withers almost choked at the mental picture of a fat Mexican *criada* on her afternoon off, galloping up and down the bridle paths of the Paseo and slapping her mount on the tail with Adele's prize bit of Mexican handicraft. But it was time to go.

"Before I leave," she said, "I don't suppose you would care to play Truth for a moment?"

Adele's eyes widened. "What?

"You wouldn't like to tell me the real reason"—Miss Withers lowered her voice to a whisper—"the real reason why you kept Dulcie from going to the Floating Gardens this afternoon and evening?"

Adele Mabie stood there, immobile. "Of course I'll tell you," she said, in a voice that had not a trace of emotion in it. "I didn't hire that girl entirely out of kindness of heart. But I must have somebody around! My husband is no help—I could be murdered a dozen times and he wouldn't know. He's a love, and he's got a great political future, but heaven knows he isn't very bright."

"Yes?" Miss Withers prompted gently.

"And the reason I want Dulcie with me every minute is because I'm scared! I'm scared to death! And I'm afraid that if I'm alone something—somebody..."

Her voice broke, but she did not sob, did not bury her head on the couch. She simply stood there, blankly. And Miss Withers knew that Adele Mabie was telling the truth.

Miss Withers said what she could, which was little enough. Then she closed the door helplessly behind her and left Adele alone with her toys—and her terror.

It was a very real terror, so real that for the dozenth time since her arrival Miss Withers wondered if there wasn't a chance that Adele Mabie knew what—or who, rather—was threatening her.

Not that she would talk, and not that Dulcie would talk. Nobody talked in this case except when in a babbling coma. And even that information had been like a tennis net, more holes than rope.

The inspector wasn't in his room. He was never in his room when she wanted him. Miss Withers stalked downstairs and through the lobby of the Hotel Georges, managing to reach the street with only one shoe-shine, a record for her.

She walked swiftly, as if trying to leave something behind her. Down Madero and along Juarez, through the green stretches of the Alameda haunted as always by a thousand peddlers selling things to each other. Then north past the busy school playgrounds, through the cobbled streets of the old quarter with their thousand glimpses of squalid courts littered with goats and dogs and children and flowers, then south again through the swarms of lottery ticket sellers that infest the Corner of Fortune, down along narrow crooked streets that ran into the great San Juan Market, where one can buy everything in the world.

She walked past stands heavy with roses, iris, gladioli, fresh scentless violets, carnations of a red that was almost black, gardenias that filled the air with perfume.

There were tables covered with broken keys, used toothbrushes, rusty hinges, third-hand and fourth-hand paper bags. There was a stand with several thousand old medicine bottles, all shining and clean, another with nothing but earrings of lovely brass, then a whole row with nothing but breasts of chicken, followed by another with the halved heads of kids and lambs. The schoolteacher moved hastily away from their accusing, pitiful eyes.

She passed another stand in the form of a great hatrack, from which dangled ropes and bridles made of hair and fuzzy as caterpillars, cinchbands of canvas decorated with beads, bits for horses' mouths and stirrups for riders' feet all chased in silver on copper, black spurs with sharp rowels three inches long, cruel and glistening.

The shadows were lengthening now along the narrow crooked streets of the old city, and here and there the red light of the western sun touched the crumbling stone of the houses with a warm unearthly glow.

The sunlight fell full and clear upon a blue tile set in an old cracked wall, a tile half hidden by the profuse blossoms of a magnificent blue-purple bougainvillea. Miss Hildegarde Withers read the ancient florid script *"Calle Violetta"*—and caught her breath.

All through the afternoon she had been unconsciously searching for this street sign. And now she was here, here on the corner of Violetta Street. Here, only last night, Dulcie Prothero had come out second best in an encounter with a taxicab. Here, within a stone's throw, must be dangling one of the loose threads of her murder mystery—for Violetta was only one block long and ended in a cul-de-sac.

She went on, and then, in a wide half-ruined gateway leading into a patio filled with goats, chickens, washing and flowers, she came upon a group of very young children playing with a ball made of rags tightly tied together.

"Hello!" she greeted them. After all, children are children in any language.

"¡Hola, señorita! Buenos tardes." They stopped their play, with the almost universal politeness of the Mexican young, and grouped around her.

"I want to find—it should be in this street or near by—the home of the American bullfighter," she said. "¿Dónde esta the house of the torero de yanquilandia?"

Seven soft voices chanted "Allá, señorita." Seven fingers pointed to a sagging tenement across the street. Seven palms accepted infinitesimal silver coins.

It was after sunset when Miss Hildegarde Withers left Violetta Street, and the glow was gone. The twilight had settled down upon the city like a solid thing. The few feeble gas flares and candles which appeared here and there served only to accentuate the darkness. The schoolteacher shivered and turned hastily homeward.

One block—another—and then she realized that someone was following her. It was a feeling, a psychic sense rather than anything definite, and yet it was as real as anything. Every time she stopped to look back she saw nothing more than the crowded streets, the homebound workers, the children playing and shouting, women packing up their offerings of wizened apples and plums to be brought back another day for sidewalk display. The streets were bare of automobiles, not a taxicab in sight anywhere.

Yet the shadows seemed to move, to merge, to deepen as she watched. The few lighted windows of the houses seemed far away, and every corner, every doorway, was waiting…

She walked faster, turned right on the next corner and then left again. "I'm nervous as a cat," the schoolteacher told herself. "I'll be seeing things yet!" All the same, she kept hurrying.

And whatever it was that followed her was hurrying too. She could almost hear the footsteps, she fancied—yet every time she looked back she was forced to admit that it must be the Invisible Man.

Some people have a faculty of knowing when they are being watched, a sixth sense that causes a little prickle along the back of the neck. This was Miss Withers' to the highest degree, and it kept signaling to her with a sharp buzzing in the back of her mind.

"It can't be bandits," she told herself angrily, "because I certainly don't look as if I had any money. And nobody would pay ransom for me, either. It can't be anyone trying to murder me, because my investigations certainly haven't cut any ice."

The street she was following suddenly twisted, ran head on into another, and stopped. And then Miss Withers realized that she hadn't the slightest idea of whether to turn right or left.

It was a time for instant decisions, and so she made one. There was no use hurrying blindly down these dark, foreign, and suddenly unfriendly streets.

There was no use trying to run away from whatever was dogging her footsteps, for long ago she had learned the lesson in life that it is usually the things one flies from that stick closer than a brother.

So, as she rounded the corner, Miss Hildegarde Withers took pains to disappear. It was not much of a place to disappear into, but it was all she could find.

She waited, watching and listening. With all her heart she wished that the inspector were here beside her. Failing that, she wished for the faithful black cotton umbrella which had served her so well in many a previous imbroglio. For it was not her imagination that had sent her hurrying from the shadows. There was the sound of light quick footsteps coming around the corner, pausing just out of view.

"Waiting to see where I went, eh? Well, I'll show them!" And from behind the swinging doors of the little neighborhood *cantina* popped an embattled spinster, face to face with her shadow at last.

It was only Julio Mendez, mopping his brow and leaning heavily upon his malacca stick.

The words which had been on Miss Withers' tongue stuck there. It was the Gay Caballero who regained his composure first. "Well, if this isn't a big surprise? To meeting you like this!"

"Surprise my aunt!" she accused him. "You've been following me for half an hour. And don't try to deny it."

"Sure," he agreed, with his usual cheer. "Bet your life I follow. Ever since I saw you go into Violetta Street—"

"You were watching that place? But why?"

"Same reason you go there, I guess," Julio admitted. "You know, I like very much this Dulcie Prothero. I interest myself in what happens to her last night."

"Of all things! Still playing detective, eh?"

"But yes! I went to school with Manuel Robles, you see? And I must doing everything I can, no?" He fell calmly into step beside her. "This not very damn-good section, maybe I better show you home. Tell me, you don't solve this murder either?"

She shook her head. "I can think of a lot of questions, but I can't think of the answers. And the inspector isn't much help. He just runs around yessing these idiotic police of yours."

"Dumbs-bells, all of them," Julio murmured sympathetically. "I know!"

They continued in silence for half a block. "If I had the answers to just six questions," Miss Withers finally burst out, "I think this case would be sewed up tight in a bag."

Julio was unwontedly serious. "Go ahead, try me," he invited eagerly. "I got nothing else to do—Miss Dulcie turns me down, and I got no date to go to the Floating Gardens."

She stared at him and then said: "What can I lose?" For a moment she was thoughtful. "First—well, first I'd like to know why Michael Fitz brought home an absolutely inedible fighting cock to eat."

Julio said he was stumped by that one.

"Second, I want to know why Adele Mabie is afraid of the little Prothero girl!"

"But—but she has been so kind to Dulcie! She takes her back, gives her the job!"

"Exactly! That's how I know she's afraid of her. Perhaps she thinks she's safer to have Dulcie where she can watch her every minute."

Julio wouldn't agree to that. "Dulcie Prothero don't kill somebody— I bet you anything. But anyway, go on."

"Third, why does Dulcie Prothero, in desperate financial straits, wear a small fortune pinned to her—pinned under her dress?"

"My guess would be, maybe..." Julio began. But Miss Withers told him that she could do her own guessing, what she needed was facts.

"I don't understand that young lady, in spite of the fact that I knew her when her red hair was in pigtails. Either her heart is broken, or she thinks it is broken..." Miss Withers shook her head. "At any rate, my fourth question is—Why does a man in a heavy rainproof coat need an umbrella in a drizzle?"

The young man thought for a moment. "You'll have to ask *Señor* Fitz that question on the ouija board, no?"

She went on. "Fifth, how could a *banderilla* get deep into a human body without being shot from a bow or fired from an air gun?"

"I understand about the bow," Julio admitted. "We both made the same experiments. But the air gun—"

"Air guns make some noise," she told him. "Besides, to shoot anything as large as that dart they would have to be specially designed. None of our suspects is a gunsmith."

They had paused outside the window of a little shoeshop on the Calle Dolores. Inside, beneath the yellow rays of a lantern hung above his bench, a gnarled old man in a big apron sent his awl through the leather sole of a *zapato* again and again, following it each time with the needle and waxed thread.

"I see what you mean," Julio agreed. "Then we got to go back to the first idea, that somebody stick *Señor* Fitz from behind?"

She nodded. "But as Captain de Silva or someone pointed out, it would take the strongest man in the world to drive a shaft of wood with a steel barb that deeply into flesh. If it had been the bullfighters' sword, the *acero,* that would be different. But a *banderilla* is just a decoration, a frill."

She was staring in at the busy little old cobbler, as if half hypnotized by the flash of his needle, the rhythmic movement of his awl.

"Unless—unless…" she murmured.

Suddenly Miss Withers turned on Julio, a new expression on her face. "Please—may I see your cane a moment?"

"My—Why, of course!" Wonderingly, he handed her the heavy malice stick, watched as she twisted and turned at the top of the handle.

"It isn't the coming-apart one," he advised her. "At home I got one with a long glass tube inside, for cockstails and things. But I don't using it much."

"I wasn't looking for a flask; I was looking for a sword," she admitted, handing the thing back. They started on again, Julio still burning with curiosity.

"Please!" he begged. "That wasn't one of your important questions, no? You think I—or somebody else—sticks a sword cane into *Señor* Fitz? But that's not how he dies! I myself saw the—the photographs in the newspaper of his body. It was a *banderilla*, sure thing you know."

"I know, I know," said Miss Hildegarde Withers impatiently. They were turning the corner near the hotel. "No, that wasn't my sixth question. I don't think I ought to tell you that one."

"But please! I am strictly positively all ears!"

"Very well, since you ask for it," she said. "Why in the name of heaven do you insist on talking like Leo Carrillo giving an imitation of a Mexican?"

"Wha-what?"

"Why the phony dialect?" she pressed. "I'm sick to death of it!"

For a long, long moment Julio Mendez stared at her wonderingly, unbelievingly. Then he began to laugh.

"You're sick of it!" he gasped. "What the hell about *me?"*

XIV

Over Niagara Falls

"MOS' CERTAINLY I recognize that photograph," said the broad-beamed lady in the purple evening dress. "That is *Señor* Hansen, the reech handsome *Americano.* I meet with him at the bullfight." She lounged enticingly in the doorway.

Captain de Silva put the photograph back in his pocket. "Mr. Hansen sat next to you in the first row on Sunday, is that right?"

She nodded.

"But he didn't stay until the end, did he?"

"Ah no, *señores.* He leave when the picadors finish with the last bull, to get some roses for me. Because I tell him I like to throw down roses to young Nicanor when he kill that bull."

De Silva turned to the inspector. "That checks, *señor,* with what you observed?"

"Absolutely," Piper said.

"But he didn't come back, did he?" de Silva went on.

"There was very much rain," La Belle Consuela explained. "I have to hurry away so I will not spoil my dress."

"And he hasn't been back to see you since?"

"Because you lock him up!" said the woman with a toss of her head. " He will come. He has promised to take me back to the United States and give me the big send-off in the movies. He says I am wasting my time here singing in cafés—that I am like Dolores del Rio only more sex appeal."

"I'd hate to hang by my thumbs until the day Al Harness gets her into pictures," Oscar Piper said to the captain as they got back into the police sedan.

"At any rate," said de Silva, "the story checks so far. Hansen left the bullfight to get flowers—"

"Saying he was going to get flowers," Piper corrected him. "But I've got an idea to test the whole thing."

Half an hour later they were rolling down Insurgentes toward the pillbox of the *toreo*. They stopped before the south gate.

"I understand," repeated Captain de Silva. "For purposes of this experiment it is Sunday afternoon at 4:36. We can set that time because it was then that the bugle sounded for the end of the affair of the picadors. Both the young lady and you agree that Mr. Hansen left the bullfight then. You, for the moment, are Mr. Hansen, in search of a bouquet of flowers."

He held up a stop watch. "All right—go!"

The Packard rolled slowly ahead, stopped two blocks ahead at a confectionery store. Yes, agreed the proprietor, he remembered very well that a gringo hurried in just before the rain on Sunday afternoon, asking for directions to the nearest flower market. He was directed north...Yes, it was the *señor* in the photograph.

The inspector, striding briskly along the sidewalk, was waved north. Another stop, and another...

Today there were flower sellers on every corner, women hunched over benches loaded with blooms and men strolling the streets like walking greenhouses. But on a late Sunday afternoon it had, obviously, been a different story. Al Hansen had gone on and on.

"Probably a point of pride with the guy not to come back and tell the dame that he couldn't find the posies he'd promised her," Piper said to himself as he trudged on.

At last, with the police sedan rolling ever ahead like a will-o'-the-wisp, the inspector came at last into the crowded and odorous streets which surround the San Juan Market. Through streets so crowded with stands, children, shopping women and dogs that there was barely room for the car to pass at a snail's cautious pace, around corners which doubled back upon themselves, past great mounds of red and green peppers, whole mountains of shiny brown-purple beans...

Far ahead the siren of the police sedan hooted, and Piper increased his pace. He was willing to bet ten dollars that Al Hansen's tongue would be hanging out a foot if he kept up with this speed for two blocks, let alone twelve.

Down the street of flowers, the block lined with sprawling booths which never close. It was a wilderness of perfume and color, an outdoor hothouse.

From either side soft-voiced women urged the inspector to stop and admire—not purchase, but just to look, *señor*—sweet miniature violets, great waxen water lilies like dinner plates...

Captain de Silva had already found the stall where on Sunday a hurried American had purchased two dozen red roses for twenty-eight cents United States currency. It had hardly been necessary to show the photograph, for customers who do not stop to bargain are few in the street of flowers.

It was 5:02 according to de Silva's watch.

"Hansen would walk while he was looking for a flower booth," the inspector suggested thoughtfully. "But once he did succeed in getting the flowers, wouldn't he take a taxi back to the bullfight, knowing how late he was?"

"Climb in!" agreed de Silva and they roared around the corner, scattering dogs and children right and left.

"No taxi ever made the time we're making," the inspector said, clinging to his hat with both hands.

But though they made top speed, when finally the monkey-like driver of the police Packard slammed on his brakes outside the giant pillbox of the Plaza de Toros, Captain de Silva looked at his stop watch and shook his head.

"It is now 5:09 of Sunday afternoon," he announced.

"Yeah," said Inspector Oscar Piper. "And the body of Michael Fitz was discovered two minutes ago!"

Back in his little office at the *jefatura*, Captain de Silva scribbled an order, gave it to a uniformed gendarme.

"A release for the man Hansen," he said, in Spanish.

"*Sí, capitán.*" The subordinate hesitated. "And for the man Lighton too?"

De Silva shook his head. "I don't see how we dare turn Rollo Lighton loose," he observed to the inspector. "He has been under questioning most of the afternoon, but all we know is that he lied when he said that he spent Sunday afternoon working."

"Any man," said the visiting New York cop, "will lie his head off when he thinks he's mixed up in a murder case."

"Innocent as well as guilty, you mean? Yes, of course. But I wish we had some way to find out if Lighton tells the truth in his corrected story about coming downtown to the Papillon bar after he couldn't sponge a free seat at the bullfight."

"He says the alderman was there and bought him a drink, but you think maybe they're supplying alibis for each other?" Piper hazarded.

The captain leaned back in his chair, folded his arms behind his head. "Would not fellow countrymen stick together?" he began. And then there came a heavy knocking at the door.

It was an officer. "The manager of the Papillon bar to see you, *Capitán*," he said.

"Show him in," de Silva said wearily. "You stay, Mr. Piper."

The fat little cock robin of a man was apologetic. "What happens when you come to my bar, I cannot understand," he said, in many words and gestures. "So many people come and go—it is only human that once I remember wrongly, no?"

"All right, all right, it was a mistake." De Silva cut him short. Piper stood back near the window, puffing a cigar in silence.

"Yes, *Capitán*. But there is also one other mistake. A mistake made by that new man I hire last week, that fool of a Ramon. He does not know…"

The cock robin was spluttering now.

"Yes, yes—what is it? Did he break a glass?"

"But no, *Capitán*. Much worse. I am going to fire him if it happens one more time. But in the meanwhile I think that perhaps it has to do with what you come to see me about. So I bring these!"

He produced bar bills for three separate rounds of drinks, dated Sunday and signed with a flourish by Rollo Lighton!

Interested in spite of himself, the inspector made a whispered suggestion.

De Silva nodded. "This Ramon, your new waiter—he worked all day Sunday?"

Cock Robin shook his head. "Only from four o'clock until closing, *señor*. And he accepted these signatures early, because some time before six one of the older waiters warned him that a chit signed by Mr. Lighton is good only for framing to hang over the cash registers."

When the little man was gone the inspector threw his dead cigar into de Silva's wastebasket. "Another suspect cleared, blast it!" he remarked. "And if you think my friend Miss Withers won't have the laugh on me when I report…"

"You're lucky," said Captain de Silva. "I have to make my report to the lieutenant colonel, and he won't laugh—not any."

Miss Hildegarde Withers, far from jeering at the inspector's afternoon, was full of an inner excitement. "I've just had a nice walk and talk with Julio Mendez," she admitted in the hotel lobby. "Don't be misled by the beret and the cane, Oscar. That young man is well worth cultivating. We haven't been giving half enough attention to Julio."

"Yeah? Well, what did you and the Gay Caballero have to talk about?"

She told him, with reservations. "Mr. Mendez was very upset to hear that Adele Mabie plans to take Dulcie away tomorrow."

He looked disgusted. "Hildegarde! You're not trying to play matchmaker again?"

"The Happy Ending, Oscar? No, nothing like that. I'll be satisfied if we can get through this case without another murder. Somehow I have a prickling at the back of my neck these days, as if—well, as if something were sniffing at my heels."

He looked at her curiously. "Relax, Hildegarde! Nothing more is going to happen, not with everybody on their guard."

She sniffed. "If I remember correctly, you were playing cards during the first murder, and you gaped at the bullfight with me during the second. So I'm taking steps of my own. When I get the answers to my six questions—no, only four now—I expect to have this case settled."

"Questions? What questions?" he demanded.

"It's a private list," she told him. "But you might be able to help me with one of them. Oscar, why would a man want to eat a fighting cock?"

"What?" Then he remembered. "You can search me. Maybe he was broke and hungry."

She shook her head. "Did you ever play bridge, Oscar?"

Piper swore that he was innocent of the charge. "Penny ante, dominoes and a fast game of cribbage are my limit."

"Well, poker then. When a man loses, doesn't he sometimes blame the cards, just as I've seen golfers smash their clubs?"

"Yeah, why?"

"Even sometimes tear up the deck of cards?"

"Gamblers will do anything," he told her. "When I was a rookie I was assigned to do guard duty up at Belmont Park, because a nag ran second in a big race. Some nut wanted to bump off the horse."

Miss Hildegarde Withers nodded, smiling like a Cheshire cat. "Another sidelight on the character of Mr. Fitz," she said. "And an answer to another of my moot questions."

"Now you're changing sides, Hildegarde! All along you've been saying that Fitz was killed by mistake for Adele Mabie!"

Miss Withers' answer was lost as the dim lobby was suddenly flooded with light. There was a commotion behind the hotel desk, cries of delight from the pretty girl at the switchboard, and the manager came out looking as if he were about to turn handsprings. "It works!" he cried in boyish delight. "The new lighting plant—it gives light! Hotel Georges service!"

"Yeah," Piper said in an aside to Miss Withers. "If we only had this much light on our mystery…"

"Before this night is over we will!" she promised him. And then she saw the inspector rise suddenly.

"There comes de Silva," he said wonderingly, "looking stern and important!"

But the captain barely paused to greet them. "I have a message for you," he said. "But I must go upstairs first. Please do not leave the hotel during the next few minutes." Then he was gone, up the steps.

"Why, the cocky little…" Piper began. "What's eating him?"

"Just a snowball, a snowball I started rolling," Miss Withers told him gently. "But here comes somebody else."

The Ippwings were the next arrivals, arm in arm, loaded down with flowers. They expressed delight at seeing the inspector and Miss Withers, delight at the miracle of electricity again, delight at almost everything.

"We've been having the most gorgeous times!" began Mrs. Ippwing breathlessly. "A real second honeymoon, almost."

"We rode on the boat, and we bought all the flowers in the world for about fifty cents American money!" Marcus Ippwing joined in. "It's the loveliest place—you ought to go there before you leave. Everybody who comes to Mexico City goes out to Xochimilco."

"What is it, a greenhouse?" Piper asked.

"The Floating Gardens! Only of course they don't float anymore. But there's a sweet little village with an old church, and you go on through to the canals and ride for hours on sort of flat gondolas through miles and miles of crisscrossed waterways, and other boats full of musicians follow you…" Mrs. Ippwing was beaming.

"You just must look at the pictures!" she insisted. "Marcus, show them!"

Nothing loath, her husband produced a long envelope, drew out a sheaf of brownish postcard size prints. "There was a little man with the weirdest old camera at the boat landing," Mrs. Ippwing went on. "He took our pictures as we started—this is the one. See? There's Father and me on the little chairs in the front of the boat. And a bower of real flowers overhead—for a sunshade!"

Miss Withers and the inspector saw, willy-nilly.

"And when we were halfway down the canal," Ippwing continued, "up came the photographer in another boat, and he had the pictures all developed and fixed up the *craziest*!"

Miss Withers looked at the prints, saw the grinning Ippwing faces, but instead of in their rightful clothes and personalities they had been transposed by some dark magic of the finisher into other, more glamorous settings.

They smiled down from the cockpit of a plane piloted by Charles Augustus Lindbergh. They smiled at the world from the observation platform of the Empire State Building, with Al Smith behind them and a very solid-looking dirigible moored to the building's tip. They shook hands with the Presidente of Mexico, rode fiery horses in *charro* costume.

"Hildegarde, we must go to that Xochimilco place and see the world," Piper said irreverently.

"Won't our daughter just die laughing at these?" Marcus Ippwing said fondly.

There were other shots, with the same two grinning faces. One showed the Eiffel Tower as a background, another displayed the couple sliding down almost vertically in a roller coaster labeled "Luna Park," and last and most impressive, the Ippwings, their heads protruding from windows in the top of a huge barrel, were sailing over Niagara Falls!

"How interesting!" Miss Withers said, with a kindly and most convincing voice. But the inspector was restless, led her away.

"I want to know what de Silva is doing upstairs!" he declared. "If that guy thinks he is going to beat me to anything."

"We might wander upstairs and find out," Miss Withers suggested. They had not far to go. They could hear a woman's voice, raised in exasperation, as they came up the second flight. Captain de Silva was standing outside the door of the Mabies' sitting room, and Adele Mabie was facing him.

"You can just go and tell your old *jefe* that I'm not going to any meeting tonight—I'm staying right here! I've been packing all day, and I've got too much to do to go anywhere!"

"In that case," de Silva said smoothly, "we can arrange to have the *notario* come here—your room is large enough, I believe, for everybody? It will only take a few minutes, I think."

"Oh, if you insist," Adele said. "Heaven knows I want to see justice done, and if it will help any—"

"Nine o'clock, then," said the captain. He turned and came down the hall, so that there was barely time for Miss Withers and the inspector to arrange themselves as innocent passersby.

He called to them. "One minute, please! It will be necessary for everybody involved in this case to make depositions before a *notario* and myself—Room 307 at nine o'clock. The orders of the *jefe*."

"What's up?" Miss Withers wanted to know.

"Just a formality," he told them. "But necessary since certain persons are planning to leave the country."

He turned and hurried down the stairs, whence a moment later arose the excited and pleased voices of the Ippwings accepting the invitation.

"The snowball rolls," Miss Hildegarde Withers observed quietly. "And rolls…"

"What?" demanded Piper irritably. "I don't get the idea of all this monkey business. Depositions and notaries and polite invitations to attend a merry-get-together at nine o'clock! You don't happen to be holding out on me, do you?"

But Miss Withers didn't answer. "We don't know whether Dulcie Prothero was happy to accept the *jefe*'s kind invitation or not, do we? But then, I don't suppose she had much to say about it."

"Dulcie? What about her?"

"Why, nothing, Oscar—except that the party is being held somewhat in her honor, that's all."

"Huh? Oh, she'll be there," the inspector assured her.

Miss Withers shook her head. "I rather fancy not," she said.

XV

Button Button!

"IS EVERYBODY HERE?" Captain de Silva said. He was looking at his watch, which showed twenty minutes past nine.

"It's my fault about Dulcie Prothero," Mrs. Mabie confessed. "I sent her over to the express office. With all these curios there are so many formalities!" Adele waved her hand toward the boxes and baggage which had been moved to the corners of the room, toward the neat rows and piles of handicraft. "But the girl ought to be back by now."

The alderman was very much in evidence, a trifle the worse for wear. He was moving restlessly up and down the room as if unable to remain in his chair. Too, he was at the stage when he could not help touching people, gripping the lapels of the men…

It was clear to Miss Withers now why Dulcie Prothero had regretted her impulsiveness on the train platform and had made tentative efforts to return the thirty dollars which she possibly imagined had strings attached.

Rollo Lighton sat in one corner, near the piles of painted pottery and the neat row of riding whips. He looked somewhat the worse for his afternoon's grilling and lighted one cigarette after another with hands that trembled. He did not listen to Al Hansen's cheerful chat, which had to do with the money that could be made in Mexico by the importation of a few nice new handsome slot machines.

The Ippwings listened, nodding politely. First to arrive, they now perched on a settee against the wall, waiting happily as if in the intermission before the feature picture went on.

Hildegarde Withers had chosen a straight, rather uncomfortable chair with a thinly upholstered back, which she edged forward a little so that she was not far from the center of the group. Adele Mabie moved nervously around the room, pausing once beside the schoolteacher to say: "Such a shame to move everything in here when Dulcie had it all arranged ready to pack! She's a treasure, that girl. Why, she even found the riding whip, the one made of alligator. You remember?"

"Where did she find it?" Miss Withers wanted to know, and Adele shook her head.

Dulcie and Julio Mendez were still missing at nine-thirty. "We will begin without them," said de Silva. Acting a little as if he were unsure of what was coming next, the captain bent over and whispered to a dark little man with thick glasses who, Miss Withers assumed, was the notario. He produced a shorthand notebook and a pile of freshly sharpened pencils.

"What the *jefe* wants is simply this," Captain de Silva began. "The lieutenant colonel is agreed that we shall not put any unnecessary obstacles in the way of our so-welcome tourist friends from north of the Rio Grande. So if each one of you will simply make a statement— under oath, of course—to everything he or she has noticed or experienced and which may have any bearing on either of these two unfortunate murders…"

"Tripe!" whispered the inspector to Miss Withers. "This is all moonshine—and I thought these boys were smart!" She hushed him.

"The lieutenant colonel has ordered that these statements be made before all of you, so that if any details are omitted or any mistaken information be given, it can be checked at the source," continued the captain. "Our first witness was to have been the *Señorita* Prothero, and she was to have discussed a certain bottle supposed to have contained perfume, once her property."

Miss Withers nodded approvingly.

"But since she is not with us, we had better begin with you, Mrs. Mabie. Please begin at your first meeting with the Prothero girl."

"Why—she came in answer to an ad I placed in the New York papers," Adele began slowly. "I asked for an experienced maid willing to travel to Mexico. She looked so smart and neat that I hired her to take the trip. Besides, she was willing to travel for a very low salary just to get down here."

"Do you know why?" asked the captain. Just then the telephone interrupted.

Miss Withers beat everyone else to the instrument. "Oh yes—ask them to come up, please."

The alderman looked startled. "No more identification parades, for God's sake?"

"Not exactly," Miss Withers told him. "You came off rather badly in the last one, didn't you? But never mind."

There was a knock on the door, and Captain de Silva opened it. In the hall stood two gendarmes in uniform, and between them, struggling and protesting, was a young man with pale hair, a sorrowful mouth, and ears—as the inspector said later—like a taxicab with both doors open.

"Oh yes," Miss Withers said. "An addition to our little group. Mr.…"

The young man glared at her, glared at everybody.

"Tell the lady your name," rasped the inspector. "Or—"

"Not now, Oscar," the schoolteacher hastily put in. "I don't think there is any need for unpleasantness. Is there, Mr.…"

"My name, if it makes any difference to you, is Robert Schultz!" He refused the proffered chair.

"Address, top floor, number two Violetta Street," Miss Withers added.

But it was Mrs. Ippwing who seemed most impressed. "Not—not *the* Robert Schultz?"

He smiled a sullen smile. "Used to be, I guess."

"Why, Father," the birdlike little old lady was chattering, "that's Mr. Schultz, the Yonkers Matador! Don't you remember reading in all the papers a year ago about the American boy who came down here and taught the Mexicans how to fight bulls?"

"That was just newspaper stuff," he admitted.

"But I haven't read anything about you lately," Mrs. Ippwing went on.

He flushed. "I'm still around."

"Around the bullfight, yes," put in Miss Withers. "You wear a red jacket and help to haul the dead bulls away, don't you?"

"Well, it's a job, isn't it?" He whirled suddenly. "I don't have to take this, and I'm leaving. I haven't done anything!"

"Haven't you?" said Miss Hildegarde Withers softly. "What about breach of promise?"

He stopped, frozen into marble.

"What about your former sweetheart, the pretty little girl from back in New York?"

Again he smiled the crooked smile. "If you mean Miss Dulcie Prothero, she's through with me. You see, she looked me up when she got down here, and she found—she found…" He fumbled with this.

"Found that you are married and have a family? Just as I discovered this afternoon?" Miss Withers pressed. He nodded.

The silence in the room was strained, hard to bear. Adele Mabie was tapping her foot against the floor.

Miss Withers was frowning. "Thank you for coming, young man. It's been a revelation to know you. I'm sorry that I didn't find you in when I called this afternoon, but it was enough to find a Mexican girl and two or three babies rolling on your floor. It must have been into just such a domestic scene that Dulcie Prothero walked, after she got your address from the bullfight office. No wonder she was shocked."

"She'll get over it," the young man said. "She's better off if we never meet again."

Miss Withers agreed with that. "No wonder the girl came out of the house in a daze and forgot to dodge the taxicabs last night. She…"

Moving toward the door, Mr. Robert Schultz stopped suddenly, legs braced wide apart. "Please say that again!"

"Miss Prothero was struck by a taxi last night," the schoolteacher explained. "Though I don't see how it matters…"

He burst out of the door.

"I don't like that young man," Mrs. Ippwing said loudly and clearly. "I was going to ask him for his autograph, but now I won't!"

Captain de Silva, obviously bewildered at the turn events had taken, made valiant efforts to proceed. "If you have no objections," he said to Miss Hildegarde Withers, with an intended sarcasm which passed like water from the back of the proverbial duck.

"Go ahead," she said. "I was only trying to clear up some of the cloudy angles of this case. At noon today I decided that if I had the answer to six questions I would have solved this entire muddle. When I came here there were only four unanswered, and no doubt before we finish this heart-to-heart talk, the other ones will be cleared up."

She tried to look particularly wise and omniscient. The captain nodded to his assistant with the notebook, began all over again. "Now, Mrs. Mabie," he said, "will you be good enough…"

The lights flickered and went out. There was a pause, a noisy demanding of matches, and then the lights came on again.

"Hotel Georges service!" quoted the inspector wickedly.

Then the lights went off again and stayed off. There was a long expectant period during which everyone sat and waited, exchanging remarks about home-generator plants and Mexican mechanics.

Miss Hildegarde Withers heard a faint rustling movement in the pitchy dark behind her and suddenly slid out of her chair. It was a movement so automatic that it surprised even her. She remained on the floor, hardly daring to breathe.

"Hasn't anybody got a match?" she demanded at last. Finally they all realized that the lights were not coming on again, and matches and pocket lighters produced several luminous spots. There was light enough to see that everyone was in his proper place—everyone except the schoolteacher.

Adele Mabie screamed and pointed. "Look!"

The inspector hurried, helped Miss Withers to her feet. "You all right?"

"Of course I am!" she insisted.

There was light enough now that Adele had found the candles so that they could all see Julio Mendez standing in the doorway, blinking with surprise. Behind him was Dulcie Prothero.

"Playing Hide in the Dark?" the Gay Caballero inquired.

"I'm sorry I'm late," Dulcie said quickly. "I didn't know you were having a meeting—and as I came back I met Mr. Mendez in the lobby."

"She works very hard," Julio put in. "She wraps and packs all afternoon, and she even forgets to eat. So I take her over to Prendes and buy her one good meal."

Dulcie nodded. Miss Withers knew that the girl had been laughing. There were signs of laughter around her mouth, and if the eyes lacked it that might come later.

"Too bad you were not here a moment ago," the schoolteacher said. "We had a friend of yours call, Dulcie."

At that moment the lights came back on again, with a blinding glare like that of a magnesium explosion. They winked, went off, came back, and stayed.

Everyone laughed nervously. "Now if this had been a mystery on the stage," Inspector Piper said, "we'd have found one member of the party lying dead in the middle of the floor."

Miss Hildegarde Withers caught her breath. "Yes, wouldn't we," she agreed, her voice strange and tight. "If this were a mystery thriller..."

She was looking at the back of her chair. Then everybody looked and saw that through the cloth, through the fiber and upholstery of the thin chairback, there was a tiny triangular hole.

"Of course!" cried Adele Mabie hysterically. "That's why the lights went out—but why was it meant for you instead of for me?"

"Because," Miss Withers said, "I happen to know the answer to the last question!"

It was Julio Mendez who spoke first. "Bad business," he observed. "Sticking knives at people's backs. Maybe"—he looked inquiringly at the captain—"maybe we ought to be turning out our pockets, no?"

De Silva accepted the suggestion at once. "Lock the doors," he commanded. "I am sorry, but everyone in this room will have to submit to a search."

"I'm not going to have anybody pawing me!" began the alderman.

"And of course," Miss Withers suggested, "anyone refusing to cooperate will be making a sort of confession, won't he?"

There was quite a good deal said on the subject pro and con, but finally everyone was taken in turn to the bedroom and searched thoroughly. Captain de Silva took the men, and at his suggestion the ladies submitted to the attentions of Miss Hildegarde Withers. Mrs. Mabie, Mrs. Ippwing—even Dulcie went through the ordeal. But the proceeding took a long time, was embarrassing for everybody concerned, and drew an absolute blank. The men, most of them, had pocket knives, but none with a blade which was anything the shape of that triangular stiletto mark.

Then the sitting room was given a thorough once-over by Captain de Silva, while Julio Mendez looked on and made lighthearted comments.

Mrs. Ippwing sought out the schoolteacher and whispered cautiously in her ear. "That young man and the girl were in the doorway when the candles were lighted," she was saying. "I don't suppose there could be a chance that *they* got rid of the knife in the hall?"

The hall was searched, but, since it was simply a long bare stretch without furniture or any other possible hiding place, that possibility was speedily eliminated.

"I know, maybe!" Julio Mendez offered suddenly. "The window, yes?"

"Just what I was going to suggest," snapped Captain de Silva. But the window was firmly closed, and when finally it opened there was so much noise in its sliding that this possibility, too, had to be forgotten. The bedroom door, likewise, squeaked on its hinges.

"It's a cinch that knife is in this room," Inspector Oscar Piper declared. "We'll look again, eh?"

They looked again, under the rug, behind the desk, in the cushions of the davenport.

But there was no knife.

Rollo Lighton said unpleasantly that he didn't suppose anybody in the room had ever heard of a secret drawer in the furniture.

"Of course!" Miss Withers agreed. "The murderer is really a woodworker, and some time ago he sneaked into this hotel and put secret drawers into the furniture just in preparation for this evening!" She sniffed. "Well, what next?"

"Must there be more?" said Dulcie Prothero. The girl stood leaning against the table, and the color which had been slowly coming back into her face through the day was gone again.

"I think maybe we get out of these place, no?" Julio Mendez suggested. "Before the lights go out again."

"Yes, for heaven's sake," Mrs. Ippwing pleaded. "As it is, Father will keep me awake half the night muttering in his sleep about clues!" Captain de Silva had no choice but to order the door unlocked.

There was a general exodus from the place, everyone anxious to put distance between himself and that room with its dreadful potentiality. The missing stiletto was a sword of Damocles, only, as Miss Withers observed, it hung by a thread in the fourth dimension.

Even the alderman moved uncomfortably, looked at his wife. "Adele, would you mind? I—I think I need a drink, and the bar up the street is still open." His fat white hands were trembling.

She didn't mind. "I'll be back early," he promised.

"Sure, I'll see he gets back early," Al Hansen said. He was smiling his usual smile, but it was frozen on his round face. "I'll have Pedro mix up some cocktails that'll make you forget your troubles past, present and future, eh, Alderman?" He looked at Rollo Lighton. "Coming?"

"No, I'm going," said Lighton and then hurried hastily down the hall, no doubt weak from the effort of will exerted in turning down a drink.

Julio Mendez was beside Dulcie. "Just to making sure that you get there without some more monkey-shining happening, how about I take you up to your room, yes?"

"Please do!" she begged, and they went. At last everyone was gone, everyone but Miss Withers, the inspector—and Adele.

"It wasn't entirely a failure, this convocation," the schoolma'am said thoughtfully. "And the evening isn't over yet. I wonder—"

"I see the plan. I see exactly what you're driving at!" Adele Mabie suddenly blurted out. She was stalking up and down the room as if it were a cage. "What if I don't agree, what then?"

Miss Withers was very innocent. "Agree?"

"To being a lure, a bait!" Adele continued, with her voice growing shakier and shakier. "Everybody knows now that I'm leaving tomorrow, and that tonight is the last chance..."

"Yes," agreed the schoolteacher.

"You just think of catching the murderer; you don't mind risking human lives!"

"Not even my own," Miss Withers advised her. "As the inspector here can tell you."

"Yours or anybody else's. You're so sure of everything! You think you can stand by and interfere before they succeed in getting me!" Adele was almost hysterical. "Nobody interfered up at Nuevo Laredo, when that nice Mexican boy died right in front of me. Nobody interfered at the bullfight, and another man died. Twice they missed me by purest accident, and don't think they'll miss the third time."

"We'll do our best. Angels can do no more," Miss Withers told her, a little stiffly.

"If you think," Adele blurted out, "that I'm going to stay here in this room alone for even an hour—"

"Wait a moment," said the schoolteacher. "I have an idea. Oscar, this is a purely feminine matter. Would you mind leaving us alone for half an hour?"

He grumbled a little. "I don't know if it's safe."

"Then lend us your revolver, Oscar," Miss Withers suggested. "That ought to be protection enough."

Adele Mabie said, "But I don't know how to shoot very well."

"I do," said the schoolteacher, taking the pistol and holding it gingerly at arm's length. "You run along, Oscar." She followed him to the door, whispered some very peculiar last-minute instructions in his ear.

When they were alone she turned toward the frightened woman. "You are in worse danger than you realize," said Hildegarde Withers, her voice full of sympathy. "Worse than anybody realizes."

The face was drawn now, no longer pretty. "I know," said Adele softly. "I ought to go away tonight instead of tomorrow!"

"The danger you are in will follow you," Miss Withers pronounced. "It will follow you around the world. You are what the newspapers call a marked woman—unless—"

"But what can I do? Adele broke in. "It's the waiting that is so terrible."

"I'll tell you what you can do, with my help," said Hildegarde Withers. "You must…"

Adele screamed as a heavy missile struck the floor beside her, bounced across the floor. It was an inkwell, with a piece of paper fastened to it by means of a rubber band.

Both women rushed to the window, which de Silva had left open. Down at the side door of Pangborn's restaurant a man was getting into a taxicab, but they could not see who it was. They watched the taillight of the taxi disappear.

It was Adele who picked up the missile and opened the folded message.

There were only four words, written with red crayon in a firm Spencerian hand. "It is Zero Hour!" was all it said.

The inspector, walking stealthily along the deserted hall of the fourth floor, stopped suddenly and listened. There were sounds of loud and angry voices coming from the direction of the rear of the building. He frowned, turned away from the stairs, and went on back, more stealthily than ever. He turned a corner and suddenly flattened himself against the wall.

Dulcie Prothero stood at the door of her room, one of the few of these smallish top-floor rooms which appeared to be occupied. Before her in the corridor two young men faced each other, unmistakably belligerent.

"You'd better go," Julio Mendez was saying quietly, his voice without a trace of accent. "Don't be a fool."

The other, a pale young man with large ears and a determined jaw, did not move. "I'm going to talk to Dulcie," he said. "What's it to you?"

"The lady doesn't want to talk to you," Julio said.

"It's no skin off your nose, is it?" The Yonkers Matador was in a snarling mood.

"Go on, get out," the other ordered. His big pearl-handled automatic appeared suddenly in his hand. "I'm not fooling."

"Please go, Bobsie," the girl said.

He shook his head. "You've got to listen to me."

"She doesn't have to do anything," Julio Mendez said. "Go on, *vamos*! If you come any closer I'll blow you apart."

The mouth of Robert Schultz was twisted and bitter. He invited Julio to shoot and be damned to hell. Then he took a step closer.

"Oh no!" Dulcie said quickly. "Please stop, please—both of you. I won't have this!"

"He's leaving," Julio said.

"Go on, shoot," invited Schultz. "I don't care. I may be afraid of a bull, but I'm not afraid of you and your gun. You can shoot, but I'm going to knock that silly smirk off your puss first."

"One more step," Julio said simply, without expression, "and you will get it."

The inspector found himself torn between a feeling that it was his duty to interfere and a strong hunch that this meeting was important, that it was destined by fate.

Schultz took one step more, two more. Dulcie cried something, started forward, but her voice was as the wind in the treetops. Down the hall somebody opened a door, peered out, and closed it with a bang. In Mexico people learn to mind their own business, and the inspector followed suit.

Instead of pulling the trigger Julio Mendez suddenly tore off his belt and holster, threw gun and all against the wall.

"All right," he said. "Come on."

"Greaser!" vented the ex-matador, and he rushed. Mendez met the rush with a quick sidestep, caught his man in a clever jujitsu hold. The inspector nodded approvingly, for it was one that he had been taught by a Japanese instructor in police school.

But Schultz twisted, rolled suddenly on his heels, and broke the armlock. He flung a fast left, and Julio, cursed as are all Latins with an inability to fathom the brutal truths of fist on flesh, countered it awkwardly.

He left himself open for a straight right hand, and it shot to his chin. Still smiling a surprised smile, Julio Mendez went down and stayed down.

From the doorway of the cheap little room which Mrs. Mabie had thought good enough for her, Dulcie Prothero watched without moving.

"Now you'll listen to me!" the Yonkers Matador said. "It isn't true!"

She shook her head slowly, but he went doggedly on. "I'm not married or anything. When you came walking into my place—"

"I saw what I saw," Dulcie said woodenly.

"But you didn't! It was only my landlady. She always brings her kids when she comes up to sweep! But I saw you were jumping to the wrong conclusion—"

"So you let me?"

"I thought it would be the best thing in the world for you!" he protested. "The best way out of it, I mean. You see, I've been through hell in the last year."

"*You* have!" Dulcie said.

"I couldn't bring myself to write it," he said. "That's why I didn't write at all. But you see, I got hooked in the ring last season, and it left me jinxed. I can't go near a bull without trembling. I'm washed up. I'm no good for anything but the kind of a job I've got, just being a ring *mono* in a red jacket."

Dulcie didn't speak.

"For a while I tried getting drunk and staying drunk," he said. "But that didn't help much. I figured you were better off without me. That's why I didn't answer at the bullfight. I ducked out and went home, but when I saw you'd followed me there—"

"It doesn't matter," Dulcie told him.

"It does! It was crazy of me, I know. But I just couldn't do anything else but let you go on thinking what you thought. And I figured you'd go right back to New York and forget me, as I want to be forgotten."

"I had the money," Dulcie told him. "I put it in the bank every week when you sent it. That's why I came down."

He didn't want to take it. "Maybe—maybe it isn't too late!" said the Yonkers Matador, brightening. "Honey, I should have known that you wouldn't give a damn if I'd flopped in the bull ring. You wouldn't care what sort of a job I had."

"Yes, you should have known that," Dulcie said evenly. She approached his outstretched arms.

"I still love you, kid," he said.

"Hildegarde ought to be here, with her yen for happy endings," the inspector said to himself. But then his mouth dropped open with wonder, for Dulcie Prothero was not enclosed within the arms of the Yonkers Matador.

"You still love me," she told him. "When I started down here that would have been the sweetest thing in the world to hear. Now it sounds like the title of a cheap song."

She placed a wad of money in the outstretched hand of Robert Schultz. Then she stepped around him to kneel beside the fallen gladiator, lifting his head to her lap.

"If you've hurt him..." she said. "Oh, go away, go away!"

As amazed and bewildered as if a canary had spat in his face, the Yonkers Matador went slowly along the hall, too dazed to notice that ahead of him a grizzled Irishman was hurrying down the stairs.

The inspector knocked softly on the door of 307 and then grasped the knob and entered. Miss Hildegarde Withers, to his great surprise, was busily turning the key in the connecting door of the bedroom. She was alone in the big sitting room, alone with the disarranged furniture and the rows of curios.

Oscar Piper stared at his old friend. He had never claimed to be the seventh son of a seventh son and would have been the first to disclaim any clairvoyant ability. But all the same, as sure as her name was Hildegarde Martha Withers, this lady was up to something.

She barely listened to his questions, cut short his account of the battle of the century and its reverse-action finish. "Listen, Oscar, do you hear anything?"

He didn't. "Look here, Hildegarde, I don't see why you send me on such crazy errands—breaking into vacant rooms upstairs and all the rest of it. I try to play ball with you when I can, but this case is in a worse muddle than before. And if you expect me to wait here in hopes that your mysterious murderer will be fool enough to fall into a trap..."

She shook her head.

"Besides, there's a hall door to the bedroom. Anybody striking at Adele would go in that way."

"The door is locked, and I have that key too," Miss Withers said.

He stared wonderingly. "Hildegarde, I'm tired of being in the dark. If you're going to play riddles I'm going to bed. I've had—"

"Shhh, Oscar. Do you hear anything now?"

Obediently he listened again. "No, and I don't…" Then it came, the muffled spat of a pistol in the bedroom.

"I heard *that*!" he said dryly and plunged toward the connecting door. But quick as he was, Miss Withers was quicker. She barred the way, arms outstretched.

"You're not going in there," she told him. "Not now."

"Are you completely batty?" He leaned forward, staring with blank amazement in his eyes. "Somebody's been and killed Adele Mabie!"

"What if they have, Oscar?" she said simply.

XVI

Tilted Scales

THE TELEPHONE began to ring—short, angry, insistent signals.

"Will you answer it, Oscar?" Miss Withers pleaded.

"Why?"

"Oh, do hurry and answer it! It must be the desk downstairs. Somebody's reported the shot. Tell them it was a mistake, that a gun was being cleaned and went off by accident."

"I'll do nothing of the kind." It was the closest that the two old friends had come to open warfare since their meeting in the mazes of the aquarium mystery.

"I know what I'm doing," she said. There was something new and desperate in her voice. "Answer it, Oscar. We can't have the police coming in until you can think up a story to protect us both."

He shook his head, but under the insistent stare of those sad blue eyes he obeyed. Lifting the receiver, he spoke authoritatively to the night clerk. Then he turned. "Hildegarde, who's in that room?"

Miss Withers barely moved her lips. "Adele Mabie."

"Dead?"

She nodded slowly.

"But why?"

"You must listen to the whole story," she told him. "Sit down, there's no need to hurry now."

"The hell there isn't…" he started to say. But gradually he lowered himself into a chair and listened.

"It all goes back to two years ago," said Miss Hildegarde Withers, "when a pretty young woman sold out her chain of beauty parlors for a million dollars and started on a trip around the world to have some fun for a change."

"Yes, I know all that!"

"But you didn't know that, as passengers on the Empress tours have the privilege of doing, Adele Mabie left the ship at a Pacific port and crossed Mexico to rejoin it later in the Caribbean—by way of Mexico City?"

"Guessing, Hildegarde?"

She shook her head. "The proof was in that packet of photos the dear old Ippwings showed us in the lobby. Remember the one showing them sliding down a roller coaster labeled 'Luna Park'?"

"I guess so, but—"

"You didn't connect it with the picture you took out of Adele's luggage on the train, which you told me proved that she'd taken a trip to Coney Island? You didn't realize that Adele had missed that picture, which was why she was so anxious Dulcie shouldn't go to Xochimilco? She didn't want word to get back to us—she didn't want us to realize that she had been in Mexico City!"

"Good grief! Then—"

"Wait, Oscar. Adele Mabie was a visitor to Mexico City, and she met a man. Somewhat unconventionally, no doubt—she regretted it later, which was why she cut his face out of the picture."

"All right, suppose she did meet a man?"

"Suppose—suppose that the man was Michael Fitz? Who seems to have spent a good deal of his time picking up pretty tourists."

He supposed for a moment. "All right, but in the few days that she could have stayed in Mexico City while her ship went through the canal there wouldn't be time for much—"

"I wonder, Oscar. Remember, she was on a trip to forget work, to have fun. And tropical climates—or so I've been told—are very stimulating to romance. Equally stimulating must have been the money which was burning a hole in Adele's pocketbook, as far as Mr. Fitz was concerned. He was just the type to combine business with pleasure."

"You think he nicked her then?"

"Heart and pocketbook, Oscar. And Adele Mabie couldn't forgive that, Oscar. Remember that she prided herself on being smarter than men in business. She looked upon herself as a mastermind of finance, on account of her success with the beauty parlors. Her pride was wounded, Oscar. The wound rankled while she went on around the world, it rankled after she married a nice stupid politician to whom she could always feel superior.

"She seemed happy, yes. But a man had gotten the best of her. A man was laughing at her. And then she found out that her new husband was contemplating a political junket to Mexico."

Piper nodded. "Mabie told me he hoped to travel with a bunch of the boys, but that his wife sort of horned in. But you aren't trying to lead up to saying that Adele Mabie came all the way down here just to get revenge on Fitz?"

"Hell hath no fury, Oscar. Adele came for a reason. It was an accident that she hired as a maid an inexperienced girl anxious to get to Mexico and find her missing sweetheart. It was another accident that Dulcie, when discharged in Laredo, left behind her a bottle of cheap perfume because it was worthless.

"But, Oscar, it wasn't an accident that Adele Mabie had with her a quantity of prussic acid, a little gift she was taking to someone. When time came to cross the border she was carrying that poison concealed in the perfume bottle, the safest hiding place she could devise. It would have been perfect if poor Manuel Robles had not picked it up, no doubt making some joke about bringing perfumes into a country where tourists always come to buy it. He sniffed of the bottle before she could interfere—and he died!"

"But she collapsed too!" he protested.

"Fainted, Oscar. From fear that her secret was out, by an unlucky accident. She knew she was in danger of arrest. And then fate played into her hands. The Mexican doctor was unfamiliar with the poison, whose characteristic odor was partly concealed by the smell of the perfume. And you leaped to the conclusion that some veiled enemy had struck at her—and missed."

Piper said, "Yes, because of the poisoned tea that somebody smashed with a bullet before I could save it to analyze!"

"Naturally. But the tea was never poisoned, and Adele smashed the glass herself. She only wanted to lead your mind—and her husband's—to the idea that she was in danger. The bullet was to make it look more real—she took it from one of her own cartridges, threw away the gun. She knew you would search her baggage."

"She had a gun?"

Miss Withers nodded. "She told me so. But wait. Things developed to help her cloud the issue when it turned out that the discharged 'maid'— with a real grievance—was on the train. There was a suspect made to order, and a further red herring was drawn across the train when you spied on the alderman and his fumbling gesture of paying Dulcie secretly the week's salary that was due her!"

Miss Withers shrugged wearily. "It worked, Oscar! You were bamboozled by the theory she had inspired in your mind. The Mexican authorities were slow, or seemed to be, and so the party continued to Mexico City."

"Where I went to jail because somebody had pinched my papers!" he put in. "But was it Adele who did it?"

The schoolteacher smiled. "Why should Adele care if you got the girl arrested or not? I'm afraid it was young Julio Mendez, a gallant young man who had fallen for Dulcie and saw a way to keep her from being arrested on your say-so until he could dig up something to prove her innocence."

"Then he was just another amateur detective? And that was why he was prowling around all the time! That's why he popped up to shoot the snake?"

Miss Withers nodded judicially. "The snake was to have been still more tangible proof of the plot against Adele's life. It was to cinch the thing. She bought it knowing exactly what it was, produced it where it would get the most display value. There was no risk for her—if Julio hadn't shot it someone else would."

The inspector objected. "You're doing it all backwards. What about the deal Hansen and Lighton were in on with Fitz?"

"Coincidence, Oscar. But not so great a coincidence as you think. It was just that Michael Fitz was well known as the kind of a man to call upon for such sharp practice as this corner in lighting plants demanded. He had been skating on thin ice down here for years.

"But when he received the telegraphed money from Lighton and Hansen—and the alderman, who was a silent partner—he took the money to a cockfight, probably seeking to build up the fund. Instead, he lost. And he was so furious at losing that he brought home the defeated rooster, killed it if it was not already dead, and even planned to eat it!"

Piper made a wry face, as if he tasted something unpleasant. "A nice guy, huh?"

"Murder is murder, Oscar. Fitz paid heavily for his sins. But first he picked up Dulcie Prothero at the consulate. The girl suspected his intentions, being no fool. But she was in desperate need of help that she thought he could give her. She knew he would have no sympathy if she were searching for a sweetheart, so she made up the story about the brother and the emeralds. And he swallowed it, hook, line and sinker."

"Confidence men always fall for somebody else's game," said Piper. "I never knew it to fail."

Miss Withers nodded and went on swiftly. "He believed her story so implicitly that he looked upon Dulcie's 'emerald' as a heaven-sent answer to his financial troubles. He stole it, tried to have it turned into cash with which to quiet the demands of his partners—"

"Only it was glass—a good joke on him."

Miss Withers sniffed. "Life was playing its last grim, practical joke on Michael Fitz. As he sat in the front row at the bullfight, wondering why the girl he had brought had abandoned him without a word to chase after somebody in the bull ring, someone moved stealthily up behind him."

"Adele Mabie? But, Hildegarde, she was with us when Fitz died!"

"Yes? Listen, Oscar. What autopsy surgeon can tell the difference five minutes would make in a corpse? Adele knew that her husband, being a soft and kindly person unused to cruelty, would be too squeamish to watch the spectacle. She appeared early at the bullfight, keeping in the background. But she admitted seeing Dulcie jump over the rail—an event which took place some time before Adele ostensibly arrived. She waited until there was great excitement in the ring—no doubt the exact moment when young Nicanor was tossed by the bull— and struck!"

"Now, Hildegarde, do you expect me to believe that?"

"She did, anyway. Under cover of the umbrella, which would effectively hide the actual deed from those behind them."

"You mean to say that shrimp of a woman stuck a dart five inches into a man's back through his clothing when I couldn't stick it half that far into a dead pig?"

"Yes, Oscar. I'll come to that in a moment. She left the dart sticking into the back of her victim, who slumped forward against the rail. But she didn't want him discovered until she was well away, so she calmly placed her rented umbrella over the shoulders of Fitz, just as if he were holding it, and hurried away!"

"She had that much nerve?"

"Yes, Oscar, and more. Women are superior to men in many things, and certainly at murder. How about Mrs. Wharton, and Cordelia Botkin, and Mrs. Vermilya and her pepper pot—and dozens more? Adele Mabie hoped that she had convinced everyone of her being the intended victim of these crimes, and that we would jump to the conclusion that Fitz was just one more innocent bystander who had caught something aimed at her!"

"I still want to know," Piper said doggedly, "how she managed to kill a man with a dart!"

"She didn't, Oscar!"

"But you just said—"

"Not with the dart. The word *banderilla* means 'little flag' in Spanish. It isn't to kill with. It is only a frilly decoration. Just some way of insulting the bull, really, in the lovely Latin manner. In the ring, the bull is killed with a long thin blade, and Adele used the same method."

Suddenly Piper pointed to the back of a chair across the room. "The blade that made that hole?"

"Yes, Oscar."

"But was the woman a magician? Where could she hide a weapon like that?"

"A question I've been asking myself for some time. You'll remember, Oscar, that when Adele came to the bullfight she carried with her a shopping bag filled with the day's purchases?"

"Remember? Say, I lugged it home for her. But there wasn't any sword in that."

"Wait. As we left the bull ring she purchased a pair of *banderillas*. A clever dodge, to make us sure never to suspect that she had also purchased a pair on her way in!"

"But you just said Fitz wasn't killed with a dart!"

"Listen. She carried another weapon with her that day, a weapon that fooled me and would fool anybody. The clue came to me when I was watching a cobbler make sandals. He used one tool to make the hole, another to take the waxed thread through."

"You mean the dart went in so easily because it followed the track of a previous wound?"

"Right, Oscar. A blade, swiftly withdrawn and leaving only a few drops of blood—and then came the *banderilla* to fool everybody, obliterating the previous track."

"That is one on me," Piper said. "I suspected Julio."

"And I, Oscar! Especially after I got the idea of the blade that might have been concealed in an umbrella or walking stick. I might never have thought of the answer had not Adele made one of her few mistakes. She hid the weapon—then the moment I noticed it was missing from this room, she returned it—for she dared not draw attention to it."

"Well, what was it?" Piper demanded. "Do you intend to keep me dangling?"

"Dangle no longer," said Hildegarde Withers. "This was the weapon that Adele carried in her shopping bag on Sunday. It was here on the table in plain view when we searched the place this evening. See?" And she handed him the heavy riding whip of alligator leather.

He took hold of the shaft, and Miss Withers suddenly pulled in the other direction with a sidewise twist. And then the inspector found himself holding only a limp leather sheath ending in the wristloop of the crop. The schoolteacher gripped a long triangular sliver of steel which had run the full length of the whip from handle to tip, a good fourteen inches!

"Why," he cried, "that would go in like a hot knife into butter!" He tried the blade gingerly against his thumb, felt the needle point.

"Yes, Oscar. It was meant to go into me tonight in the dark, because Adele was afraid that I would again ask Dulcie a certain question—the answer to which, she knew, would damn her. It would make Dulcie a certain witness against her in court, hang her actually."

"Yeah? What question?"

"Simply this. Where had Dulcie thrown the perfume bottle she admitted discarding? The answer, of course, was that she had simply left it behind when Mrs. Mabie fired her at Laredo."

"And that's why Adele Mabie wanted to keep Dulcie so close to her, why she didn't want her to go out with Julio or to be here at the meeting tonight!"

"Right, Oscar. You see, that girl was a potential key witness. And I have an idea that had they both started home on the steamer, some night Dulcie Prothero would have 'committed suicide' by jumping overboard."

"So far so good, Hildegarde. But not good enough. You've covered everything except the reason why Adele Mabie is dead in there instead of being behind the bars."

Miss Withers stood up, walked across the room and back. "You wouldn't understand, Oscar. But I couldn't bear to think of a country-woman of mine standing before a firing squad in a foreign land or spending her days on Mexico's Devil's Islands in the Pacific."

"You mean, after all this, that you sympathized—"

"We had it out, Adele and I. While you were upstairs just now, arranging that little demonstration for me. When the inkwell came tumbling in the window, she knew that I knew. She realized that I had solved her trick of tossing the thing—and the *banderilla* too—down from the balcony above into the open window of my room."

"But I thought: you said you made an excuse to see if the inkwell was gone from the desk here? And it wasn't!"

She smiled faintly. "I never thought of looking in the bedroom to see if there was a second desk, which there is. And a second inkwell, which there isn't. But anyway, when she saw that I knew, the fight went completely out of Adele Mabie. She was just a terrified woman, caught on a trail that led downward so steeply that there was no turning. What I did was the decent thing to do, Oscar. You'll have to help me cover it up somehow."

"You don't mean—"

"I locked her in the bedroom, Oscar. And just before I closed the door I tossed your revolver—with only one cartridge in the chamber—onto the bed." The schoolteacher was defiant. "She knew what to do with that one cartridge, and you heard her do it!"

The inspector rose slowly to his feet. "You're a funny woman, Hildegarde. I suppose—oh, we'll cover you somehow, though de Silva and his chiefs will raise bloody hell." He held out his hand. "Give me that key."

He unlocked the bedroom door, opened it, and then closed it firmly behind him. There was a moment of silence, and then the schoolteacher heard his agonized, incredulous yell.

"Hildegarde!"

She was through the door and beside him in a moment, steeling herself for the sight that she must see.

But Adele Mabie did not lie on the floor, a confessed murderer and suicide. Adele Mabie was gone.

Together they stared down at the broken lock of the hall door, a lock smashed under the impact of a heavy 38-caliber slug of lead.

"And as you say, I *heard* her do it!" the inspector muttered.

XVII

The Last Mile

"OH, OSCAR!" wailed Miss Hildegarde Withers from the utter depths of despair. "How was I to know?"

But he wasn't listening. He dashed down the stairs, with the school-teacher close at his heels. At the desk he pounded with his fist, awakened the drowsy night man.

"Did you see a lady go out of here? Which way did she go?"

The man shook his head. "No lady, *señor*. Nobody go out for a long time, not since midnight." That was more than two hours before.

"Asleep, eh? And of course she sneaked right by you!"

But the Mexican grinned, a very wise grin. "Nobody comes or goes after midnight without I know, *señor*." He reached behind his chair, took up a great brass key fastened to a stick. "For the door," he explained happily. "Somebody goes out, they wake me. Somebody comes in, they have to ring and wait."

The inspector and Miss Withers stared blankly at each other. "Then she's hiding somewhere in the building, Oscar! Quick, get the police!"

But he shook his head. "No time, Hildegarde." He was running up the stairs, as he had not run in twenty years. "Dulcie—one witness against the woman…" They rounded a corner. "Adele is probably half crazy now—maybe she'll try…"

Second, third, fourth floor.

Down the hall, around a corner, then to a half-open door. "I think it's there," Piper said.

They both had stopped, waiting, listening. For some reason neither was anxious to explore what lay beyond that narrow oblong of light. Then they heard the voice of Dulcie Prothero.

They stood in the doorway, before them a picture that neither was ever to forget.

There was Dulcie, alive and unhurt, speaking into the telephone. "But isn't there anybody at the *jefatura* who speaks English?" she was pleading.

There was Adele Mabie, wild with fury, her hair Medusa-like over her eyes and her red lips gray now, drawn back to show the canine teeth. Her dress was torn from her shoulder, her cheek was bruised, and in bitter, furious silence she knelt on the floor, fighting against the grip of a handcuff.

The other link of the cuff was held by Julio Mendez, who leaned weakly against the side of the bed and with his free hand mopped at the blood pouring from a short gash in his forehead.

"Hello!" he greeted them happily, a world of relief in that one word.

Piper went into action, pinioned the woman's arms neatly and cuffed them behind her. Miss Withers was beside Julio.

"How bad?" Piper demanded.

"It's nothing," Julio said. "When she knocked on the door I didn't see that she had a sliver of glass in her hand—piece of a broken tumbler, I guess. I found out soon enough, though."

"Look out, Oscar!" gasped Miss Withers.

Adele had lifted her pinioned arms, trying to strike at the inspector's head with the heavy manacles. He dodged, gave her the elbow in the pit of the stomach so that she rolled back on the bed, gasping and writhing. Dulcie went calmly on telephoning.

"My prisoner, Inspector," said Julio in a weak voice. "I have had my eye on her all along—and downstairs, I noticed that she was the only one to point to Miss Withers on the floor and cry bloody murder. She expected to find a corpse there!"

"Good work, boy," Piper said. Then he stopped, frowned. "You talk differently," he accused. "And where did you get the handcuffs?"

"Yes, Oscar," Miss Withers put in. "It's time you knew. Meet Lieutenant Colonel Mendez of the *Securidad Publica*. He's been playing the part of the Gay Caballero while he investigated this case, but after I accused him of it we had a good laugh and he obligingly helped in some of the arrangements for the evening."

The inspector's jaw dropped. "Well—well—so that was why—"

"It was," Julio said cheerfully. "I started talking that way and then I had to keep in character." He looked older now, far more serious. "She's the murderer, of course?" he said, pointing to the captive.

Miss Withers told him everything. "And if it had not been for your somewhat informal call, I'm afraid Dulcie might have been the third victim."

"What?" Dulcie Prothero gasped, putting down the telephone in the middle of a sentence. She was blushing. "Oh, please! Do you think— why, I dragged the poor boy in here! Look at his head!"

Julio turned, to display a lump like a half orange. "From landing on the tile floor outside when I got knocked down. I can't stand very well yet, which was why the lady nicked me with the sliver of glass. Dulcie had just brought me to when the knock came."

Finally the girl at the telephone got through to the proper parties, and the wheels of justice began to move.

"You see," Julio Mendez explained, "I understand your compunctions, Miss Withers. But I do not share them. I really did go to school with Manuel Robles, which was why I flew up to Villadama to take on the case personally. I was godfather to Manuel Robles' son," he added grimly. "So I am happy to see this woman captured; I will be happy to see her stand trial. I don't care what happens to Mrs. Mabie!"

"I care what happens to *this* one, though," Miss Withers said, looking down at the tumbled red hair of Dulcie Prothero. "Have you any plans, child?"

Dulcie shook her head.

"One small minutes, please!" Then Julio stopped, shook his head. "There it goes, that damn dialect. But what I mean to say is—she *has* a plan."

"Oh yes," she agreed. Dulcie smiled, all over her face. It was the best, the very best and happiest, smile that Miss Withers had ever seen her give. "Of course I have one plan. I'm going to Xochimilco to see the Floating Gardens by moonlight!"

"With *me*!" added Julio. "Don't forget that."

Inspector Oscar Piper turned to the schoolteacher. "You know, there must be something in that place. We'll have to take a trip there before we go back. How far is it?"

Miss Withers was watching the young couple. "What?"

"I said—How far is it to the Floating Gardens?"

"About twenty years, Oscar," the schoolteacher told him sadly.

THE END

About The Rue Morgue Press

The Rue Morgue vintage mystery line is designed to bring back into print those books that were favorites of readers between the turn of the century and the 1960s. The editors welcome suggests for reprints. To receive our catalog or make suggestions, write The Rue Morgue Press, P.O. Box 4119, Boulder, Colorado (1-800-699-6214).

Rue Morgue Press titles as of August 2004

Titles are listed by author. All books are quality trade paperbacks measuring 6 by 9 inches, usually with full-color covers and printed on paper designed not to yellow or deteriorate. These are permanent books.

Joanna Cannan. This English writer's books are among our most popular titles. Modern reviewers have compared them favorably with the best books of the Golden Age of detective fiction. "Worthy of being discussed in the same breath with an Agatha Christie or a Josephine Tey."—Sally Fellows, *Mystery News.* Set in the late 1930s in a village that was a fictionalized version of Oxfordshire, both titles feature young Scotland Yard inspector Guy Northeast. *They Rang Up the Police* (0-915230-27-5, $14.00) and *Death at The Dog* (0-915230-23-2, $14.00).

Glyn Carr. The 15 books featuring Shakespearean actor Abercrombie "Filthy" Lewker are set on peaks scattered around the globe, although the author returned again and again to his favorite climbs in Wales, where his first mystery, published in 1951, *Death on Milestone Buttress* (0-915230-29-1, $14.00), is set.

Torrey Chanslor. Sixty-five-year-old Amanda Beagle employs good old East Biddicut common sense to run the agency, while her younger sister Lutie prowls the streets and nightclubs of 1940 Manhattan looking for clues. The two inherited the Beagle Private Detective Agency from their older brother, but you'd never know the sisters had spent all of their lives knitting and tending to their garden in a small, sleepy upstate New York town. *Our First Murder* (0-915230-50-X, $14.95) and *Our Second Murder* (0-915230-64-X, $14.95) are charming hybrids of the private eye, traditional, and cozy mystery, published in 1940 and 1941 respectively.

Clyde B. Clason. *The Man from Tibet* (0-915230-17-8, $14.00) is one of his best (selected in 2001 in *The History of Mystery* as one of the 25 great amateur detective novels of all time) and highly recommended by the dean of locked room mystery scholars, Robert Adey, as "highly original." It's also one of the first novels to make use of Tibetan culture. *Murder Gone Minoan* (0-915230-60-7, $14.95) is set on a channel island off the California coast where a rich Greek magnate has recreated a Minoan palace.

Joan Coggin. Meet Lady Lupin Lorrimer Hastings, the young, lovely, scatterbrained and kindhearted daughter of an earl, now the newlywed wife of the vicar of St. Marks Parish in Glanville, Sussex. You might not understand her logic but she always gets her man. *Who Killed the Curate?* (0-915230-44-5, $14.00), *The Mystery at Orchard House* (0-915230-54-2, $14.95), *Penelope Passes or Why Did She Die?* (0-915230-61-5, $14.95), and *Dancing with Death* (0-915230-62-3, $14.95).

Manning Coles. The two English writers who collaborated as Coles are best known for those witty spy novels featuring Tommy Hambledon, but they also wrote four delightful—and funny—ghost novels. *The Far Traveller* (0-915230-35-6, $14.00), *Brief Candles* (0-915230-24-0, 156 pages, $14.00), *Happy Returns* (0-915230-31-3, $14.00) and *Come and Go* (0-915230-34-8, $14.00).

Lucy Cores. Her books both feature one of the more independent female sleuths of the 1940s. Toni Ney is the exercise director at a very posh Manhattan beauty spa when the "French Lana Turner" is murdered in *Painted for the Kill* (0-915230-66-6, $14.95) while she's a newly minted ballet reviewer when murder cuts short the return of a Russian dancer to the stage in *Corpse de Ballet* (0-915230-67-4, $14.95).

Norbert Davis. There have been a lot of dogs in mystery fiction, from Baynard Kendrick's guide dog to Virginia Lanier's bloodhounds, but there's never been one quite like Carstairs. Doan, a short, chubby Los Angeles private eye, won Carstairs in a crap game, but there never is any question as to who the boss is in this relationship. *The Mouse in the Mountain* (0-915230-41-0, $14.00), was first published in 1943 and followed by two other Doan and Carstairs novels, *Sally's in the Alley* (0-915230-46-1, $14.00), and *Oh, Murderer Mine* (0-915230-57-7, $14.00).

Elizabeth Dean. In Emma Marsh Dean created one of the first independent female sleuths in the genre. Written in the screwball style of the 1930s, *Murder is a Serious Business* (0-915230-28-3, $14.95), is set in a Boston antique store just as the Great Depression is drawing to a close. *Murder a Mile High* (0-915230-39-9, $14.00) moves to the Central City Opera House in the Colorado mountains.

Constance & Gwenyth Little. These two Australian-born sisters from New Jersey have developed almost a cult following among mystery readers. Each book, published between 1938 and 1953, was a stand-alone. The Rue Morgue Press intends to reprint all of their books. Currently available are: *The Black Thumb* (0-915230-48-8, $14.00), *The Black Coat* (0-915230-40-2, $14.00), *Black Corridors* (0-915230-33-X, $14.00), *The Black Gloves* (0-915230-20-8, $14.00), *Black-Headed Pins* (0-915230-25-9, $14.00), *The Black Honeymoon* (0-915230-21-6, $14.00), *The Black Paw* (0-915230-37-2, $14.00), *The Black Stocking* (0-915230-30-5, $14.00), *Great Black Kanba* (0-915230-22-4, $14.00), *The Grey Mist Murders* (0-915230-26-7, $14.00), *The Black Eye* (0-915230-45-3, $14.00), *The Black Shrouds* (0-915230-52-6, $14.00), *The Black Rustle* (0-915230-58-5, $14.00), *The Black Goatee* (0-915230-63-1, $14.00), *The Black House* (0-915230-68-2, $14.00) and *The Black Piano* (0-915230-65-8).

John Mersereau. *Murder Loves Company* (0-915239-69-0, $14.95. Young Berkeley professor James Yeats Biddle finds love and murder while looking into a murder at the 1939 San Francisco World's Fair. First published in 1940.

Marlys Millhiser. Our only non-vintage mystery, *The Mirror* (0-915230-15-1, $17.95) is our all-time bestselling book, now in a seventh printing. How could you not be intrigued by a novel in which "you find the main character marrying her own grandfather and giving birth to her own mother."

James Norman. *Murder, Chop Chop* (0-915230-16-X, $13.00) is a wonderful example of the eccentric detective novel. Meet Gimiendo Hernandez Quinto, a huge Mexican who once rode with Pancho Villa and who now trains *guerrilleros* for the Nationalist Chinese government when he isn't solving murders. At his side is a beautiful Eurasian known as Mountain of Virtue, a woman as dangerous to men as she is irresistible. First published in 1942.

Sheila Pim. *Ellery Queen's Mystery Magazine* said of these wonderful Irish village mysteries that Pim "depicts with style and humor everyday life." *Booklist* said they were in "the best tradition of Agatha Christie." Beekeeper Edward Gildea uses his knowledge of bees and plants to good use in *A Hive of Suspects* (0-915230-38-0, $14.00). *Creeping Venom* (0-915230-42-9, $14.00) blends politics, gardening and religion into a deadly mixture. *A Brush with Death* (0-915230-49-6, $14.00) grafts a clever art scam onto the stem of a gardening mystery.

Craig Rice. *Home Sweet Homicide* (0-915230-53-4, $14.95) is a marvelously funny and utterly charming tale (set in 1942 and first published in 1944) of three children who "help" their widowed mystery writer mother solve a real-life murder and nab a handsome cop boyfriend along the way. It made just about every list of the best mysteries for the first half of the 20th century, including the Haycraft-Queen Cornerstone list.

Charlotte Murray Russell. Spinster sleuth Jane Amanda Edwards tangles with a murderer and Nazi spies in *The Message of the Mute Dog* (0-915230-43-7, $14.00), a culinary cozy set just before Pearl Harbor. "Perhaps the mother of today's cozy."—*The Mystery Reader*.

Sarsfield, Maureen. These two mysteries featuring Inspector Lane Parry of Scotland Yard are among our most popular books. Both are set in Sussex. *Murder at Shots Hall* (0-915230-55-8, $14.95) features Flikka Ashley, a thirtyish sculptor with a past she would prefer remain hidden. It was originally published as *Green December Fills the Graveyard* in 1945. Parry is back in Sussex, trapped by a blizzard at a country hotel where a war hero has been pushed out of a window to his death, in *Murder at Beechlands* (0-915230-56-9, $14.95). First published in 1948.

Juanita Sheridan. Sheridan's books feature a young Chinese American sleuth Lily Wu and her Watson, Janice Cameron, a first-time novelist. The first book (*The Chinese Chop* (0-915230-32-1, 155 pages, $14.00) is set in Greenwich Village but the other three are set in Hawaii in the years immediately after World War II: *The Kahuna Killer* (0-915230-47-X, $14.00), *The Mamo Murders* (0-915230-51-8, $14.00), and *The Waikiki Widow* (0-915230-59-3, $14.00) .